PASSION AND PLUNDER

Highland Heather Romancing A Scot Series

COLLETTE CAMERON

SOUL MATE PUBLISHING

New York

PASSION AND PLUNDER

Copyright©2017

COLLETTE CAMERON

Cover Design by Rae Monet, Inc.

This book is a work of fiction. The names, characters, places, and incidents are the products of the author's imagination or are used fictitiously. Any resemblance to actual events, business establishments, locales, or persons, living or dead, is entirely coincidental.

Published in the United States of America by
Soul Mate Publishing
P.O. Box 24
Macedon, New York, 14502

ISBN: 978-1-68291-413-7

ebook ISBN: 978-1-68291-377-2

www.SoulMatePublishing.com

The publisher does not have any control over and does not assume any responsibility for author or third-party websites or their content.

Beta Babes, this one's for you!

LB, MD, DF, JM, KG

Hugs and Kisses

xoxo

Collette

Acknowledgements

I wrote PASSION AND PLUNDER during an extremely trying time in my life, and if it hadn't been for a handful of people who held me up in prayer, as well as encouraged me to keep writing, despite my heartache, I might not have finished the book. Or kept on writing at all.

So to you who held my hand, witnessed my tears, interceded for me, and pushed me to keep doing what brings me the greatest joy, I humbly and gratefully thank you.

Chapter 1

Tornbury Fortress, Scottish Highlands
January 1819

Life's never predictable.

Lydia Farnsworth forced her stiff lips into a sunny smile and, smoothing the heavy russet counterpane across her father's once muscular chest, refused to acknowledge the sorrow clawing at her ribs.

For his sake, and the clan's too, venting her grief would have to wait until she sought her chamber. Future lairds, especially female chiefs, controlled their weaker emotions.

She inhaled deeply, longing for the crisp outdoor air rather than the stuffy sickroom's fug.

Wasting disease. Heart failure.
My God.

She'd lost Mum scarcely three months ago. Her brothers six months prior to that. And the man she loved too, though he hadn't died. He might as well have for the grief she'd suffered. And if that wasn't chaos enough, mere weeks ago, her orphaned, American second cousin had arrived.

Unannounced.

And now this awful prognosis?

Wretched, bloody unfair.

Like something from one of Mum's gothic novels she'd kept stashed behind her half-boots within her wardrobe.

Lydia had devoured several as well, in utmost secrecy, of course. Chiefs didn't read risqué novels. Rather, they didn't get caught reading them.

"I'll see Doctor Wedderburn out, Da." She brushed a lock of gray-threaded, bright red hair from her father's pale, slightly damp forehead before kissing him.

Her hair, secured at her nape with a lavender ribbon a shade lighter than her gown, billowed forward.

Da's lips tipped up at the corners, and love glinted in his still brilliant hazel eyes, so like hers. He playfully tugged a tendril of her almost black hair.

"Nae need to look so solemn, lass." He winked. "I dinna plan on cockin' up me toes just yet, ye ken. I still intend to see ye wed and to bounce yer bairns on me knees."

A coughing fit interrupted his raspy chuckle.

Sorrow squeezing her lungs, Lydia passed him a fresh handkerchief.

Doctor Wedderburn waggled his grizzled eyebrows at his long-time friend. "Aye, Bailoch, yer too stubborn and contrary to point yer knobby toes heavenward without a fight."

Da grunted and scowled, but his feet wiggling the bedding belied any actual annoyance.

Would he live long enough to play with her children?

Doubtful.

Besides, she wasn't even betrothed. Hadn't any prospects either.

Anymore.

Stop it!

Dredging up *that* heartache was pointless and just plain stupid, particularly with Da's looming health crisis. If she also ruminated on her broken heart, she might splinter—fracture into a thousand jagged, miserable pieces.

Lydia had neither the time nor the strength to lose her composure and indulge the pain she'd resolutely suppressed since last spring. Besides, she quite detested moping females, and sulking about in a fit of the blue devils benefited no one.

If hell had a season, she'd just borne several long, unrelenting months, and her torment didn't look to be over soon.

How much more could she endure?

Da stirred again and, though he winced, managed a puny smile.

For him?

I'll endure as much as I have to.

She and Da only had each other now. But God help her, at nineteen, though educated right alongside her brothers and often surpassing them in academics, Lydia wasn't prepared to be the clan's chieftain yet.

Would she ever be?

Did she want to be?

Not now. Not like this.

Even before Colin's and Leath's deaths, Da had trained her, took her into his confidence, asked her opinions, insisted she speak the King's English with a cultured lady of the realm's accent.

So why did feelings of inadequacy still plague, sharp and frequent?

The harsh, even scathing, whispers about a female chief, that's why.

But proving a woman worthy of such a lofty role as laird?

Well, that intrigued her mightily.

She'd love to prove the naysayers wrong.

Of course, Da had assumed she'd marry a high-ranking Scot to help her lead, not fall in love with a titled Sassenach. Nevertheless, to honor Da, as well as her brothers' memories, she would accept the role.

If Da did, indeed, name her his successor.

Lydia had made no provision for otherwise, and that included any notion of nuptials.

By God, she'd do well by the position. She would.

She'd have a purpose then, a focus, something to work toward since her dream of marriage—at least a love match—had been ground to dust and the specks blown across the moors by the Highland winter's wild gales.

As she'd sobbed in his embrace after confessing Flynn had married another, Da had gently advised, "Only after a tree's weathered a fierce storm can it claim strength, Liddie lass. Didna give up on love yet. Yer too young. Given time, a wounded soul can heal and learn to trust again."

Not hers.

Grief's cumbersome weight pressed cripplingly, and she rotated her stiff shoulders, then kneaded her sore nape.

However, humoring Da couldn't hurt.

"Of course you'll play with my children." Lydia drew one velvet bed curtain closed against the room's piercing chill despite the hearty fire snapping a few feet from the bed's footboard.

She grinned and skewed a brow upward playfully. "All eight of them."

"Och, eight, ye say?" Da laughed and slapped his gaunt chest when he started coughing again. "We'd best find ye a husband soon, and get started then. Ye've nae time to waste. A big, strappin' Scot, like one of those McTavish twins. That Alasdair McTavish, now he be a braw fellow. Keen too."

Flynn hadn't been Scottish.

Mayhap destiny had played a part in his marrying another, since Lydia could no more have abandoned Tornbury after her brothers' deaths than Flynn could've forsaken his marquisate.

"A fine, honorable man," Da rattled on, oblivious to her ruminations. "A warrior who can protect ye and Tornbury when I be gone."

She didn't need a man to protect her. Far past time for Da to accept a woman could, and should, be allowed to do what men had presumed was their exclusive rights for centuries.

The doctor canted his head toward the Italian baroque nightstand. "Take the medicines I left ye, follow me orders, and Tornbury may yet have the pleasure of their cantankerous laird for a goodly while." He rolled his eyes heavenward. "The guid Lord preserve us all."

"Wheesht." Da wagged his hand at Doctor Wedderburn, a faint smile pulling at his mouth. "Stop flappin' yer tongue, and get on with ye. I'll outlive ye by a decade."

An absurd exaggeration, if Lydia had ever heard one. Still, she summoned another valiant smile. "Da, I'll be back in a few minutes, and I'll bring you a tray. Cook made you cock-a-leekie soup and custard. Also fresh oat rolls."

"I'd rather have a dram or two of whisky, beef collops, and mutton chops," Da grumbled, a scowl contorting his ginger brows. "Me pipe too."

She could use a tot of whisky-laced tea herself.

On second thought, never mind the tea and the teacup.

"No tobacco or whisky," Doctor Wedderburn admonished, shaking his finger before snapping his worn-about-the-seams bag shut. "But each evening, ye may have a half glass of red wine before ye retire."

"I'm nae a confounded half-wit or a droolin' invalid." Da made a disgusted noise, sounding very much like his familiar, disgruntled, bearish self.

Bernard, a rather spoilt tabby and one of the mansion's best ratters, cracked an amber eye open at having his nap disturbed at the bed's foot. He stretched his lanky form and sank his claws into the coverlet before leaping to the floor.

Perhaps her father did feel better. His temper, as fiery as the thatch atop his head, hadn't waned a jot.

Da pounded the counterpane. "I be Bailoch Farnsworth, laird of Tornbury Fortress. And I'll tell ye right now, I winna be stayin' in this confounded bed."

In the process of adding wood to the fire, Lydia dropped

a log, launching a cascade of angry sparks. "But Da, you must—"

"My tribe needs their chieftain, daughter. Tornbury canna be seen as weak. I canna be seen as weak.

"Neither of ye breathes a word about me heart, ye ken? Not even to yer Uncle Gordon or cousin Esme, Liddie. I'll be up and about in a day or two. Ye tell anyone askin' ye, I've naught but a wicked bout of influenza."

As she swept ashes from the hearth, Lydia pressed her lips into a grim line. He asked much of her.

His eyes sunken and circled by purplish shadows, Da wilted further into his pillows, yet his commanding gaze held their attention, demanding their compliance. "I mean it."

"Yes, Da," Lydia half-heartedly agreed as Doctor Wedderburn gave a reluctant nod.

Not that keeping silent would do much good.

Concerned murmurs and worried glances had followed the laird these past few months already. A few of the more daring servants and clan members had asked probing questions which she'd answered with platitudes and half-truths.

And, by George, she didn't like lying. Even for a compelling reason, as if that excused dishonesty.

Auburn brows pulled tight, Da jutted his square jaw in proud defiance. "I'm nae as feeble as ye think I be."

Yes. He was.

"That's wonderful to hear." His bravado nearly undid her, and she blinked way hot moisture as she escorted Doctor Wedderburn from the chamber.

"I'll be back tomorrow, ye cross old boar. Get some rest." Doctor Wedderburn's gentle insult earned him a rude gesture.

Shutting the heavy door, Lydia drew in a steadying

breath. Drawing every ounce of mettle she possessed, she squared her shoulders and faced the doctor.

Hopefully, she appeared collected. Weeping and histrionics wouldn't earn the clan's admiration. Scots honored strength and forbearance almost as much as loyalty.

As they neared the stairs, she slowed her steps, and Doctor Wedderburn raised a bushy gray eyebrow expectantly.

"How long does Da actually have, Doctor?" Swiftly scanning the corridor and stairway, she lowered her voice. "You must understand the gravity of our situation and the clan's precarious position right now. We've no war chief since Lundy drowned."

He'd been on the same ill-fated boat that sank, snuffing her strapping brothers' lives far, far too early.

Doctor Wedderburn's half nod confirmed his agreement.

"And Da hasn't chosen another, nor named his successor as laird. None of us dreamed both his sons would die before him, or that he'd fall ill so early on. And though he's all but told me I'll be the next laird . . ."

The doctor rubbed his nose and puffed out his florid cheeks. "A year at most, lass. Likely less. Six months would be me best guess."

Anguish lanced Lydia, and for an endless moment she couldn't speak or draw even a spoonful of air into her lungs.

Her entire family gone in less than twelve months.

Either she'd been cursed, or she had the most confounded bad luck. She'd better never wager a shilling at the gaming tables.

Tornbury might be lost with the toss of a die.

Stop feeling sorry for yourself.

"And?" She blinked against the hot tears stinging behind her eyelids. "Yer sure? There truly be nothin'—" She sucked in a shuddery breath. "Nothin' at all that can be done?"

Misery thickened her brogue and stilted her speech.

Da would scold her until her ears glowed red if he overheard. Why must her speech mimic a lofty lady's when his brogue was thicker than congealed porridge?

"Nae." Doctor Wedderburn shook his head. "I'm afraid nothin', except to reduce yer father's stress. Keep him calm and try to prevent upsettin' him."

Far easier said than done.

He suddenly chuckled softly, covering his lips with a forefinger. "I ken Bailoch, though, and he winna be a biddable patient. Ye should be prepared fer him worsenin', perhaps rapidly, if he refuses to follow me directives."

He'll follow them, all right. Even if I have to tie him to his bed, the ornery dear.

Nodding, she swallowed the lump mounting in her throat.

Neither spoke as they descended the stairs and made their way across the parquet floor to the grand entrance.

Gordon Ross, Lydia's maternal uncle, emerged from the study, carrying a short stack of thin books in his gangly arms. He stopped, appearing startled upon seeing her. He cut a troubled glance to the stairs. "How fares Uncle?"

Straight to the point, as always. No "Hello," or "How is your day," or "Such lovely spring weather we're having."

"Da's resting and should be up and about in a day or two," Lydia said. Not precisely the truth, but not an outright lie either.

"Nothing serious, then? He'll recover?" A frown wrinkling his forehead and crunching his black eyebrows, his pewter gaze swung between Lydia and the doctor. He slid the ledgers under an arm, holding them close to his chest. "There nae be need fer concern?"

"Rest assured, laddie, the laird isnae ready to topple into his grave, just yet." Firming his grip on his medicine bag, Doctor Wedderburn exchanged a conspiratorial look with Lydia. "I'll see ye on the morrow, lass."

He took his leave, and Uncle Gordon's scowl deepened, but whether from the doctor calling him laddie, or he'd detected the nuance of untruth in Doctor Wedderburn's words, she didn't know.

At the moment, she didn't care, truth to tell.

Not a thing new about Gordon's darkling temper, and today, she wasn't in the mood, nor had the patience, to cajole him out of his pout.

"Please excuse me, Uncle Gordon. I promised Da I'd fetch his midday meal. He didn't eat much breakfast and is quite famished."

Slight exaggeration there, but he must eat. He'd grown far too thin in recent months.

"Lydia, ye do ken I want to help ye in any way I can, didna ye?" Uncle Gordon touched her shoulder, his eyes filled with compassion.

His concern moved her, and she softened minutely.

"Ye've born much, and a woman be fragile. Your delicate constitution isnae made to carry such heavy burdens."

And there went her pathetically short-lived empathy. "I assure you, I'm neither fragile nor delicate, Uncle."

He bristled, and quickly masked irritation flickered in his eyes before he schooled his angular features. "I'm nae a fool, Lydia. I ken Uncle be ailin', has been fer a wee while. Time he named a successor, but with yer brothers dead . . ."

Chapter 2

Lydia stifled the vulgar retort thrumming against her teeth. She didn't typically curse or have a hot temper, but at this moment, unleashing her tongue sorely tempted.

Uncle Gordon's broad hint hung suspended, awkwardly filling the silence. He'd always coveted the chief's position, but even as the laird's brother-in-law and steward, he didn't stand a clooty dumpling's chance in the soldiers' barracks at mealtime of an appointment to the position.

The men didn't respect him.

Never had, and since coming to live at the Keep fifteen years ago, he'd done nothing to remedy their ambivalence.

In fact, they'd resented his promotion to steward four years ago, and had made no bones about their objection to Da elevating him to war chief.

Which was one of the reasons the clan, yet, lacked one.

That, and none of the clansmen possessed the skills Da demanded to train his men and defend the Keep. With an ailing laird, the situation left Tornbury entirely too vulnerable.

Slender, actually thin to the point of scrawniness, Gordon didn't wrestle, couldn't wield a sword well, and those deficits, combined with his volatile temperament, added substance to the clan members' opposition.

"Thank you for your concern and your offer of help. I'm sure when Da feels the time's right, he'll announce his successor."

Da hadn't confided his intent to name her laird with anyone, and it wasn't her place to do so. From the mutterings she'd overheard, some mightn't be altogether keen about the selection, her uncle included.

Da had probably heard them too, or at least heard of them.

True, Scotswomen had carried the title before her, but Farnsworth clan hadn't. She'd be the first *The Lady Tornbury Fortress*, and that troubled Lydia.

Gordon's drivel about a woman's delicate constitution also rubbed more than a little. She could out-ride, out-swim, and even with her eyes closed, out-perform her spindly uncle with a bow and arrow. And although not a large woman, she could out-eat and out-drink him as well.

She eyed his hanging coat. Probably could out-arm wrestle him too, if permitted to compete.

Maddening, how many things men prohibited women from doing. That would change when she became laird, at least as much as the law allowed.

"Now, if you'll please excuse me, I really must see to Da's meal."

"Of course." After a slight dip of his head, Gordon disappeared back into the study.

He must've forgotten something.

A few minutes later, carrying the tray, Lydia made the return trip through the polished walnut-paneled corridor. Unlike the stone floors at Craiglocky Keep, the colorful oriental red and blue runner beneath her slippers muted her footsteps.

Candle flames danced in the wall sconces as she passed, and glancing upward she met the black, sightless eyes of a dour-faced, bearded ancestor.

Savage fellow, her three times great-uncle Donell had been. Or so family legend held. He'd always given her the shivers too.

Not as much as the suits of armor displayed at Craiglocky Keep, however.

A medieval stone castle, Craiglocky was far older and in some ways grander than Tornbury. Colder, too, than the E-shaped manor house her ancestors had called home for five generations. Tornbury possessed a cozy warmth she'd never found in any of the opulent mansions she'd visited during her single London Season.

Where she'd met Flynn, the Earl of Luxmoore.

No, he was the Marquise of Bretheridge now. And he was married.

Blissfully so.

Lydia was glad for him. Truly, she was. He was an honorable, decent man.

Flynn had never looked upon her with the same absolute adoration he'd shown his wife, and she wouldn't begrudge him his happiness. Even if it meant he'd never be hers, and she'd never know the same joy.

"Miss Lydia." McGibbons, the butler, hurried along the corridor, his haste emphasizing his pronounced limp.

Foot poised atop the bottom riser, Lydia paused. "Yes?"

"An invitation arrived. Should I place it in the study, or do ye want to deliver it directly to the laird? I ken he prefers to read his correspondence promptly." McGibbons held up a creamy, scarlet-ribboned parchment bearing the McTavish seal.

An event at Craiglocky this time of year? How unusual.

"Thank you, McGibbons. I'll take it. I have his midday meal, anyway. Just place it on the tray, beneath the serviette." Gordon snooped, and Da ought to know the contents before her uncle.

After doing so, McGibbons folded his hands before him and peered at her with his one remaining pale blue eye, the other having been lost in a long-ago battle and now covered with a patch. "How be our chief, if'n ye dinna mind me askin'?"

Da's closest chum, McGibbons had come to work as Tornbury's butler the same year Da had become laird. Hard to believe the now entirely proper servant had ever cavorted and whooped his way across the Highlands with her rapscallion father.

"Of course, I don't mind. I'm sure it will be no surprise to you, he's determined to be up and resume his duties."

Probably to his health's detriment.

Bernard wound his way around Lydia's lower foot. His loud rumbles as he rubbed his scent on her ankle vibrated his lean form.

McGibbon's face broke into a lopsided grin. "Aye, that sounds like Bailoch." His attention fell to the tray once more. "Do ye wish me to carry the tray fer ye?"

"No, it's not heavy, but thank you." Such devotion and loyalty her father had earned. How could she possibly replace him? How could anyone? "Could you please find Esme, and tell her that I'll have to postpone her archery lesson until tomorrow?"

"At once, miss." He scooped Bernard into his arms. "I'll also take this fellow to the kitchen before he trips ye. Och, and miss, Sheba whelped eight healthy pups this mornin'."

"Da will be so pleased." Da had a particular fondness for Border collies, especially Sheba. He'd never roam the moors with her trotting at his heels again.

Lost in grim ruminations, Lydia swiftly arrived at Da's chamber then scowled at the partially cracked doorway. He'd better not have taken it upon himself to ignore the doctor's orders and leave his bed.

Obstinate fool.

She *would* tie him to the posts.

Nudging the door open further, Lydia marched inside.

"Da—" She faltered to an unsteady stop.

Her gaze vacillated between her father propped against his pillows and Gordon looming beside the bed.

"Uncle Gordon. I didn't know you were here. Doctor Wedderburn wants Da to rest."

Gordon offered a sheepish grin and his gaze shifted away. "I wanted to see fer myself how Uncle Bailoch be, and I had somethin' I needed to discuss with him."

"Something urgent? Enough to disturb his rest?" Gordon's measure of urgency typically proved much different than Lydia's. He sent for the doctor if he had a corn or a blister.

"Nae, nothin' like that." He waved his hand and had the grace to look abashed while delivering an apologetic smile that didn't quite reach his eyes.

Glancing into Da's sitting room, she squinted then frowned. The small servant's door stood slightly ajar. Only Da's man ever used it, and rarely at that.

"You thought it necessary to use the domestic's access? Why?" Unfamiliar irritation pricked her.

At this rate, she'd be a harpy by her first-and-twentieth birthday.

Did he think she'd lied earlier? Whatever he'd needed to discuss might have waited a day or two, and his sneaking in the servant's entrance made no sense.

Looking properly contrite, he offered a closed-mouth smile. "I didna want to knock and wake Uncle if'n he slept, so I thought I'd use the staff door."

Suspicion niggled, but Uncle Gordon's excuse was feasible, if somewhat shallow.

"I assured Gordon, I'll be fine as a fiddle tomorrow." Da gave her a telling look before happiness wreathed his face and he sniffed, scooting back into the rumpled pillows. "Och, the soup smells delicious."

Lydia eyed the disheveled bedding. What had he done whilst she'd been below? Wrestled boars?

"Uncle Bailoch might ride with me to the village on the

morrow, Lydia." Gordon rested a shoulder against the bed poster and folded his arms.

A man who could barely sit upright in bed—supported by pillows, no less—wasn't soon gadding about atop a horse.

To keep from snapping at Uncle Gordon and revealing just how weak Da was, Lydia bit her tongue and set the tray on a small oval table near the roaring hearth. The movement jostled the contents and the invitation's corner poked out from beneath the serviette.

After pushing her hair behind a shoulder, she lifted the parchment. "An invitation has arrived from Craiglocky. Naturally, we'll send our regrets."

"Nae so fast." Da extended his hand, his expression animated. His thick, coppery hair stood on end, giving him a somewhat demented appearance.

What *had* he been doing while she'd been below?

"Let me see it, lass." He donned his spectacles, the lenses magnifying his eyes. "I've been contemplatin' a reason to send ye to speak with the McTavish on me behalf."

"Uncle Bailoch, really, isnae that a duty fer yer steward?" Gordon helped himself to an oat roll, earning him a censured look from Lydia as he took a large bite.

"That's for Da. If you're hungry, I'm sure Anice would be happy to prepare you something to hold you over until dinner." Lydia handed Da the crisp parchment then urged him to lean forward before placing another pillow behind him.

She flinched upon brushing his bony shoulder.

So horribly thin.

Uncle Gordon swallowed his mouthful. "Besides, Lydia be in mournin', so attendin' affairs widnae be proper. I'd be happy to take any message ye have to Ewan McTavish."

His lenses balanced on the tip of his nose, Da glanced up from reading the invitation. "Dinna tell me protocol, son. Did ye forget yer also in mournin'?"

Hand at his mouth, Gordon faltered. "Nae, I just thought it be more fittin' fer me to go in yer stead than a woman."

More of his *women being inferior* hogwash again.

Gordon finished the roll and slid a hungry glance at the remaining two.

I don't think so.

Lydia retrieved the tray and then in four strides reached the bed. She waited for Da to finish perusing the invitation, and when he'd refolded the paper, removed his spectacles, and smiled at her, she placed the tray onto his lap.

"Lydia, order yerself and Esme new gowns, fallalls, fripperies, slippers, anythin' ye need. Ye'll be attendin' the McTavish's week-long Valentine house party." He winked conspiratorially as he dipped his spoon into the soup. "There be a ball, too. Bound to be a few eligible chaps in attendance. Ye can look fer a husband while yer there."

Chapter 3

Lydia snapped her gaping mouth shut. She should've tossed the invitation in the fire when she had the chance.

Da scooped a mouthful of soup then closed his eyes and sighed. "Nae finer cook than our Anice."

"Da, Esme and I cannot possibly attend. Why, the weather alone is worrisome, but Mum's only been gone three months. What would people say?"

Besides, she wanted to spend every precious moment she could with him, and she'd imposed upon the McTavishes too much already.

"I agree, Uncle. Most imprudent."

Gordon sank into a high-backed chair. Crossing his thin legs, he cupped the arms with fingertips sporting overly-long nails and stared covetously at Da's luncheon.

Before taking another sip of soup, Da's attention brushed over Uncle Gordon.

"She nae be attendin' to have a grand time, me boy."

Resentment flared Uncle Gordon's nostrils and whitened his mouth. He resented any inference to his lack of maturity.

Da's keen gaze rested on her, and a proud smile lit his wan face. "Ye'll be performin' yer first task as me potential successor, lass."

~ ~ ~

Ribald laughter echoed off the lichen and moss covered crags as Alasdair McTavish led the small hunting party the last stretch toward Craiglocky Keep.

Though windy, bitingly cold for February, and ominous, pregnant clouds shrouded the twilight sky, the weather had mercifully held.

And there'd be fresh venison for the house party as well as a stiff dram of whisky to reward his cold, tired men. He might enjoy his drink in his eagerly anticipated bath. Might also snatch some of those special salts Seonaid recommended for muscle aches, as long as no one knew.

Couldn't have his fellow Scots thinking he'd become a soft, pasty-skinned Sassenach.

Kicking Errol's sides, he urged the huge gray into a trot and grinned at his twin, Gregor. "Canna keep up with me, ye great gollumpus?"

"Aye, I can, brother, and I'll beat ye to the Keep too, ye dotty old crone."

Gregor's horse lunged forward, and Alasdair threw back his head, releasing a *whoop* as he charged after.

Their hooves churning the sodden ground, the horses tore down the road, bordered by Scots pine on one side and plunging cliffs leading to jagged rocks and boulder outcrops on the other.

Laughing and bent low in his saddle, Alasdair inched past his twin.

"Bloody hell." Gregor's blue-gray eyes widened and alarm streaked across his features. He pointed, his expression grim. "Look."

Alasdair whipped around just in time to see a coach and four farther along the road.

Having lost a wheel, it tilted at a precarious angle before spilling onto its side and launching the coachman from his perch. The conveyance's momentum yanked the rear horses off their feet and also sent the postilion astride the lead mount hurtling to the soggy ground.

Terrified shrieks, neighs, and hoarse oaths filled the air.

The lone horseman accompanying the vehicle reined sharply around before thundering back toward the carriage. Amid the sharp crack of wood and glass shattering, the vehicle rammed into a cottage-sized boulder a few feet off the trail.

Thank God, else the entire conveyance and team would've plummeted over the steep cliff.

Certain death for the passengers and the horses.

As the other clansmen rounded the bend, Alasdair yelled over his shoulder and gestured. "A coach has tumbled off the road."

This near the Keep, the occupants were likely guests for Craiglocky's house party. He squinted, attempting to make out the coat of arms on the coach's black side.

Impossible given the conveyance's perilous angle.

The other Highlanders immediately surged forward and in moments, the Scots arrived at the chaotic scene.

The downed horses had managed to gain their feet, and the equine quartet stood lathered and trembling, but seemingly unharmed.

A pair of good-sized trunks had tumbled onto the road— one sporting a jagged crack—and the splintered wheel's debris lay scattered in all directions.

The coachman moaned and cradled his shoulder while the postilion, despite the blood running down his face, attempted to climb atop the sideways coach.

Hushed, terrified feminine sobbing echoed from within the vehicle.

Cursing, the tall rider accompanying the coach slid from his horse. But rather than assist either of the injured men or the passengers, like a petulant child, he swore and kicked at a piece of wheel across the road.

"Guid-damned, incompetent smithy. I be havin' his head. I told him to check the wheels, myself. Farnsworth will be furious."

Farnsworth?

Alasdair's stomach plummeted to his mud-caked boots, and he speared the carriage a desperate glance. Was Lydia Farnsworth a passenger?

Since Searón Neal, no other woman except Lydia had breached his guarded heart—a secret he protected as fiercely as he did his clan.

The man swore again and pushed his hat higher on his forehead.

Gordon Ross.

No surprise that maggot concerned himself with cursing the blacksmith instead of helping the injured.

Alasdair sprinted toward the wrecked vehicle. "Be yer niece inside?"

His expression leery, Ross jerked off his plaid tam and gave a short nod. "Aye."

Why the hell hadn't Farnsworth sent other outriders along? That mewling twit Ross couldn't stand upright against a strong breeze. What if they'd been set upon by rogues or highwaymen?

"McLeon, ye help me with the travelers. Gregor and Taggart, see to the hurt men, and McKinnely, ride to the Keep. We'll need a wagon for the luggage and anyone who's too hurt to ride. Take the stags with ye. Burness, make haste to Craigcutty and collect Doctor Paterson."

Bring the doctor here, or should Doctor Paterson make straight for Craiglocky?

Unless the injuries were life-threatening, Gregor could treat them. Besides, the Keep lay less than three miles away.

"Have the doctor meet us at the castle." Alasdair climbed onto the coach.

Giving a terse jerk of his head, McKinnely accepted the venison-laden mount's reins.

Before he and Burness had galloped more than a few yards, the sulky clouds chose to release their burden, and icy raindrops pelted Alasdair as he wrenched open the crested door. Peering into the bottle green interior, he braced himself for what he might see.

The faint aroma of wild roses and spice wafted upward, mixing with dank earth and sweaty horses.

Huddled at the shadowy bottom, her bonnet askew and a nasty lump discoloring her forehead, Lydia Farnsworth cradled a weeping woman.

"Ah, I thought I heard your voice, Alasdair. I must confess to being greatly relieved."

She graced him with a breathtaking smile, a droplet of blood trickling from her sweet mouth's corner. "As you can see," she swept her hand to indicate the toppled coach, "we're in a bit of a pickle."

Chapter 4

The ground trembled with the thunder of approaching riders. Recognizing Alasdair McTavish's rumbling brogue, immediate calm beset Lydia, and she nearly wept with relief.

He was no stranger to mayhem, and he'd know just what to do. Unlike Uncle Gordon, loudly railing about the blacksmith's stupidity instead of rushing to help her and Esme.

A petulant wind blasted giant, chilly raindrops into the door's opening, and Esme shivered.

Lydia tightened her embrace, setting her teeth against the tremors also racking her.

"A pickle, lass?" A honey blond eyebrow launched skyward above his twinkling bluish eyes, and his strong mouth hitched into a practiced grin. "I'd say yer in a mite more trouble than that. But I've seen ye in worse."

He had. Just once.

Lydia glanced at her cousin's reddish-blonde head as she softly wept against Lydia's bosom. "This is my cousin, Esme Adams. Her leg is hurt, but I don't know how badly. And I suspect she has other injuries too."

Having the starch scared out of their chemises didn't help either. Lydia's heart still beat frantically. She'd believed she was about to die a terrifyingly, painful death.

"And yerself, Miss Farnsworth?" Alasdair leaned farther into the interior, his broad forehead, framed by the same golden hair as his eyebrows, wrinkled in concern as he assessed her. His unique manly scent, combined with sweat and leather, drifted into the opening. "Are ye hurt?"

"I think I'm fine. A few cuts and bruises, but nothing pains me terribly. Except my head aches like a tippler's the morn after Hogmanay." Lydia touched the throbbing above at her hairline. She'd smacked the coach's side when it piled over, and truth to tell, she couldn't say which was worse— the waves of dizziness or the nausea assailing her.

She swallowed and shut her eyes for an instant.

Lord, she thought for certain they'd perish, and all she could think of was what her death would do to Da.

What it would mean for the clan.

Who would be laird?

Alasdair shifted his position, and angled lower. "The last time I saw ye, Miss Farnsworth, ye'd dispensed of three scurvy Blackhalls." He switched his attention to Esme. "Never seen a more gifted archer, man or woman. Her shootin' was somethin' to behold, I tell ye."

Warmth infused Lydia at his praise, even though she'd tried to block that day from her mind.

Attacked by rogue Scots, she'd done what needed to be done. Nevertheless, she couldn't summon a morsel of pride for her actions. No one should be proud or boastful of killing another human.

"Lydia, you killed *three* men?" Shock rounded Esme's treacle-brown eyes and left her delicate jaw slack.

"She did indeed. Her bravery saved lives that day." The admiration in Alasdair's gaze launched another rush of scouring heat up Lydia's cheeks.

"My side hurts," Esme whispered, pressing a palm to her ribs.

"Aye, lass," Alasdair assured her. "We'll be gettin' ye out of there, straightaway."

The coach wobbled again, and another giant Scot appeared at the opening—one Lydia had seen at Craiglocky but had never spoken to.

"I be Douglas McLeon, ladies." He gave them a rakish grin. "I didna ken I'd be privileged with rescuin' fair damsels today."

As dark as Alasdair was fair, the handsome Highlander winked.

"Likely a *brounie* caught sight of ye two bonnie lasses, and he be so captivated, the wee fellow risked bein' seen in the daylight and tried to climb inside the coach. Broke the wheel right off in his eagerness, he did."

Esme raised her head and smiled feebly. "Plumb rotten manners if you ask me."

"Och, he be smitten, so ye canna blame him, lass." Mr. McLeon winked and grinned again.

Charming behemoth.

And from Esme's dazed countenance, she was fast on her way to succumbing to his charm. Either that or she'd suffered a far more severe blow to her head than Lydia realized.

"McLeon, enough of yer twaddle. One of us needs to climb inside and lift the women out." Alasdair straightened and curtly motioned with his hand. "Ross and Taggart. Get over here. We need yer help."

A few moments later, amidst Esme's soft cries, the men's smothered oaths, and Lydia's tattered dignity—her bosom had been brushed and her leg exposed to her knee—the women had been safely extricated.

She wanted to throw her arms around Alasdair's neck and give into the urge to cry and be comforted by the gentle man, but Uncle Gordon would tell Da her weakness.

Lairds didn't cry.

Ladies scared spitless do. Even ones determined to be as strong as men.

She'd never really believed in curses before, but after this . . .? No family had a streak of bad luck this long.

Taking a deep breath, she attempted to straighten her bonnet and surveyed the scene. One of the men had unhitched the team, and someone else had moved their trunks to the roadside. The other luggage had been removed, too, and was now stacked neatly beside the crippled coach.

Gregor tended Esme, while George, the postilion, held a reddened cloth to his head.

"Miss Farnsworth." The coachman, his face pale as death, limped her way, one hand wrapped protectively around his upper arm. He scowled at the wrecked carriage before meeting her gaze. "Forgive me, but there was nothin' I could do. The wheel shouldnae have shattered like that."

He swayed and Alasdair steadied him. "Sit down, mon. There be no shame in restin'. Yer shoulder be dislocated."

He managed a grateful smile as Alasdair eased him to the ground.

What a woeful and filthy lot would present themselves at Craiglocky.

Lydia almost smiled at the mental image of the bedraggled, mud-caked, injured entourage's arrival, more closely resembling gypsies than house guests.

Driving rain deluged the miserable travelers, and she hugged her shoulders and clenched her chattering teeth. Couldn't the storm have held off another hour? To her pounding head, the pattering raindrops echoed like miniature explosions.

The coachman peered up at her, worry lining his haggard face. "Be ye and Miss Adams all right?"

"We'll be fine, and I don't blame you at all. I'm just grateful none of us is hurt worse than we are." Lydia quirked her mouth upward on one side, and pain instantly lanced her face. Salty warmth trickled from her mouth, and she dabbed where it stung worse. Her fingertips came away tinted red. What a sight she must be.

Where was her reticule? She needed her handkerchief.

Drat it all. Had she left it in the coach? It also contained Da's letter to Ewan McTavish, Laird of Craiglochy.

She touched Alasdair's arm. "I'm sorry, but I think I left my reticule in the coach. There's an important epistle inside for your laird."

Uncle Gordon's eyes narrowed. "I'll fetch it."

No.

Lydia clenched Alasdair's forearm in silent entreaty.

"Nae, we'd have to lift yer skinny arse out too. Why dinna ye make yerself useful and help with the horses?" He pushed past Gordon who turned an accusing stare on Lydia.

She lifted her chin.

Da had commissioned her with this task, and Uncle Gordon wasn't going to jack the mission. He'd been peevish and distant since Da announced his intention to possibly name her laird.

More than once, she'd caught Gordon staring at her with an odd expression on his face. Part envy, part irritation, and something which appeared disturbingly like cunningness. Gone was the concerned uncle, and the stranger in his place unnerved her.

After examining Esme, Gregor stood and pushed sodden blond strands off his forehead. "The lass got pummeled mightily, but nothin' be broken. She'll be sore for a few days though."

"I hope nae too sore to grant a humble Highlander a dance at the ball." McLeon extended a hand and helped her to stand.

Despite the pouring rain and her obvious pain, Esme blushed and smiled. "If it's permissible."

He cocked his head. "Yer American?"

Her expression guarded, Esme nodded. "Yes, I was born in Salem."

"*Hmph.*" His grunt could be taken as displeasure or approval.

Confusion flitted across Esme's bruised face, and she slid Lydia a questioning glance.

She lifted a shoulder to indicate she hadn't a clue what caused McLeon's stilted behavior.

In the distance, a wagon accompanied by several riders barreled in their direction.

"Here ye be." Alasdair appeared by Lydia's side and passed her the reticule. He nodded toward those approaching. "I suppose I should've asked fer a coach too, except I nae be certain of yer condition when I sent the men fer help."

Lydia smiled as she slipped the bag's cords over her wrist. "The Keep isn't far. We should manage it."

"I'm afraid ye ladies will have to ride before us. We'll make better time, and this tempest has only begun to release her fury." He shot a wary glance skyward indicating the churlish, steely clouds. "Besides, neither of yer drivers is capable of sittin' a horse, and ye've so much luggage, there isnae room for ye in the cart. Are ye sure ye only meant to stay a week?"

Humor crinkled the corners of his blue eyes.

Da had insisted on a wardrobe worthy of a British lady, though why Scots always felt they had to prove their worth to the English peeved a mite.

"Aye. Atop a horse will do." She didn't relish a bone-jarring journey in the wagon bed in any event.

In short order, the luggage was loaded and the postilion and coachman settled somewhat comfortably in the wagon beneath a blanket and tarpaulin.

"We'll send a crew to repair the wheel and retrieve the coach." Alasdair mounted his impressive horse. "Miss Farnsworth, I'd be pleased if ye'd ride with me."

She'd be pleased too.

Well, either him or Gregor. Amongst the men, she knew those two the best.

"I'll take Miss Adams," McLeon quickly volunteered, earning him a teasing grin from Gregor and another of Uncle Gordon's habitual scowls.

He didn't volunteer to take either woman, however.

Color lined Esme's face again.

Hmm, was a romance blooming between her and McLeon already? Esme could do far worse than the burly Scot, but she intended to return to America once she became of age. She'd a vast estate and a considerable fortune at her disposal.

Perhaps a word with her later was in order. At seventeen, Esme was naive and impressionable, and though Mr. McLeon seemed like a decent enough chap, Lydia didn't see him scampering off to Massachusetts, trading his trews for buckskins, or his whisky for ale.

Gregor helped the women onto their respective horses, and then wearing a silly grin and shaking his head, leapt into his saddle. "Seems to me, somethin' more than a storm be brewin', bairn brother."

"Ye only beat me into this world by four minutes, and that be because ye elbowed yer way out first, ye codshead." Alasdair wrapped one oak-like arm around Lydia's waist and clicked his tongue. "It be the only thin' ye've ever done first."

Gregor chuckled and after yanking his tam lower, trotted his horse away.

Lydia clutched the huge gray's mane as the animal heeded his master's kick to his sides. Spine straight, she tried to keep from sinking into Alasdair with each gentle bump of the horse's gait.

"Be at ease, Lydia. Yer goin' to be sore from bein' tossed around in the coach, and ye dinna need to add overworked muscles to yer discomfort."

Her muscles did, indeed, object to the awkward posture.

He leaned down and whispered in her ear, sending a most inappropriate, but utterly delicious, tremor coursing through her. "I promise I'll be a gentleman."

Most disappointing.

At the unprompted thought, she lurched straight up.

"Relax." Alasdair pressed her against him.

Sighing, she slouched against his chest's hard, wide planes and closed her eyes. For these few moments, she'd let someone else take care of her, pretend that her whole life hadn't been upended. That if she hadn't already given her heart to another, this enormous, kind, and considerate man might have tempted her to set her cap for him.

"I'm surprised ye are attendin' the house party, Lydia. Especially accompanied only by Ross. Yer the first guest to arrive, too."

"Originally, two other clansmen were assigned to accompany us, but just as we were to leave, Uncle Gordon got word of an issue that needed immediate attention. He sent the men to oversee the situation." She snorted and snuggled a mite nearer to escape the pelting rain and intrusive wind. "He's always smugly confident he can handle everything, and the journey between Tornbury and Craiglocky isn't terribly long. Plus the road is well-traveled."

"That be true, but Ross nae be exactly a robust, brave sort."

A cowardly, knock-kneed, craven better described her uncle.

"I suppose I should've insisted on waiting for a new guard, but I didn't want Da to catch wind and worry. I have business with McTavish of Craiglocky and wanted to arrive before the other guests." Even to her ears, she sounded utterly worn out.

Alasdair nudged her head with his chin. "I heard about yer mother. Ye've suffered much of late, lass."

"Yes, and I fear there's more grief to come. That's my real purpose for journeying here." She hadn't meant to tell him that yet. Certainly not looking like a half-drowned puppy, and amid an ugly winter storm.

"Humph." He made the rough sound in the back of his throat. "Can I help?"

Lydia turned her head, meeting his gentle gaze. "Yes. You can agree to return with me to Tornbury and act as our war chief."

Chapter 5

Alasdair choked on a strangled curse.

Tornbury's situation was that precarious then?

Of any number of things Lydia might have requested, he wouldn't have ever guessed she'd ask him to return to Tornbury Fortress with her.

And certainly not as the acting war chief.

Farnsworth must be truly desperate, or something else went on that he'd not revealed to his daughter.

With the deaths of her brothers and mother, and having been the target of a deranged Scot's intent on abducting Lydia to acquire the gold discovered on Tornbury's lands, she'd endured enough already.

Devil take it and dance a hellish jig.

Alasdair silently ground his teeth. He'd wager his coveted whisky, Cousin Ewan would agree to the request. At least temporarily.

Had Farnsworth specifically asked for Alasdair?

Probably.

As Craiglocky's war chief's son, he possessed the skill and knowledge to train the allied tribe, and he boasted unusual size and strength for a Scot. So did his twin, but as a gifted healer, Gregor was needed at the Keep, unlike the more dispensable Alasdair.

Exceeding six feet herself, Mother's Norse heritage had contributed to his and Gregor's immenseness.

Alasdair skewed his mouth sideways. Rather convenient when engaged in hand-to-hand combat or other tests of power. Few men, except perhaps McLeon and a handful of others, could hold their own against him and his brother.

Alasdair dropped his focus to the petite, exhausted bundle slumped in his arms.

Lydia shivered, and he drew her closer, offering her his body's warmth. He dared imagine the delicate ribs he cradled beneath her plaid mantle and traveling costume, as well as the slope of her waist and hips and the curves of her small breasts.

Fierce protectiveness gripped him.

She made a contented noise and snuggled nearer, murmuring drowsily, "I fear, I'm half frozen."

No wonder either, since angry sleet now mixed with the unrelenting rain. "Aye, my toes be complainin' too, but we'll be at the Keep soon enough, lass."

He'd never met a more courageous woman, or one he admired more. Yet, he couldn't do a hellfired thing about his attraction. Just as well since he knew she'd been desperately in love with Bretheridge before the marquis threw her over.

The months Lydia had lived at Craiglocky last fall had extracted a toll on Alasdair's studiously built buffers, and he didn't relish the idea of suffering more of the same sense-battering assault if he resided at Tornbury.

Precisely how long would he be expected to stay and train the Farnsworth clan members?

He screwed his face into a frown.

When had her brothers and Lundy drowned?

Five—no, six months ago?

Hell, Tornbury's men had really gone half a year without regular training? With daily practice, make that two sessions, morn and afternoon, it would take that long to bring the undisciplined men up to battle readiness once more.

And living with Lydia all that time?

God help him.

And it wasn't as if he could avail himself of willing females at Tornbury. It seemed a betrayal of her in some perverse way. Besides, he'd also heard Farnsworth strictly forbid shagging the servants.

Mulling over Lydia's impossible request, he flexed his back. True, he'd could sleep in the barracks. Still, he'd have to report to Farnsworth regularly. Why hadn't the laird just sent Ewan a letter rather than require Lydia deliver the message?

She shifted restlessly, and her sweet fragrance billowed upward, tormenting him. Something musky and floral, blended with a spice he couldn't quite name, but which tantalized unmercifully.

He sniffed lightly, and his groin pulled in response.

Blast, he couldn't even adjust his position to relieve the pressure. Pray God Lydia couldn't feel the telling lump beneath her taut buttocks.

Nae.

He bloody well wasn't putting himself in the torturous position of having her nearby for months. Farnsworth would have to find another man to train his men. Surely there must be a Scot or two amongst his clan capable of the task.

Alasdair's attention gravitated to Ross hunkered in his saddle, still occasionally grumbling about the blacksmith's ineptitude.

Not him. Never.

McLeon could do it though.

Alasdair sought out the object of his ruminations.

A bemused expression on his craggy face, McLeon tenderly embraced Miss Adams. Indeed, the perfect solution.

He might suggest the notion to Ewan and give McLeon a little nudge in the romance department too.

A guffaw bubbled up Alasdair's throat.

Ye gods. Now he played Cupid?

He, who'd failed so miserably at being a husband, his wife had left him after a humiliatingly short time?

At once a mixture of relief and remorseful longing assailed him. Relief Searón hadn't stayed and disrupted his life further, and yearning he'd never know a woman's—a wife's—love.

Make up yer bloody mind.

His thoughts swung back and forth like a flag in a storm.

Ye ken what would happen if ye went to Tornbury.

Aye, he'd end up a smitten buffoon. Again.

Besides, he'd been discontent with his lot, hankered for a change, and had been on the verge of announcing his departure from the clan for a spell. Somewhere out of Scotland. Perhaps America or Rome. Wasn't that where wrestling—his favorite pastime besides whisky and wenches—originated?

Damned poor luck to discover his dead heart could still feel. He'd preferred enjoying what a woman's soft curves offered in the way of comfort and physical release without the entanglement of emotions.

As a young, gullible lad of nineteen, he'd indulged his softer sentiments and stupidly married a tailwag, though he hadn't known her whorish ways at the time.

Searón's desertion after two scant months of marriage, scarcely long enough to conceive the child she brutally aborted when she decided she didn't want to be a wife and mother after all, had left him a scarred and bitter man.

For the past eight years, his carefree manner and bawdy humor hid the burbling woundedness he'd buried. But he'd forbidden anyone to so much as mention Searón's name or his disastrous nuptials—in and out of his presence.

The few who knew of his impulsive marriage in Edinburgh remained loyally tight-lipped.

So, now he found himself with a tempting armful; a

brave, steadfast woman whose spirit equaled his own. But she loved another.

Fate, most definitely, was a malevolent, coldhearted bitch.

In the distance, Craiglocky Keep rose majestically against the steely, foreboding horizon. He had lived his entire life there, hadn't even gone off to university. God knew he loved the place and her people, but for months now, a restlessness had pricked him.

Actually, since Lydia had departed for Tornbury months ago.

Savoring the last few moments with her enfolded in his embrace, something he wasn't likely to be gifted again, he redirected his musings.

"How fares yer father, Lydia?"

Her sudden tenseness answered as surely as if she'd shouted the news. Tilting her head, her pain-filled greenish gaze roved his face, lingering a jot too long on his mouth.

"Not well." Lips pursed, she exhaled softly but audibly. "However, I've given my word not to speak of it. Even Gordon doesn't know, and I must beg you to keep my confidence."

"Aye, lass. I winna breathe a word."

Though, little good it would do.

Rumors regarding Farnsworth's deteriorating health had reached Craiglocky weeks ago, and Alasdair had worried for Lydia, particularly given the clan unrest of a few months prior. If the gossip proved true, her father hadn't long for this world.

She'd soon be alone with no one to protect or advise her.

Ross didn't count any more than a midge in that regard.

Her focus gravitated back to Alasdair's lips before she slanted a sideways look at her uncle. "Uncle Gordon is none too pleased Da may name me laird. This," she made a little circle in the air, "asking you to oversee our warfare training, is my first official task. I cannot fail."

Jesus.

How could Alasdair say nae?

How could he say aye?

He couldn't. So he did neither.

Instead, as the horses and wagon clattered across the drawbridge, he scrambled for a distraction.

"Have ye heard Seonaid be betrothed?" Another love match for a Craiglocky Keep resident. So far, he was the only sot whose nuptial had ended disastrously.

Lydia twisted to stare at him, her battered face wreathed in a huge smile. She winced and touched her swollen lower lip. "I didn't know. I'm thrilled for her. Who's the fortunate man?"

Alasdair chuckled and released her waist long enough to wipe a strand of her wet hair off his cheek. "Monsieur le baron de Devaux-Rousset."

Her mouth dropped open, and her lush lashes fluttered a few times as she digested the information.

"No? Truly? I quite thought they loathed each other." Brow elevated and skepticism scrunching her pert nose, she poked his chest. "You're teasing me. Who is he really?"

Though wholly inappropriate, he hugged her to him for a fraction, and bending his neck, whispered in her ear. "I'm nae teasin' ye. They'll announce their betrothal at the Valentine ball. It's almost enough to make me believe in that inane, fools' adage, *love conquers all.*"

"My, for someone who's never been in love you sound most cynical." Her countenance grew solemn, and she presented her profile. "There's something to be said for being spared that heartache."

Despondency resonated in her now husky voice as if she struggled against tears, and Alasdair wanted to kick himself in the arse for his thoughtlessness. She still wasn't over Bretheridge, and why the knowledge lay heavily in his gut, like tainted meat, he didn't know.

Hard to be jealous of a chap so confounded likeable. Which chafed Alasdair's arse all the more.

Lydia had a valid point, nevertheless.

He'd suspected from the beginning Searón didn't love him as much as he cherished her, but his young, pompous, *randy* self had been convinced that in time, his wife would grow to love him. All he had to do was shower her with affection and gifts—cater to her needs.

He'd been bloody damned wrong.

His pride still stung at moments like this when his stupidity—superior and taunting—glared him straight in the face.

Ten minutes later, the weary travelers entered the Keep. The injured men and exhausted ladies were promptly hustled off to their bedchambers with promises of a visit from Doctor Paterson, hot baths, and dinner trays.

Lydia had entrusted the letter for Ewan into Alasdair's keeping. "Please convey this to the laird. Tell him I'll seek an audience in the morning when I'm presentable and my head doesn't ache quite so unbearably."

"Aye lass. I'll see it delivered fer ye."

She'd disappeared up the stairs, and yet, he remained staring at the cold stones where moments before she'd stood exhausted and shivering. And never looking lovelier.

Think of something else.

Giving himself a mental shake, he heaved a sigh and pivoted toward the great hall. A much-anticipated long soak and a leisurely bottle awaited Alasdair as soon as he'd reported to Ewan.

"You've had quite an adventuresome day, and a successful hunt too." Tankard raised, Ewan beckoned him to the great hall's trestle table. "I saw the stags earlier. They're fat as hogs this year."

"Aye, they be good eatin'." After arching his back in a welcome stretch, Alasdair accepted the ale-filled tankard Ewan offered then jerked his head toward the hall's entrance. "Lydia be damned lucky to have survived the coach overturnin'. If the accident occurred a few feet in either direction, the lot would've plunged to their deaths."

All except Ross.

Hooking an ankle across his knee, Ewan scrunched his forehead and toyed with the mug's handle. "I'm surprised to see anyone from Tornbury, actually. Naturally, Mother insisted they be invited, but so soon after Lady Tornbury's death?" He leveled Alasdair a sidelong glance. "Though I suspect you don't mind Lydia's arrival in the least."

What exactly did he imply? Did he suspect Alasdair's interest in Lydia? *Better put him off that trail.* "Nae more than any other guest to Craiglocky."

Ewan cocked his head and, eyes narrowed, made a pretense of thoroughly scrutinizing Alasdair.

Alasdair returned his perusal with a bland stare. Ewan couldn't possibly have guessed his interest in Lydia.

"You have a rather cow-eyed, woebegone, down-in-the-mouth, I've-been-kicked-in-the-ribs look about your eyes every time you glance at her, Dair. Which is whenever you can sneak a peek. About every two seconds or so. Perhaps it's time you sought a divorce—"

Alasdair's infuriated growl muffled the rest of Ewan's words. Itching to wipe the sardonic grin from his cousin's mouth, he balled his hands. "I've bade ye not to speak of *that. Ever.*"

"True." Ewan took a deep drink. "But, as your cousin and friend, I have opted to override your wishes." Once more his keen gaze skimmed Alasdair, then he shrugged.

"There's nothing wrong with opening your heart to another woman, Dair."

Rather than make an uncouth suggestion about what smallish, dark recess Ewan could shove his preposterous suggestion into, Alasdair gulped his ale, trying to cool his temper.

Ewan's knowing chuckle vaulted it upward again. Swiftly.

Deliver Lydia's letter and depart your brattish cousin's prattling advice.

That was what he'd do before drowning his feelings in Ewan's fine Scotch.

"Farnsworth dispatched Lydia to deliver this to ye." Alasdair fished the letter from inside his plaid. "They want our help. Specifically, me to return and stand in as war chief."

"What say ye?" Ross's strident voice grated from the entrance. Still wearing his sodden traveling clothes, he marched across the stone floor, his heels reverberating with each angry stomp.

Dismay flickered across a maid's pretty face at his muddy footprints trailing the stone floor she'd just swept.

Ewan leisurely raised his gaze to Alasdair's before murmuring, "I presume he wasn't privy to the letter's contents?"

Alasdair barely had time for a subtle head shake before Ross was upon them. Shoulders hunched, ready for confrontation, fury lined his face and shook his voice.

"Did ye say McTavish may be Tornbury's war chief?" He shot Alasdair a contemptuous glare. "I should've been consulted. I be steward after all. There be nae need to brin' in outsiders."

"But you aren't laird, Ross, and your chieftain has every right to make such a request, however unusual it might be. And perchance you need reminding, he doesn't need to consult you. Ever." Frost at dawn held more warmth than Ewan's mien.

Ross drew himself upright, notched his considerable nose in the air, and puffed out his thin chest, which unfortunately, made him rather resemble a starved raven. "The men winna like it." The hostile glower he sliced Alasdair would've withered a lesser man. "They winna take to ye."

Alasdair plopped his tankard down a more forcefully than he'd meant to. Ross was a prickly spur in a bruised arse. He slapped Ross on the back, grinning when the blow sent the smaller man stumbling sideways a couple of steps.

"Ach, sure they will, my friend. Ye ken everybody loves me, dinna they, Ewan?" *Except Searón. She loved cock— more.* "Besides, I haven't agreed to the task."

"Aye, but I suggest you do. The McTavishes have always sworn allegiance to the Farnsworths, and if I had a need, I've not a doubt Farnsworth would be the first to volunteer his clan's help." Ewan stood, his piercing turquoise eyes sending a clear message. "You and a dozen other McTavish clan's members will accompany Ross and Miss Farnsworth on their return to Tornbury."

Like hell I shall.

Alasdair scratched his nose while drawing in a steadying breath, and all too aware Ross watched the exchange with acute interest. Ewan only suspected Alasdair's interest in Lydia, and probably couldn't conceive why the notion of trundling off to Tornbury would disturb him.

"I'd rather nae go, Ewan." That ought to give Ross fits. "Send McNeal. He's more than capable. In fact, I'm convinced he'd enjoy it."

Ewan examined a fingernail. *Too casual, by far*. "Aye, he's a wise choice, but I must insist you go too, cousin."

God's blood.

Ewan only called him cousin when the hammer was about to drop.

Hard and heavy.

And inflexible.

Crossing his arms, Alasdair notched a brow upward in challenge and spoke very softly. "Och? And if I refuse?"

Chapter 6

Excitement shining in her eyes, Lydia straightened a burnished curl beside her right ear as she gazed at her reflection in the floor length oval mirror. An amethyst and diamond teardrop earring winked at her between the dark strands.

The set had been her mum's, and were her most cherished jewels.

Though she wore a gown of deep violet edged in ebony lace with a black gauze overskirt, she barely conformed to mourning protocol.

"Ye look just like a princess, Miss." The maid Bradana, assigned to her and Esme, beamed, justly proud of her workmanship in styling Lydia's thick, and at times, unruly hair.

Arthritic Grizelda didn't possess the same skill, but the dear had been Mum's abigail before she became Lydia's. It didn't seem right to trundle her off to a retirement cottage and retain a younger lady's maid. Not yet, anyway.

Grizelda's unfortunate tumble down the stairs the week before their intended departure for Craiglocky had almost been a relief since Lydia had already determined the journey too rugged for the aged woman.

She just hadn't told anyone else of her decision yet.

Afterward, confined to her bed with three broken toes, there'd been no question of Grizelda accompanying Lydia and Esme.

The abigail had been contentedly knitting a fifth pair of nubby stockings when Lydia bade her farewell.

Neither she nor Esme required a lady's maid, and rather than tote an untrained servant with them, they'd opted to assist one another. However, Lady McTavish insisted they permit Bradana to serve them, and rather than insult their hostess, Lydia and her cousin had agreed.

Bradana proved sweet and capable, and her sunny disposition soon had Lydia in lighter spirits. She welcomed that more than any assistance the competent maid provided.

Tonight's dinner officially launched the house party, and her stomach periodically knotted in nervous anticipation. A surprising number of guests had braved the rutty roads and shrewish weather for the four days of entertainment.

All told, an additional four-and-twenty gentlemen and six-and-thirty ladies now flitted about the austere castle.

Lydia knew none of them.

Other than in her chamber, she hadn't had a moment alone since her arrival. She'd spent the better part of the morning attempting to avoid a young whelp, who'd presented her with a rather syrupy, poorly rhymed sonnet. Not to mention an overly-cologned Frenchman who'd hinted, quite frequently and lewdly, he'd like a private *tete-a-tete*.

Other than those boors, another time she might have enjoyed the festivities and meeting new people, but worry for Da combined with her not-so-long ago losses shrouded her, dampening her spirits.

She should be home with him, but duty to the clan must come first. Always.

Did she possess the character and strength, the fortitude, to be a good chieftain? To put aside her personal wants for the benefit of the tribe?

She must, at all cost.

As a woman, she couldn't afford to show any hint of softness or weakness.

Lydia rotated her hips slightly, causing the gown's skirts to sway. A gown perfect for waltzing. For certain, dancing—

one of her favorite pastimes—was prohibited until her mourning period ended.

She hadn't indulged since that fateful ball at the Wimpleton's when Flynn learned of his father's death.

Perhaps if she kept to the shadows, she might avoid tattle and enjoy the other couples who took to the floor at the Valentine's ball in three days.

Catching her contemplative expression in the mirror, she scoffed.

Who did she think to fool? Nothing about being here was proper, except, perhaps, acting as her da's emissary.

How was he anyway?

She fretted about his health daily. However, she'd be home inside a week, and then she'd have a candid conversation about both their futures.

If he did, indeed, intend to name her his successor, better he do it sooner than later. That gave everyone, including her, time to adjust.

Maybe Uncle Gordon would stop his darkling sulks too.

If he continued to pout, he'd find himself bereft of his steward position. A surly, uncooperative overseer wouldn't do.

She'd grown disgusted with his barbed comments and sly looks.

God's toenails.

He should count himself fortunate Da had agreed to take Mum's illegitimate half-brother in when he'd been arrested for petty theft all those years ago. Her parents had hoped Uncle Gordon would follow in Leath's and Colin's footsteps. Da never said so directly, but his somber gaze often revealed his disappointment in his wife's nephew.

Satisfied her hair, jewels, and attire would pass muster, Lydia dabbed perfume at her throat and behind each ear.

A soft knock preceded Esme poking her stunningly coiffed head in the door. A huge smile covered her face when her gaze lit on Lydia. "Oh, you are ever so lovely, Lydia. Like an exotic orchid. You've quite recovered from your headache?"

Lydia's artfully arranged hair hid a spoon-sized lump. She crooked her mouth and collected her feathered fan and black gloves. If she was an orchid, Esme was a most perfect rose. "I pale in comparison to you, dearest. And yes, if I don't touch where my head struck the carriage, I'm quite well."

Esme fairly glowed in her virginal white gown, but the red roses embroidered along the hem, across the gold satin beneath her breasts, and along her sleeve's edges, reflected the fire in Esme's coppery hair. She wore rubies in her ears and at her throat and the most elegant red and gold, beaded slippers.

Even her lips glowed crimson.

Lydia donned a glove, wiggling her fingers into each finger hole. She rather hated wearing the silly things. They made her all thumbs, and she was forever taking them off to nibble a sweetmeat or other dainty. And then she forgot to put them on again.

Her browned hands would send the whole of the Polite World into apoplexy should they have seen them.

"How's your leg this evening, Esme?"

"Much better. The swelling around my knee is nearly gone, but I have a bruise as wide as a fat hog's behind on my thigh." Esme raised her hem to her shapely knees and stuck her foot out revealing intricate red clocks at her heels.

Not an ounce of bashfulness in the girl.

Chuckling, Lydia pulled on her other satin glove. Esme did have a colorful way of speaking. The bold Scots found her mannerisms amusing, but Lydia fretted the stuffy *haut ton* mightn't be as easily charmed.

"Are you ready?" Esme peered around Lydia's chamber, taking in the rustic stone turret and diamond-paned windows. "This is quite an ancient castle, isn't it? Very rustic, but also quite intriguing. Are there any ghosts lurking in the corridors or turrets, do you think?"

"The original Keep's ruins are across the loch, and I imagine if any spirits are roaming about, it would be over there." Lydia finished tidying her dressing table before looking up and giving Esme a reassuring smile. "I've never explored them though, nor have I ever heard mention of any unusual goings on here."

"America doesn't boast anything as old or majestic as this. At least not where I live." She scrunched her nose and shuddered. "We're famous for those horrid witch trials."

"Yes, I've read about that nonsense. I cannot imagine why people allowed themselves to be so deceived." Lydia opened the door and waited for Esme to finish gawking.

Esme flitted out the door and heaved a great sigh. Her shoulders slumped as she fidgeted with her ivory handled fan. "I confess, I'm nervous as a mare in season. I've never attended a grand affair."

Lydia looped her arm through Esme's and guided her down the stately passageway. Likely generations old, beautifully woven tapestries detailing castle life hung suspended along the walls. Who had the men and women been who created the masterpieces? Alasdair's relatives?

"Really? I would've thought you'd have plenty of opportunities in Salem."

"I was too young before Papa died, and when Mama fell ill shortly thereafter, I spent the next two years attending her." Esme shivered and briskly rubbed her hands over her arms. "This place gives me chicken skin." She glanced warily up and down the severe passage. "It's cold and almost eerie. Are you quite sure there aren't any spirits loitering about?"

Lydia laughed softly. "It is a bit daunting, and I admit, I prefer Tornbury's coziness, but Craiglocky possesses its own appeal."

"You still didn't answer my ghost question," Esme grumbled. "I felt certain someone has been watching me. My nape hair has been standing on end all day."

Probably McLeon. A more besotted man, Lydia had never seen.

A few minutes later, they paused at the great hall's entrance.

Guests mingled about the room, a few chatting and laughing before the enormous, stately fireplace. Others sat upon the needlepoint covered benches before the mullioned windows, and several small, animated clusters gathered here and there.

A celebratory atmosphere permeated the hall, and Esme gave a tense giggle.

"My, everyone looks splendid, don't they? And the Highlanders are so dashing in their dress kilts." Her gaze fell on Douglas Mcleon before she quickly glanced away. "Lydia," she whispered beneath her breath, "did Mr. McLeon just wink at me? Awfully bold of him, I must say."

Drawn to Alasdair's commanding form the moment she crossed the threshold, Lydia hadn't noticed. Such anticipation brimmed in Esme's eyes, however, Lydia couldn't crush her cousin's hopes.

"I shouldn't be the least surprised," Lydia said. "He's been most attentive. And he's quite a handsome devil, isn't he?"

Not as handsome as Alasdair.

Although not handsome in Flynn's polished, jaw-dropping manner, Alasdair's arresting strength and size, nevertheless, shouted masculinity. His tawny hair—much too long for London's glittering parlors—suited him, and devilish humor usually glinted in his startling bluish-gray eyes, the sky's color over the ocean at dawn.

His was a raw, untamed, manly beauty, and why the

devil she continued to ruminate on it—*him*—vexed to her carefully plucked eyebrows.

Still, a whoosh of unexpected delight tripped across her shoulders when he and Mr. McLeon excused themselves from the group they'd been conversing with.

More than one attractive lady's face puckered in momentary displeasure, before their pert noses elevated, and they turned their attentions to dazzling the other gentleman at their elbows.

Confused disappointment swiftly replaced her bewildering elation when Alasdair crossed to speak with his father rather than join Mr. McLeon as he strode in her and Esme's direction.

Mr. McLeon bowed gallantly, his focus trained on Esme. "From the way the room suddenly brightened, I ken the moment ye fair lasses entered."

Esme's muffled snort earned her his face-splitting grin.

"You are full of hogwash, Mr. McLeon, for I saw you whispering in that stunning brunette's ear." She inclined her red-blonde head briefly. "And you no more noticed our entry than a dog knows a tick's latched to its arse."

Chuckling and shaking his head in disbelief, Mr. McLeon's eyebrows vaulted to his hairline, and Lydia gave a rapid glance around.

No one had heard Esme, thank goodness.

"Esme, a lady doesn't use that word in public." To soften her reprimand, Lydia leaned in and murmured, "Though I quite agree with your assessment."

Esme pursed her lips, impishness fairly leaping in her eyes. "I beg your pardon. Our entry was as unremarkable as a parasite on a canine's posterior."

McLeon's loud guffaw drew several guests' attention, and even Alasdair sent a fleeting glance in their direction, a ghost of a smile playing round his mouth's edges, before he pointedly directed his attention to his father once more.

Lydia's spirits deflated faster than a cooling soufflé.

What did she care that he obviously intended to ignore her tonight? Come to think of it, she hadn't seen him yesterday either. Not since their arrival, actually.

He avoided her.

What had she done to pique him?

She edged her chin upward.

Never mind.

She wasn't here for entertainment anyway, most especially not of the gentlemanly type. Her interest in Alasdair McTavish was purely mercantile. He possessed a skill necessary to Tornbury and naught else mattered.

Yesterday, her meeting with the laird had gone well—very well, truth be known—and he'd assured her he'd provide his assistance until summer.

Perhaps longer.

He hadn't specified which man he had chosen for the interim war chief, but he'd also promised two score of his finest soldiers would be at her disposable for an extended period.

That knowledge had lifted a considerable burden, and she'd thought she might actually enjoy the next few days. Her wayward gaze strayed to the room's opposite side once more.

Alasdair's aloofness oughtn't to sting. But he was so easy to talk to, she could be perfectly candid with him in all things.

What *had* she done to put him off?

Flicking her fan open, she peeked over its feathery edge at his broad back, the cloth of his evening jacket pulled tight across rippling muscles. Everything had been quite genial and comfortable until she'd bade him present her letter to the laird.

He hadn't spoken to her since.

A minute frown pulled Mr. McLeon's brows together as he followed her focus. "Don't fash yerself, Miss Farnsworth. Alasdair's been a disagreeable brute since the laird told him he'd either make himself available to train yer regiments, or he could take his leave of Craiglocky."

Chapter 7

Good God.

Lydia only just managed to prevent her jaw from sagging wide. As it was, she gasped loudly, earning her concerned looks from Esme and Mr. McLeon.

Why had Ewan McTavish made such a preposterous stipulation? Had Alasdair protested the assignment?

Perfectly wonderful. Now she'd have to deal with a reluctant, and perhaps uncooperative war chief along with everything else she had to juggle at present.

Gordon would likely dance a jig in delight, crowing *I told ye so* the entire while. Someone ought to put him in his place, and she was in precisely the mood to do so.

She didn't need any more dissention at home, and she was of half a mind to impose a similar ultimatum to Uncle Gordon. Either he committed to restoring Tornbury Fortress to her previous power and status, without selfish motives, or he could take himself off permanently.

Craiglocky's laird climbed the dais, and the chatter hushed a trifle. "Dinner is served, ladies and gentleman."

Mr. McLeon extended both his elbows. "May I escort ye lovely lasses to the table? I'll be the envy of every man present."

"But where's Lady McTavish?" Lydia craned her neck, looking for Yvette. Witty and intelligent, she'd been exceedingly kind to Lydia on her previous visit.

"Ah, her ladyship is confined to bed until her bairn comes." He looked down at Esme. "Ye are seated to my right, Miss Adams, and ye, Miss Farnsworth are seated between Mr. Brownly and Alasdair." He winked. "Brownly is a chatty flirt, but he be harmless."

How did he know where they were seated? Had he perused the seating arrangements in advance?

He was smitten, though no good could come of it.

"I do apologize for Alasdair's churlish behavior." Mr. McLeon led her to her seat first. "He'll come 'round. He's just obstinate, and of late a mite techy. I think a change of scenery would do the surly sot good."

He made no attempt to quiet his voice as he delivered her to her assigned seat beside Alasdair's.

He speared McLeon a heated glower as he stood. "Aye, I could use a break from yer ugly face, to be sure."

McLeon laughed as he guided Esme away.

Over her shoulder she gave Lydia a worried look, and Lydia managed an encouraging upward tilt of her mouth.

For pity's sake.

The world wouldn't end just because Alasdair was in a masculine sulk.

She'd deal with far more important and much more difficult situations as laird. Ironic that men criticized women for being so emotional, yet from what she'd observed, males far more often let their passions rule them.

Sinking onto the chair, she murmured, "Thank you, Alasdair."

At first he didn't respond, simply pushed her chair in then stood behind her, his strong hands still gripping the posts. Tension radiated off him in strained waves.

His gusty sigh warmed her scalp.

"I've been a rude ar—um, cull. Forgive me, please." He came around and slid into the chair beside her, giving her a sheepish grin. The boyish action, the humility behind it, caused a queer pull against her ribs.

"No one likes being forced into something, Alasdair.

Would you like me to speak with the McTavish, and suggest he ask someone else?"

Who? No one was more qualified that she knew. Unfolding her serviette, she canted her head slightly and surveyed the burly Scots assembled along the table's length.

How well trained was Douglas McLeon?

Alasdair followed her lead, draping his cloth square across a broad thigh. "Nae. I've been promised a much-coveted reprieve once I'm finished."

"Oh, and what might that be?" She returned Seonaid's cheerful smile and friendly little wave.

He relaxed against his chair, one hand atop the table and the other resting on his kilt covered thigh. His muscled knee and calf drew her naughty focus once more. Why must he have such spectacular, light golden-hair covered legs?

He flicked a large, callused finger upward, rotating it. "Six months away from this damp, moldy clime. Truthfully, I mightn't ever return. Just spend the rest of my days soakin' in the sun along some tropical shore or barren desert."

"You're not serious?" Lydia stopped fussing with her silverware to gape. "You might be restless and discontented at present, but you love Scotland as much as I do. You could never leave her permanently." She grinned and poked his trunk-like arm. "You favor your whisky, Scotch pies, and haggis too much."

"While ye speak truth, lass, there also be hellish memories here I'd rather leave behind." All trace of the usually glib Highlander disappeared as he twisted his mouth in derision and stared across the hall.

His sarcasm couldn't disguise the hurt lacing his words.

What had happened to him that left such a profound and lasting scar?

The chattering and laughing of his family and clan snared her attention momentarily. The McTavish clan laughed much more than Tornbury's.

"You would be missed, Alasdair. Quite terribly, I think." Everyone adored him.

He turned his penetrating gaze on her, now the color of the sky after a summer thunderstorm. "Would *ye* miss me, lass?"

Like the sun's warm caress on a winter's day, I would.

The simple question oughtn't to have sent Lydia's pulse to tripping or dried her tongue to such an extent she required a sip of wine to moisten her mouth. Fine then, a gulp. Which she choked on indelicately, causing a humiliating and robust round of coughing.

Face flaming from the concerned looks darted her way, she swallowed several times. When she dared speak once more, she bent a trifle closer. "Everyone would miss you, Alasdair, and I confess, I'd hoped you'd be the one to come to Tornbury."

Not grudgingly or as the result of a bribe. She slumped slightly in her chair, catching Uncle Gordon's curled lip from the corner of her eye.

Lairds didn't slump.

Up went her spine, stiff and straight. She edged her chin upward too.

"It's true Tornbury isn't all that different from Craiglocky"—*it was, actually*—"but at least you'd be away from whatever haunts you here."

It must have been something quite tragic for his family and the servants to have never breathed a word of it. Maybe they didn't know either.

He blew out a long breath and shook his shaggy head. "Nae distance can scrape the memories from my mind."

"I'm a good listener if you ever want to talk to someone about them." She dared lay her hand atop his rigid forearm but immediately snatched it away when he stiffened. To hide the heat suffusing her face, Lydia took another sip of her wine. "I beg your pardon. That was much too forward of me."

"Nae a bit." He leaned back as a servant placed a bowl of cullen skink chowder before him. "I like a bold, saucy wench."

"I don't doubt you do." Jealousy most definitely *did not* cause her tone's dryness.

Probably had more than his share of such chits.

Even tonight, plenty of willing and brazen lasses had turned an interested eye his direction more than once.

Truthfully, she rather liked one particular bold, saucy Scot herself. A blond giant of a Highlander, but this sensation was more of an easygoing, trusting comradery than a whisked-off-her-feet-with-giddy-emotion as she'd experienced with Flynn.

She wouldn't describe her feelings as brotherly either, more of a deep, abiding, familiar friendship. It had always been thus between them.

Lifting her spoon, Lydia managed to keep from wrinkling her nose as the chowder's aroma drifted upward. She didn't favor haddock, but years of politesse drilled into her made her take a dainty sip, nonetheless.

She even managed to suppress the automatic shudder that followed. Almost.

Alasdair answered a question put to him by a much-too-pretty red-head on his left. Miss Reid, if Lydia remembered correctly from their introduction yesterday.

Sweet and cordial, if a bit of a consummate flirt.

The girl pouted prettily when he promptly turned his attention back to Lydia and spoke softly.

"As laird, Lydia, ye'll need boldness, courage, and confidence. Nae all men will take to a female chief in the beginnin'. Ye might want to consider acquirin' yerself a husband soon."

He sounded like Da. Did men think women were incomplete unless secured within the bonds of matrimony? *Bonds* being the key offensive word.

"Why, so he can tell me what to do, and try to usurp my position? He winna be laird. I shall be." Well, she would if Da appointed her. Most men didn't take easily to having a woman lead in any capacity. It threatened their masculinity or some other nonsense. Utter hogwash.

"Aye, and I didna mean any offense. I just meant that ye'll need someone at yer back, and yer twiddlepoop of an uncle—" Alasdair jerked his head to his left. "Well, he has his own motives and agenda, I be thinkin'."

She couldn't agree more.

Finger to her chin, Lydia sent Uncle Gordon a sidelong, speculative glance.

His eyebrows cinched tighter than a parson's purse, he applied himself to his food, ignoring the guests on either side.

Though she hated to admit it, even to herself, she didn't entirely trust Uncle Gordon. For certain she watched him more closely in recent weeks, and she didn't like what she saw.

Suddenly, Gordon peered past the fiery haired beauty and consternation lined his face as his dark gaze shifted back and forth between Lydia and Alasdair. Etiquette prevented him from addressing either down the table, but given his compressed mouth and the message fairly screaming from his eyes, he had something he couldn't wait to say to her.

Or Alasdair.

"I have a suggestion, Alasdair."

She swallowed another mouth of soup and managed not to grimace. Wasn't the next course about to be served? How much more chowder did she have to gag down?

No more.

She laid her spoon against the bowl's rim. "Agree to come to Tornbury for a short while, say a fortnight, and train me in weaponry. And then if you find it's not to your liking, you can be on your way to your spectacular escapade."

Wish I could go away too. For a time, at least.

Traveling the world did rather appeal more than mediating disputing tenants, collecting taxes, or cajoling disgruntled clansmen.

Disbelief swept Alasdair's face and for an instant he appeared to have swallowed something terribly foul.

The soup, perhaps? She well understood his aversion.

"Train ye? But yer already an expert archer." He stared at her as if she'd gone daft.

Was the notion so repugnant?

She kicked her pride and consternation under the crowded table. A chief must be able to defend the clan as well as herself.

"Yes, but a laird should know how to shoot and wield a blade or two proficiently as well. Most particularly a female chief. I'm thinking I might quite enjoy the short sword." She canted her head and shifted her gaze to Seonaid. She'd always fancied wielding a sword. "I happen to know all of the Ferguson woman have weapons training, and I'll wager my monthly allowance you helped with their instruction."

Touché.

From his immediate, shuttered expression, she'd hit the mark square on.

"Train ye," he muttered again, more to himself than her. "God help me."

Irritation's bevy of little pointed barbs stabbed her. He needn't sound so blasted incredulous or put upon. It wasn't as if she were a pox-ridden hag or failed to bathe or cleanse her teeth daily, for pity's sake.

What she'd do if he left after the fortnight, she couldn't—*wouldn't*—begin to speculate. So preoccupied with the distressing notion, she absently raised her spoon, almost gagging as the tepid soup met her tongue.

Gads.

Time to deal with the obstacle of Alasdair leaving later.

In any event, she had to persuade him to come first. She slid a glance toward the dais. "Your laird didn't specify how long you had to stay, did he?"

"Nae. He didna." As he took her meaning, Alasdair slowly shook his head, an even slower, shrewder grin lighting his face and eyes. His focus, too, shifted to the laird. "I like yer way of thinkin', lass. I do, in truth."

"Well then, he couldn't object if you decided to depart sooner, rather than later, could he?" She arched her eyebrows knowingly.

"Aye, I could stay fer a shorter while, and he'd have to fulfil his promise." A low, triumphant chuckle rumbled forth, and he tore a piece from his roll. "He'll be absolutely furious. That alone prompts me to say aye."

"Good. It's settled then." Brilliant. She hadn't a doubt her broad smile revealed her relief and pleasure. Two weeks to tempt him to stay longer.

How?

Money?

No. She didn't have access to a sum large enough to tempt anyone besides a pauper.

A promise of a position? Land?

Could she finagle either? Both?

She'd think of something.

She had to.

"You look extremely pleased, Miss Farnsworth." Mr. Brownly finally turned his attention from ogling the buxom widow seated on his other side.

Lydia's modestly covered, less-than-impressive bosom met with his insultingly brief scrutiny.

She didn't care a whit.

"Indeed, I am." She nodded and smiled wider. "Mr. McTavish and I have entered into a most exciting agreement."

Fishy odor assailed her nostrils.

Drat it all. Mr. Brownly had distracted her, and she held another spoonful of scaly wretchedness to her lips.

Inhale deeply.

She filled her lungs.

Mr. Brownly struck a dramatic pose and clapped his hands. "How splendid."

Hold your breath.

The air lodged in her chest, she tentatively edged the spoon nearer.

"Let me be the first to offer my congratulations!" he chirped, overly loud.

Sip quickly.

She shoved the offensive liquid between her pursed lips.

"When do the nuptials take place, or perhaps haven't you settled upon a date? I suppose those details have yet to be decided." He clapped again. "Oh, this is most exciting."

Swallow—

"Another wedding at Craiglocky."

WHAT?

Chapter 8

Lydia choked on her chowder, and only by slapping her serviette across her mouth prevented the soup from spewing forth and spraying the table and other guests.

At Mr. Brownly's giddy pronouncement, several nearby diners' heads whipped toward them, and Seonaid's jaw gaped for an instant before she snapped it shut with an audible click.

Alasdair dropped his knife, and the utensil's abrupt clattering onto his plate drew everyone else's attention.

Gregor snorted into his soup.

Lady Ferguson's roll slid from her fingertips and plopped into her bowl.

Craiglocky's laird completely missed his mouth and dumped wine onto his lap.

Her serviette still pressed to her mouth, Lydia shot Alasdair a panicked sidelong look.

Murder simmered in the stare he leveled Mr. Brownly.

"What are ye babblin' about?" Gordon practically shoved the petite Miss Reid flat against her chair as he rudely leaned across the table and glared at Alasdair.

Miss Reid huffed her displeasure and, with a furious glare, shoved his arm away. "Uncouth brute. Remove your elbow from my person at once."

"Lydia isnae marryin' McTavish," Uncle Gordon denied, his voice strident.

Lydia had heard of rooms growing quiet as death, but never experienced the phenomenon before. However, at the moment, an ant's tiny toot would've resonated cannon-blast loud in the great hall.

Several of Alasdair's family exchanged shocked or confused glances, and surely granite was more malleable than his stony expression. Awkward scarcely described the palatable tension hovering round the table. One of the Keep's ancient lochaber axes wielded by a pict couldn't have sliced it.

"Ye. Be. Mistaken in yer assumption. Sir."

Each word of Alasdair's clipped speech slapped sharply against Lydia's tender pride.

Of course, Mr. Brownly was incorrect, but Alasdair's keenness to set the chap straight bordered on belligerent.

Uncle Gordon laughed and whacked the table, rattling the dinnerware and earning him reproachful glances. "I'll say he be. Lydia has nae choice in who she marries. Farnsworth has arranged a competition for her hand. The announcements and invitations were sent the day we left. Any mon who can afford the ten-pound entry fee can contend."

A wave of rage sluiced through Lydia, so intense, her vision blurred for an instant, and she thought she might swoon. She gripped the table's edge, determined to maintain her composure.

Chiefs did not have fits of the vapor or cry when outraged.

Da wouldn't do that to her. *He wouldn't.*

Unless some demon taking human form—namely one uncle seated two chairs to her left and now openly gloating—had suggested the ridiculous farce.

Oh, if only she were a man, she'd call Uncle Gordon out, family or not. He'd be the first to find himself a new position once she was named laird. He'd proven where his loyalty lay, the traitorous cawker.

She darted Alasdair another peek, and found him sending frigid warning glances round the table.

Hounds' teeth.

What kind of bloody competition had Da arranged? And apparently, Craiglocky hadn't been sent an invitation. Most interesting, considering the McTavish clan was known far and wide for their physical strength and prowess. No need to speculate who'd been behind that particular oversight.

Gordon, God curse the vermin.

Worry about that later.

"Uncle Gordon, this isn't the place, and during dinner certainly isn't the time. We shall discuss that matter in private later."

My, she sounded quite chieftain-like.

Settling her serviette atop her lap once more, she squared her shoulders and swept the table with a cool gaze.

"Mr. Brownly." Lydia forced a genial smile. "Mr. McTavish has merely agreed to act as Tornbury Fortress's temporary war chief. I assure you there has never been any discussion of marriage between us."

"Aye. Never." Alasdair shook his head fervently. "Nae once."

His enthusiastic agreement had her reaching to pinch him before catching herself and snatching her fingers away to serenely clasp her hands upon her lap.

How utterly degrading.

Soundly rejected.

In public.

No worse than having her hand won at Highland games, though. That she wouldn't acquiesce to as mildly, no indeed. Too bad she couldn't compete herself.

~ ~ ~

Alasdair clamped his teeth until pain shot along his jaw and squeezed the chair's edge so tightly, a less sturdy piece of furniture would've snapped under the pressure.

Damn Brownly and his bloody assumption.

What a hellfired nincompoop for jumping to such an inane conclusion.

Few members of Alasdair's family knew Alasdair's situation, but those that did knew better than to utter a word contradicting Brownly's supposition.

However, Lydia didn't have a notion why Alasdair had vehemently denied the conjecture, and her set jaw and stiff posture clearly revealed her offense. And he couldn't explain anything. Not at this moment, in any event.

That discussion wasn't one he'd ever anticipated having with her, and he honestly didn't know how to broach the subject.

By the by, Lydia. I'm married, so ye see why the notion of us marryin' be bloody preposterous.

Awkward as hell.

And what purpose would there be in telling her?

She hadn't given him any reason to indicate her feelings toward him were anything other than cordial friendship.

Another wave of ire battered him, thinking her father would hand her over like some trophy to the man who won her in a goddamned Highland game. What kind of contest did Farnsworth plan? One of those medieval fetes of skill and muscle?

Ross had put Farnsworth up to the ludicrous suggestion, or Alasdair would eat the man's malodorous socks. Given Ross couldn't lift a clamor with both arms, let alone wield the sword with any skill, a contest of strength was all the more absurd.

Normally the salmon in whisky cream sauce was one of Alasdair's favorited dishes, but as he sat chewing the tender fish, he might as well have gnawed charred parchment.

How many men had Farnsworth invited? More importantly, whom?

Wait, Ross had said an announcement went out too.

Did that mean any cull could attend as long as he paid the entrance fee? Damned dangerous, that.

Though outwardly composed—magnificently poised, truth to tell—the tautness of Lydia's shoulders, slight flare of her delicate nostrils, and chagrin lingering within her astute gaze testified to her true state.

She'd do well as laird.

The rest of the diners resumed their meal, though an occasional perplexed glance slid his way. Lydia too, turned her attention to the peppered salmon, except she mostly poked at the coppery fish with her fork and pushed it around her plate.

Brownly, all contriteness, attempted a charming smile. "I beg your pardon, Miss Farnsworth. Please forgive me for my outspokenness. My tongue frequently leads my wit."

Lack wit, was more apt.

"No need to apologize. It was a simple misunderstanding." Lydia obligingly pooh-poohed his apology.

Her perfunctory forgiveness didn't fool Alasdair one iota. Her retreat into contemplative silence suggested Gordon's revelation had astounded her as much as it had Alasdair.

Took the wind right out of her sails, it had.

As if possibly taking on the lairdship wasn't enough stress, to learn her father planned on offering her up like a trophy was utterly galling, even to a seasoned competitor such as himself.

Intent on securing the coveted position of her husband, no telling what sort of despots and riffraff would compete. For not a doubt existed that though Lydia was a spectacular prize, Tornbury Fortress and her lands were the more tempting reward by far.

"Ye didna ken yer da's plans?" He asked the question in Gaelic knowing full well he breached decorum since neither Miss Reid nor Brownly, both Sassenachs, spoke the dialect.

"Nae." Hurt swirled in Lydia's eyes, deepened to the

shade of a forest floor at twilight. "I canna believe he didn't speak to me about it first. I'm so angry. What else has he plotted behind my back?"

Her voice shook with repressed emotion, and Alasdair brushed his fingertips across the hand lying atop her thigh.

Sensual awareness, undeniable and penetrating, swamped him.

"I know Uncle Gordon's behind this farce. What I don't know is, why? How does he benefit if I marry? I suppose I have to someday, but not in such a demeaning manner. Like some feudal maiden."

This time he distinctly detected tears and a trace of fear in her husky voice.

Devil take it.

Alasdair shouldn't get involved.

Wisdom, his very bones, shrieked he'd regret it.

"All will be well, lass." Short of biting the unruly appendage off, he couldn't halt his determined tongue.

"How can you say that when I'm not even permitted my choice of a husband? I might be forced to join with an absolute stranger."

"Aye, ye'll have yer pick. I'll see to it. I give ye my word."

Alasdair mightn't be able to claim her for himself. After all, the kirk frowned strongly on bigamy, but he could grant her the right to select her husband.

If, and when, she decided she was ready.

The hopeful, watery gaze she turned on him tumbled his heart arse over head. He was a bloody, besotted fool about to commit to a much longer stay at Tornbury than a mere fortnight.

"How can you possibly promise that?" She idly pushed a glazed carrot around her plate.

He smiled and winked. "I'll win the contest, and then gallantly decline to marry ye."

Chapter 9

Tornbury Fortress
One Month Later

Absorbed in the sparring men in the courtyard below, Lydia narrowed her eyes and snorted loudly. Tugging her berry and charcoal plaid shawl snugger, she rested a shoulder against the south solar's oak window sash.

Pathetic.

God help Tornbury if anything larger than *brounies* or fairies or mice decided to attack.

She snorted again as a Tornbury warrior's sword went flying, clanging along the worn stones. She'd seen doddering village crones fight over a bread loaf with more enthusiasm and skill than her clumsy, out-of-shape clan.

How had they become so unfit in a few months?

No one to drive or challenge them, that's why.

Oh, a few exceptions stood out. Very few.

With a critical eye, she scrutinized Farnsworth's warriors.

Mayhap two dozen in all still nudged her chieftain's pride upward.

Not chieftain yet.

But Da had hinted just this morning, he planned to make the announcement soon. Just after he'd doggedly insisted she must marry and produce an heir.

Or two. Or three.

"Ye did say ye wanted eight bairns." His jest carried more than a little seriousness.

She elevated a skeptical brow. "Like a brood mare?"

No, a prize sow. Birth an entire litter and be done with the matter.

"Ye'll marry the man who wins the tournament, or I'll name another me successor, Liddie lass."

Pig-headed, obstinate, mulish—

Behind the hard glint of his whisky-tinted eyes, irrefutable love glinted. He worried for her future as much as he did Tornbury's.

She drew part of her lower lip into her mouth.

If Alasdair did win the contest, and she prayed he would, how would Da react when her champion refused to marry her? Would the disappointment further jeopardize his already frail health? And, God help her if Alasdair didn't triumph.

What then?

Hadn't Da considered that whomever she married— particularly if the Scot wasn't of her choosing—the man quite likely would attempt to wrest the lairdship from her? Perchance even plunder and pillage the estate, peasants, and village?

Then where would Tornbury Fortress and its people be?

Lydia's practiced gaze skimmed the feinting scrappers again. Slower, less finesse with their weapons—and from what she'd witnessed, tiring far sooner—Tornbury's fighters, even after three weeks of rigorous, daily training, stood little chance against the adept McTavish warriors.

One of her clansman stumbled and fell to his knees, his shoulders rising and falling with his labored breathing.

Or anyone else, for that matter.

She exhaled a frustrated sigh. Should she suggest longer practices? Would that make any difference or only serve to stir resentment?

It wasn't her place, in any event. Alasdair knew what he was about. She'd just have to trust him in this area.

What would she have done if he'd kept to their original plan and left after a fortnight?

Lydia shifted, transferring her weight to her other leg while rubbing her sore arm. Lucky she hadn't broken it during her tumble from her gelding two days ago. She couldn't remember the last time she'd been thrown.

Poor Liath.

He hated the new saddle's fit, and only after being tossed on her arse, did Lydia discover the horse's sore withers.

Despite Uncle Gordon's objection that future lairds had an image to protect, she'd instructed the groom to use her old saddle in the future. Gordon had insisted the dated saddle was hazardous—complete rubbish, of course—and had ordered new tack for her, Da, and himself.

Another foolish waste of funds.

Just an excuse for Uncle Gordon to gain himself a fancier saddle.

She knew perfectly well what he'd been up to. As estate steward, oughtn't he to be more thrifty and mindful of unnecessary expenditures instead of plundering the coffers?

A hoarse shout rose to her jolting her from her reveries.

Alasdair pointed and gave directions to one of her men, struggling against his McTavish opponent.

Though she loathed the idea of a tournament for her hand, at least Alasdair's promise to participate guaranteed additional training for her men for several weeks yet.

Da had set the contest date for May first, and absolutely wouldn't hear a word about cancelling the event.

Lydia had scarcely spoken to him for a week upon her return, she was so incensed. Then another attack laid him low, and fear of losing him had softened her heart.

Some laird she'd make if she went soft and malleable every time her emotions were tweaked.

"I only wish to see ye and Tornbury cared for, lass," Da had wheezed between harsh coughs. "I still ken what's best fer ye both."

He thought he did, but within the past few days, her misgiving had arisen more than once as to his continued competency. Moments of confusion seized him, and his patience, none too abundant to begin with, had diminished too.

Dr. Wedderburn had warned Da would fail rapidly if he refused to heed the doctor's instructions—which he had, blast his blessed soul—and his deteriorating health substantiated his folly.

Expressions intense, and arms folded across their broad chests, Alasdair and Douglas stood to one side observing the score of cursing, lunging, and thrusting men.

Sweat drenched the fighters' fierce faces and once-clean shirts.

Alasdair made a sharp gesture, cutting the air with his arm, and yelled something.

At once the men stilled.

Unbuckling his belt, he spoke to them. Despite the mid-morning winter's grudging sunlight, the wind whipping across the Highlands stole his words.

The men mopped their faces and moved to the sides. Several gulped the water an eager lad offered.

Alasdair swiftly disrobed to his waist, and then pointing at one of Tornbury's few burly chaps, Lennox, took a defensive stance.

Lydia straightened, her mouth gone dry as mowed August hay.

Above Alasdair's rippled torso, a fine matting of golden curls dusted his sculpted chest. His cudgel-like arms bulged with muscles, as did his massive shoulders.

Lord, but the man boasted a beautiful physique.

Power and protection.

If only he could remain Tornbury's war chief.

Forever.

Shaking her head, she stepped farther into the curtain folds. Gads, she mooned over him like an enamored chit. Her conscience gave her an annoying prod.

Flynn hadn't intruded upon her thoughts in . . .?

She puckered her brow and hugged herself.

Well, truth be told, she couldn't quite recall when her old love had last distracted her.

Alasdair raised his sword, and his muscles flexed.

Of their own accord, her fingers clenched on the woolen shawl. An instinctive reaction, duplicating gripping his manly form, which every part of her yearned to do.

Over and over. *And over.*

Astonishing, and not a little troubling, that she should be so physically drawn to him when her heart held another's image dear.

She splayed her fingers over the soft wool.

How would Alasdair's flesh feel beneath her fingertips?

Would it also be warm and smooth?

Velvety? Firm?

What about that tantalizing hair carpeting his glorious chest? Crisp and wiry or soft and silky?

As he and his opponent warily circled each other, Lydia squinted. Even at this distance, she could make out whitish ridges and raised, irregular ribbons revealing scars.

From battles?

Uncle Gordon strolled from the house, munching on what looked to be a handful of shortbread biscuits. Would do him good to participate in the twice daily training, and it would earn him a degree of respect with the clan that he badly needed.

She'd suggested as much to Da, and though he'd heartily agreed, Gordon had yet to set foot in a session.

In his typical fashion, he disappeared into the study or library, or toddled off to the village, rather than partake in the exercises. Perching his left hip on a barrel, he continued to eat, his expression mocking and bored.

Careful there, Uncle, lest you fall even lower in the men's estimation.

For the most part, the men ignored him, their attention locked on the pair taking each other's measure in the courtyard's center.

Built similarly, Lennox and Alasdair were fairly evenly matched.

Alasdair boasted a couple of inches on Lennox, but the latter weighed at least a stone more. The biggest difference, which soon became increasingly noticeable, was the manner in which they moved.

Alasdair was light and agile, a concert of grace on his feet, swiftly gliding or dancing away, twisting and turning with elegance and ease.

Lennox lumbered, heavy and awkward. Giving a skin-prickling shout, he swung his sword, repeatedly striking Alasdair's, only to have each powerful, bone-jarring blow deterred.

Lennox thought to use brute strength, but Alasdair fought with keen cleverness and fleetness of foot. Alasdair made his move, and in a flash, Lennox lay on his back, a sword tip tickling his flexing Adam's apple.

Lydia leaned in, smiling her approval.

Alasdair would have to teach her that nifty trick.

His finesse even took her by surprise.

Rather than erupt in rage, Lennox grinned and accepted the hand Alasdair offered. Talking animatedly, he slapped Alasdair's back before tossing a remark over his shoulder at the onlookers.

A few nodded and smiled, some men looked skeptical, and others shook their heads in apparent rejection or disbelief of whatever he'd said.

Dratted wind. Why must it pick up now?

She pressed closer to the cool glass, as Alasdair and Lennox chatted. Her movement, or perchance her bright wrap, caught Alasdair's attention.

He raised his head, his captivating gaze spearing straight to her.

Something in her middle turned squishy and flopped about clumsily.

Must be hunger.

To take advantage of the charitable weather and also enjoy a brisk walk, she'd skipped breaking her fast this morning. The exercise helped clear her head and often, a solution to a problem came to her while striding along the crags.

Alasdair acknowledged her small, self-conscious wave with a nod before redonning his shirt and addressing the warriors.

The men promptly fell into parallel lines.

A shiver, more of a long-fingered icy nudge, shook her, and she shifted toward the source.

Uncle Gordon, his face turned upward and an obstinate scowl contorting his features, glowered at her. He tossed his remaining biscuits onto the ground, and a pair of hounds immediately gulped them down. With a final withering glare at her, he swiveled and stomped in the stables' direction.

Hands on his hips, Alasdair watched him tramp away. He scratched his head as he directed a contemplative glance at her.

Across the distance, their gazes meshed, and Lydia couldn't break the magnetic hold.

Her attraction to him, for even she was honest enough to admit that was what she felt, grew stronger daily.

Douglas said something, and Alasdair broke their visual bond.

"There ye be, lass." Leaning heavily on a cane, Da shuffled into the solar.

His once vibrant hair seemed to have dimmed in recent weeks. Hollows emphasized his cheekbones, and eyes.

"Watchin' the men, are ye? Good." He nodded his approval. "McTavish approached me yesterday about givin' ye lessons. He said ye'd asked him to train ye."

Lydia slid her hand through her father's crooked elbow. So frail. Even more so than a mere week ago.

Not long now.

"I did. I think it wise for me to be able to defend myself." She left off the *If I'm to be laird* part. The implication hovered between them, and her father wasn't a fool.

"Here, Da, sit beside me on the window seat. The view isn't quite as good, but you can still see most of the maneuvers."

She guided him to the window where a pair of stone seats faced each other. Long, bottle green velvet cushions padded them, but he still winced as he settled his feeble form.

He truly hadn't much time left, and grief twisted her stomach.

Every day he faded a bit more. She prayed that when the time came, he'd slip away peacefully in his sleep, as Mum had.

"I'll agree to allow yer trainin' under one condition." Both bony hands gripping the cane's silver lion's head handle, he rocked forward slightly as he peered at her, his cheekbones clearly defined beneath his papery skin.

Lydia angled her head and smiled. Lord, she loved the stubborn, crusty man. "And what might that be?"

His keen gaze bored into her. "Ye give me your word, you'll marry the tournament winner without a fuss."

Impossible.

Alasdair had agreed to compete only so that she could

choose her husband. A spark of irritation flickered, but as fast as it jumped to life, it fluttered and died.

How could she say no to her dying da's request, if it brought him a degree of peace?

But what if Alasdair didn't win?

What if he did?

What a pickle.

"Da, shouldn't we wait to see the contest's outcome?"

"Lass, ye must think of the clan first. Always. Ye canna have what ye want when ye are laird. I need to ken ye be strong enough fer the position, that ye be willin' to sacrifice all fer yer clan, ye ken?"

I know, and I am.

He smiled, his eyes crinkling at the corners lovingly before giving her a secretive wink. "And I be fairly certain I ken who the winnin' contender will be. A man I heartily approve of."

Alasdair?

Had Da another, a more duplicitous, reason for specifically requesting Alasdair's presence at Tornbury?

Did Alasdair know? Had they discussed it? He met with Da daily, so the notion wasn't absurd.

Yes. It was.

Alasdair wasn't conniving, nor was he dishonest. His reluctance to travel here had been real.

Maybe he'd been offered an incentive he couldn't refuse.

Cease your mental prattling this instant, Lydia Alline Therese Farnsworth.

As Da observed the tussling men below, he rubbed his jaw, and his shoulders slumped. A raspy chuckle rattled against his chest, sounding hollow against the rock wall behind him. "There be a day when I could've whipped the lot of 'em."

"I remember, Da."

He'd been a fierce warrior, as had her brothers.

"What say ye then, daughter?" His crepey hand covered hers, and he gave it a firm, but gentle squeeze. "Will ye give me yer word, so I may go to me grave in peace? Ye'll marry the victor?"

Chapter 10

In the crowded, smelly barracks late that evening, Alasdair polished his sword and subtly studied his men. Only for Lydia would he endure these accommodations, and he'd be a liar if he didn't acknowledge a comfortably appointed bedchamber in the mansion didn't tempt mightily.

He'd declined a room in the Keep, preferring the company of the troops rather than a comfortable bed which he'd lay upon, awake, pondering Lydia.

Legs spread, his sword lying atop his bare knees, and a half tankard of dark ale within arm's reach, he ran an oiled cloth along his blade's sharp edge.

Around him, the boisterous men, made more so by full stomachs and plentiful drink, joked, played cards or chess, or like him, attended their weapons.

McLeon, staring into the fire's flames, coaxed mournful tunes from his bagpipe, which in truth sounded more like a bawling Highland heifer.

Miss Adams had refused his request for a walk earlier today, and he moped about like a lovelorn lad.

On the long room's opposite side, a small crowd had gathered around Lennox and the Scot he arm-wrestled. Alasdair hadn't been challenged to a match since his first night at Tornbury—after easily winning a half dozen contests and the unfortunate last chap had suffered a fractured arm.

The Farnsworth's clan might not be the fiercest or mightiest fighters, yet—or ever—but they diligently tended their weapons as well as kept their barracks fairly tidy.

However, regular bathing wasn't a priority for more than a few, and the place stank more than a little.

His nostrils switched as a particularly malodorous chap, his trews stiff from filth, strode past. Wouldn't surprise Alasdair if some of the men weren't harboring vermin in their untamed beards and oily, untrimmed hair either.

He hadn't broached that subject yet, but he wasn't commanding a regiment of ripe Scots in dingy plaids either. Still, they were an amiable lot with ready smiles and always quick to extend a hand; even quicker to offer a flask.

Except Ross, the sour-faced, squawking raven.

The man grumbled more than an increasing fishwife whose foxed husband never cast a net. And he was a lazy cull too.

Rather than calling on tenants and tending to estate business, he spent his time in the local pubs or at a certain disreputable cottage on the village's edge.

Was his behavior new, since Farnsworth fell ill, and neither Lydia nor the laird were aware? Or was Ross's slacking habitual? If so, then why hadn't it been addressed or his service severed without character?

Couldn't hurt to nose around a trifle and find out. The dour fellow made Alasdair wary. Ross watched Lydia too closely, and behind his hooded eyes, occasional glints of what appeared suspiciously like animosity flickered.

Alasdair finished downing his ale just as the outer door swung open. Over the tankard's rim he spotted the subject of his musings.

Speak of the devil.

Ross's beady gaze flitted around the room until his crow eyes rested on Alasdair. Resentment simmered there. He jerked his head. "McTavish. Yer wanted in the solar—"

"Och, Ross. Ye want to have a go?" Waving his oak-thick arm, Lennox indicated the now vacant chair opposite him. "I promise to go easy on ye." He tapped his thumb against his forefinger. "I'll only use me thumb and finger."

Undisguised ridicule dripped from each mocking word and resulted in a chorus of guffaws from the other men.

"Ye'd still snap his bony wrist like a crossbill's leg," someone said between snickers.

Clapping his mouth shut, and without waiting for Alasdair's response, or answering Lennox, except with a crude gesture—which resulted in a louder round of catcalls and hoots—Ross, his upper lip slightly curled, tromped from the barracks.

After putting his basket hilt sword away, Alasdair donned his belt and black leather vest then slid his stag antler dirk into his stocking.

A request this time of night, in the solar, no less, didn't bode well. He'd thought the laird and Lydia already abed and was soon for his humble, too narrow and too short, cot as well.

In overly-tired bemusement, he dared let his mind travel down a trepidatious path.

What did Lydia wear to bed?

How did she look in slumber?

Did she plait her shiny, raven hair with its teasing hint of curl, or wear it loose?

Did she talk in her sleep?

Enough lewd musings.

Searón had plaited hers, but she'd always slept nude as a nymph, her plump, white body, on its way to fleshy and fat even at her young age, ever ready for a tryst. With any man who'd promise her a satisfying tumble between the sheets, he'd later learned.

That rather chafed his young man's esteem until he understood some women's carnal urges—much like a glutton's for food or a tippler's for spirits—couldn't ever be satisfied.

She'd claimed an imaginative and voracious sexual appetite that no innocent miss ought to have knowledge of. No surprise, really, she'd turned to selling her favors to fancy cits in Edinburgh.

Hell, Alasdair didn't even know if she still lived.

He hadn't had any word about her for over three years now, though rumors had circulated a year and a half ago that she might have been one of several prostitutes who died in a brothel fire.

A whorehouse that offered every kind of perverse, carnal vice known to men, and for which Searón was a rumored favorite because she enjoyed the more depraved activities.

He pursed his lips in distaste.

The proprietor couldn't be sure she'd been a victim since several of his ladies of the night had assumed fictitious names, and more than one given to stoutness had perished that night.

Wouldn't that be a convenient solution?

Guilt speared his gut. No one deserved to die in such a fashion, even the likes of her. He'd thought he'd loved her once, so a morsel of compassion wouldn't be amiss. Even if he couldn't comprehend her choices.

Alasdair heaved a hefty expanse of air as he planted his dagger-weighted foot on the floor. Perhaps he'd seek Ewan's council on hiring a man to explore Searón's whereabouts. If she yet lived, if disease or her depraved existence hadn't killed her, he'd consider petitioning for a divorce.

Something he should've done years ago, though God only knew why he hadn't. He'd known she wouldn't return, and he hadn't wanted her to. His pride stung, but not enough to prevent him from seeking a divorce, and he readily admitted his mistake in wedding her.

At the door, he swung back to face the jovial men. "Be in the bailey at half past four in the morn."

Grinning and ducking as several men groaned and McLean tossed a leftover oat roll from dinner at his head, Alasdair dashed out the door.

A few minutes later, he strode into the solar's open entrance, and faltered to a stop.

Lydia sat in a fern green high back chair, her feet tucked beneath her as she drowsily stared into a hearty fire. An open book, its charcoal-hued spine facing upward, balanced on the chair's arm, and a pair of bedroom slippers, hastily kicked off from their haphazard appearance, lay on their sides.

The muted rumbling purr of the black, gray, and orange patched cat curled in her lap mixed with the fire's crackling and popping. Lydia's hair, a shiny sable cloud, hung about her slim shoulders, covering her velveteen cerulean robe.

Had she sent for him? In her nightclothes?

He'd have expected as much from Searón. Actually, he'd heard she entertained stark naked.

Lydia generally exhibited much more modesty. However, she thought of him as a brother or cousin, so mayhap receiving him in her bedclothes didn't concern her overly much.

Then again, perhaps she deemed the matter urgent, or given the late hour—the great clock in the corridor had chimed half past the tenth hour as he passed—she hadn't wanted to redress for a few moments of conversation.

Alasdair couldn't blame her.

He'd be hard pressed to drag his sorry arse from his too-small bed before dawn tomorrow. Served him right for making a point with the men earlier and demanding their presence before the birds left their nests.

So why had he been summoned?

Perhaps she wanted to discuss her weaponry training. He'd managed to put her off, claiming the troops were his first priority, but she'd grown quite persistent in recent days.

Other than two double tapers burning atop the elaborate, carved mantle, darkness shrouded the comfortable room. Shades of green, soft browns, and poppy red added to the solar's welcoming ambiance.

He'd never been invited to the family's private chamber before. Most audiences took place in the long study, Tornbury's meeting hall, or the laird's sitting room.

"Ye sent fer me, Lydia?"

Chapter 11

Alasdair really ought to address her as Miss Farnsworth, but the social formality added a barrier he didn't want, despite the impropriety.

And hypocrisy.

He was married to a light-skirt. Couldn't get much more scandalous than that.

Lydia started and yanked her focus from the flames, her expressive eyes rounding in surprise as she pressed a hand to her breast.

A soft, self-conscious laugh escaped her as she drew her neckline closed.

"No. Yes. That is, I asked Uncle Gordon to tell you I wished to speak with you in the morn after the clan's drills." She looked behind him before her gaze drifted back to his face. "Did he retire already?"

Probably pelting his way to the village whore's cottage.

After rising from his brief bow, Alasdair lifted a shoulder. "I'm not sure. Once he delivered the message, he left the barracks."

In a girlish huff.

"I apologize for the confusion, Alasdair. You needn't have come tonight. The matter isn't pressing."

Her soft voice caressed his weary senses and aching body.

Truth to tell, he was sore as hell from the pounding he'd taken sparring with a dozen men eager to show him their prowess. *Or lack thereof.* He'd have welcomed a long soak, but instead had settled for a quick dip in the icy river bordering the meadows.

Edging farther into the chamber, he searched the shadowy corners again. Neither Miss Adams nor a maid sat sewing in a discreet nook.

He and Lydia were entirely alone.

Not exactly proper. Not wise either.

At least on Alasdair's part.

"Ross failed to mention the appointment was fer tomorrow. I came straightaway, fearin' somethin' had arisen that caused you or the laird alarm." He scrubbed a hand across his stubbly chin.

Her soft mouth bent into a smile, and she shook her head, her loose raven tendrils caressing her shoulders like giant glossy fingertips. "Partially true, but it certainly might have waited until the morrow."

He'd intended to avoid seeing Lydia like this.

Her long neck glowed ivory pale in the dimly lit room, and his imagination needed no encouragement picturing what she wore, or didn't wear, beneath her simple robe. Nonetheless, his curious gaze probed the fabric, seeking the treasures hidden within.

Her intelligent eyes met his squarely. She trusted him, and he'd never give her cause to regret that trust.

The task her father had set for her was difficult for a man, and Alasdair couldn't fathom how hard it must be for a young woman. A grieving lass still reeling from multiple losses, to boot.

Eyes half-closed, she petted the cat, her long, delicate fingers gliding through the calico fur. "Father's made an impossible request of me. I couldn't say no outright. He's quite weak and tires so easily now. I'm not sure how much longer—"

Her throat worked as she struggled to control her emotions, and Alasdair longed to gather her in his arms, tell her he'd make sure she never had to worry or be afraid again. She could rule her people, and he'd stand behind her—beside her—ready to lay low anyone who dared look at her crossly.

"Well, I be here now, lass, so what do ye need?"

A long sigh whispered past her lips and, resting her head against the chair's back, she closed her eyes all the way. Her lashes, dark and thick, feathered across her cheekbones, a glaring contrast to her smooth, pale skin.

Defeat radiated from her.

"Father demands I marry the tournament winner within a fortnight. If I refuse, he's threatened to either not name me laird or else pick another man. One he deems worthy. He wants my word I'll comply."

~ ~ ~

Lydia kept her eyes firmly shut, not wanting to see Alasdair's expression.

He'd vowed he'd be the victor, but that was before Father had extracted the blasted half-promise from her. How she longed to defy him, tell him she'd marry who she wanted when she wanted.

Why must women always be subjugated to men's authority?

Perhaps if illness hadn't weakened him so, she might have summoned the nerve. However, dread, that he might suffer a fatal attack, had stilled her rebellious tongue.

The same couldn't be said for her defiant thoughts.

She hadn't exactly agreed, but neither had she adamantly disagreed to his ultimatum. Changing the subject seemed wiser, but Father knew she'd conform. 'Til now, she always had, and he'd have the oath from her lips before the tournament.

Unless by some grand, unfeasible miracle she were betrothed by then. Fustian codswollop. Dragons attired in ribbon and lace trimmed petticoats would call for tea first. And bring shortbread too.

"Och, that dis throw a blasted wrench in the cog, disna it?" Alasdair's mouth tipped upward as he slanted his head.

He looked particularly dashing. Though, in her groggy state, perhaps she but imagined his increased allure.

Marrying Alasdair wasn't as objectionable as being shackled to a stranger, or worse, one of the unsavory Scots that had started trickling into Tornbury over the past few days.

True, attractive men numbered amongst the eager, early arrivals, but outward appearances didn't reveal a man's heart or character. God forbid she wed and weeks, months, perhaps even years into the marriage, her husband's true nature emerged.

Her carefully calculated plans for the contest's outcome had been tossed noggin over bum. This whole affair was unjust and infuriating, and though she loved Da dearly, his manipulation had stirred deep resentment. She might not have refused him verbally, but in her thoughts she screamed *no*, over and over.

She gestured toward the adjacent chair. Hopefully, Bernard's fur didn't litter it too awfully. "Have a seat, Alasdair, and warm yourself. I know the room's parameters are cold, though you may be accustomed to the chilliness. Craiglocky is always far colder than Tornbury."

He joined her before the fire, but instead of taking the chair she waved him to, he rested his forearm on the mantel and drummed his large, rough fingers atop the polished wood. His strong profile, straight nose and chiseled jaw, stood out vividly from the reddish-golden glow silhouetting his large frame.

His stark manliness drew Lydia as surely as if he'd been a magnet and she a sewing pin. Warm permeated her which couldn't be attributed to the fire. Beleaguered annoyance and desire battled for supremacy. Best to redirect her wayward thoughts before she said or did something foolish.

Or humiliating.

"It's rather a larger pickle this time, isn't it?" Her pathetic attempt at humor met with a dry chuckle.

"It be rather more than a pickle, Lydia." Alasdair slid her a mocking look beneath his bent arm. "I made ye a promise too, one which I intend to keep."

She lifted Bernard and placed him on the floor before standing and touching Alasdair's back. "You cannot. I winna hold you to the commitment. Besides, how can you be so certain you would be the victor?"

He elevated an incredulous brow.

Not unjustly cocky, only self-assured.

She crossed her arms and ducked her head.

Of course he would. She'd seen his physical prowess.

His confidence wasn't undeserved.

No opponent came close to matching his skill, and unless some foreign behemoth appeared, Alasdair would seize the day. How could she expect him to give up his desire to escape Scotland, for a time at least?

He dropped his arm as he faced her. The aroma of soap and the leather he wore wafted downward. He tenderly touched her cheek, the gentle, one-fingered stroke stealing her breath and sending a spark of sensation streaking along her face.

And lower.

Mustering her courage, she reluctantly raised her focus from the soft, worn leather encompassing his ridiculously broad chest.

"Dinna look so woebegone, lass."

"What are we to do?" She stared up at him, refusing to permit her surge of tears to fall. "Da wouldn't have forced either of my brothers to marry before assuming the lairdship. This stipulation reveals his lack of faith in me. In my gender."

"Nae, he wouldn't, but I think he believes he be protectin' ye." A throaty quality deepened his voice as he drew her into his arms. One large hand framing a shoulder and the other cupping her waist, he pressed her near.

God help her, his strong, comforting embrace felt splendid, like a long overdue homecoming. So secure and safe.

And a bit terrifying too.

She wanted to wrap her hands around his large frame, bury her head in his shoulder, and stay snuggled there for hours.

Perchance days.

Forever.

Desire blazed in his eyes as he tilted her chin upward at the same moment he dipped his lower. Her woman's intuition recognized the passion bubbling beneath his composed demeanor.

She inhaled a short, quick breath.

Would he kiss her? No man had ever kissed her. Well, no man she didn't share blood with and who made her flesh pucker in anticipation.

Her breath hung suspended, and when she didn't voice an objection or pull away—why would she when she'd wanted his mouth on hers for weeks?—Alasdair brushed her lips with his.

Amazingly petal soft and firm at once.

Lord Almighty. Sagging into him, her knees came unhinged, and she clutched his vest in order to remain standing.

Lifting her higher, he groaned, and his tongue edged between her parted lips.

If he hadn't been holding her upright, she would've melted into a pool at his feet.

Who knew a kiss could turn your bones to pudding?

He tasted slightly of ale, and the warmth of his full mouth sent her senses spinning every which direction, making thinking impossible.

His breathing ragged, he broke their kiss, but kept her tucked into his embrace. "Och, ye be a heady distraction, Lydia Farnsworth. I beg yer forgiveness fer takin' liberties."

"I kissed you too." No sense pretending false modesty. She had and she'd quite enjoyed the experience. So much so, she'd have liked to continue.

Why had he stopped anyway?

Was she too inept and untried for a man of the world such as Alasdair?

Despite the flush heating her face, she forced her gaze to meet his. He still held her in his unyielding embrace, and she could no more find the strength to move away, than the snapping flames in the hearth could turn to straw. "I wanted to know what it would be like. Just once."

To kiss a man she found desirable, for Flynn had never kissed her.

"And?" Alasdair's smug self-assurance conveyed that he already knew the answer.

"If you think I'm going to discuss kissing you—" She hunched her shoulders and shook her head once, plucking at her robe's satin cuff. "I've got no business dallying. I must come up with a plan, but God only knows I can keep my word and still not exchange vows." She pulled a face and sighed deeply. "It's a rather hopeless plight, isn't it?"

He touched her nose, though she had the distinct impression he wanted to plunder her mouth again.

If only he would.

"Things nae be as glum as they seem," Alasdair said, seductive flames still flickering in his eyes.

"You would marry me then?" Hounds' teeth, she'd just practically proposed. "If you win, that is."

"Och, ye can count on me winnin', but we'll nae have to wed." An unexpected gruffness edging his words caused her to lift her head and peer at him curiously.

A log tumbled, sending sparks exploding up the chimney. A small ember shot from the grate. It glowed hotly on the stone hearth for a moment before dying.

"How can you be so certain, Alasdair?"

She leaned away, and he promptly released her. An odd sense of abandonment engulfed her.

Silly.

They'd hugged just this once, and only for a few short minutes at that. "I've all but given my oath, and my honor requires me to keep my word, unless I can justify why doing so would cause the tribe harm. A chief must exemplify integrity, or they cannot lead with any authority. The people won't follow me if they don't trust me."

Alasdair raked a large hand through his fair hair, and a blank, unreadable expression descended upon his striking features.

Nonetheless, undisguised pain glinted in his arresting eyes, framed by surprisingly thick, dark eyelashes. What happened to cause such lingering woundedness in this tough warrior?

"Aye, lass. I can win, and yer father canna force ye to wed me."

"But—"

He covered her lips with a forefinger. "I already be married."

Chapter 12

Married?

As in, exchanged vows before a cleric?

With a woman?

No, with a duck.

Lydia would never be sure how long she gaped at Alasdair, questions and accusations clanging about in her head louder than a full tinker's wagon careening over uneven cobblestones.

She'd never heard the slightest whisper.

Ever.

And she'd lived at Craiglocky for months.

Who was this mystery woman that Alasdair kept so well hidden? Was she so very scandalous, the family abhorred speaking of her?

"And yet you kissed me, Alasdair? Why?"

Had receiving him in her nightclothes given him cause to think she'd invited his attention? *Flim flam.* The Alasdair she knew wasn't an opportunistic cull.

"Call it an impulsive lapse in my judgement or stupidly yieldin' to a moment of temptin' insanity. Forgive me, please." Genuine contriteness shadowed his face and words.

She'd reached to trace the lines bracketing one side of his mouth as Bernard rubbed against her leg, his loud purrs vibrating his sleek length.

He gently dug his needle-sharp claws into one bare foot, jerking her back to full awareness, and she swiftly let her hand drop to her side.

She shouldn't encourage Alasdair but admitted he intrigued her in a way no other man had Not even Flynn. Perchance he enthralled her because he was such an enigma.

Who was he, really?

A loyal McTavish clansman? Good-natured brother and cousin? Fierce warrior? Cuckholded husband? Discontented wanderer?

Or an aggrieved soul like her, trying to put a broken heart behind him and forge a new destiny, perhaps even reinventing himself?

She'd rather yearned to do that, too. But the unbridled truth was, the matter was altogether out of her hands. As a dedicated daughter of the laird, Lydia knew her duty.

Blast loyalty and conscience to hell's bowels.

Those double yokes permitted her no reprieve. Her wishes, wants, and dreams had no bearing.

"Yes. Well." She pulled the vee of her robe together, feeling more bereft and vulnerable than she could recall.

Not a speck of room for compromise.

Married. He ought to have told her. Before she—

Never mind, fool.

Her laughter rang hollow and brittle even to her ears.

Bernard must have thought so too, for he stopped his contented rumbling and rubbing, and plopping his haunches onto the warm hearth, stared up at her. His citrine, almond shaped eyes glowed as his gaze shifted between her and Alasdair.

"I'd say the tournament matter is neatly settled then."

"Aye, in a manner of speaking, I suppose." Alasdair pulled at his ear, another inscrutable smile quirking his mouth to the side.

"Why . . .?" Lydia clinched her teeth together, refusing to pry.

His marriage wasn't any of her business, and obviously not something he wished to speak about, or she would've known he was married. And still, her determined tongue formed the questions.

"Why don't you ever speak of her? Why doesn't anyone?"

Alasdair lifted a broad shoulder, his attention once more focused on the cavorting flames. A muscle ticking in his jaw contradicted his casual manner. "I haven't seen her in eight years, and I forbid anyone to mention her name. Only a half dozen family ken."

"Why?" She clenched her hands.

Damned, cursed curiosity.

"Searón said she wisna content to suckle bairns, wipe their shitey bottoms and snotty noses, or stay faithful to one man. She wanted more excitement and adventure from life. She left me after two months." Bleakness deepened the lines creasing his forehead and framing his mouth. "After abortin' our bairn."

Good God.

Tears welling hot and swift, Lydia clasped his arm, her horror compelling her to comfort him.

"I don't know what to say, Alasdair. Sorry seems so very inadequate and trite." Stupid, selfish woman. Children were a tremendous gift. "I cannot imagine what it's been like for you all this time."

"Och, one gets used to the pain, and the memories fade in time," he said with a cynical twist of his molded lips.

Not really.

A person just forgot how life was beforehand. Before suffering changed them, stripped them of hope, expectation, anticipation. Made them leery and skittish, and fearful of trusting again.

She nibbled her lower lip as Bernard meowed softly then jumped into her vacated chair. "You must have loved her terribly to still be so injured."

And she'd thought Flynn's actions hurtful, though certainly not deliberate in intent by any means. He'd never even declared himself, let alone married, then cruelly abandoned her.

Alasdair, on the other hand, was a compassionate man; a man who cared and felt deeply, though he strove to hide his gentle side beneath his soldier's steely exterior or sarcastic, sometimes scornful humor.

Except, if one examined him closely—really scrutinized him as she did now—devastation lurked in his gaze and ravaged his face.

"I thought I loved her. But I was a scarcely more than a horny whelp, and she be a verra, verra bonnie lass. I ken she nae be an innocent when I took her to my bed, but I naively thought she loved me." He reached for the thick lock of Lydia's hair draped across her left shoulder. "Her hair be bright red, more orange like a baby carrot than coppery."

Lydia chuckled and shook her head, accidently tugging her hair loose. "Not the most romantic description I've heard."

"Ah, but yer hair, lass, has the richest sheen. Sable soft, sweet smellin' and warm as molasses," he murmured, his voice a low, husky rumble.

That description combined with his throaty tone caused her pulse to take wing and flitter about like an intoxicated moth.

Dangerous business, this. He's a married man. Remember that.

She ought to be furious he'd taken advantage of the moment and sneaked a kiss. That she wasn't, couldn't in fact muster a jot of outrage, proved quite troublesome.

Better to turn her idle musings elsewhere.

Any nonsensical, miniscule notion she might have imprudently entertained regarding him—*them*—died as speedily as the ember had earlier when he announced he was married.

Lydia wasn't a slut who wagged her tail to entice a married man to her soiled sheets. Nor was she content to be a man's mistress, available whenever he'd the urge to make use of her body, but never give her his name or afford her respectability and honor.

That sort of glorified prostitution, of which many in Society indulged, had always baffled her. And more on point, she quite abhorred selfish, conscienceless women who dallied with married men.

Had they no consideration of the anguish their treachery caused the poor wife? Or his children, later on? Surely God reserved a special, especially vile, *very hot,* place in hell for the like.

When Lydia married, she would remain faithful to her husband and whether the standard was fashionable or not, she'd expect the same from him.

Or she'd divorce him. Simple as that.

Another way Scotland surpassed England. Divorces were possible here.

The first time her husband took another to bed, she'd take a dirk to his privates and see him to the door. Naked and castrated.

She surveyed Alasdair through the sweep of her half-lowered lashes. True, he'd likely not honored his marriage bed or vows, but his wife had left eight years ago, and Alasdair was young and brawny.

Odd that she excused his immoral behavior.

Why did she?

Because he was a slighted man? True, but he'd chosen to remain married.

What did that say about her character that she could so easily excuse his adultery?

Why hadn't he divorced this Searón creature anyway? She sounded positively wretched. Though dying to know the whole of it, Lydia couldn't very well ask. She wasn't a busybody or a snoop.

She'd seen the wenches ogling him, seen the sensual smiles exchanged, had heard the titters at Craiglocky about his tussled sheets, caused by vigorous nightly bed sport.

So preoccupied had she been with her infatuation of Flynn, she hadn't paid the *on dit* any real mind. Scots by their very nature were a passionate lot, and her brothers hadn't been monkish in the least, much to Mum's chagrin.

Her parents had shared a bedchamber, even during Mum's illness. And more than once as a child, Lydia had accidentally interrupted their intimacy when she'd climbed into their great bed after a nightmare had awoken her.

Mum had always blushed and tutted with embarrassment, but Da had laughed heartily and tucked Lydia between them, mindful that the sheets covered his nakedness.

The Farnsworth men made no apologies about their bedroom prowess, yet Lydia was expected to remain chaste until wed. Such hypocrisy rankled, not that she'd sought a man to warm her sheets. Though, God knew she'd welcome another body in bed during winter's fiendishly frigid nights to keep her frozen feet warm.

She'd not pretend ignorance or girlish reticence about what went on between men and women either. Livestock and barnyard fowl aplenty wandered Tornbury's lands, and animals weren't discreet when they coupled.

Not quiet either.

Then again, neither were people. Entirely.

So now, why did penetrating disappointment wash her, its icy tendrils coiling about her limbs, chilling her to the core to learn Alasdair wasn't available?

Available for a respectable union, that is.

He had provided her a perfect, unarguable reprieve from marrying, despite her reluctant promise to Da. And for certain, the empty feeling in her stomach had nothing to do with the tiniest, most remote notion that marriage to him wouldn't have been unbearable.

Might have been most acceptable, in fact.

More likely the slight upset could be attributed to worry about Father's reaction to the news that Alasdair had essentially tricked him.

Chin against her chest, she fiddled with her robe's belt. "I can't deny this turn of event is most providential, but should you triumph, Da's response when he learns you can't marry me troubles me greatly."

Alasdair nodded, his compassioned-warm eyes fanning at the corners. "He'll want ye to select a husband. Straightaway if possible. But, at least ye'll have a choice in the matter."

She raised a skeptical brow and hitched a shoulder upward, the simple movement impeded by exhaustion and discouragement. "We'll see."

He frowned but remained silent.

Weariness engulfed her, and she hid a wide yawn behind her hand. "I'm done in, Alasdair. And I'm sure you are soon to bed as well. I know you run the men through their exercises most mornings before I arise. Still, I should like to start my training at your earliest convenience. Have you any time on the morrow?"

"Och, at one of the clock." He cocked his head and lightly tugged her lock again.

The wanton tendril curled round his hand, binding them together.

"I can see the questions burnin' in yer bonnie eyes, lass. Go ahead. Ask me. I'll answer as best I can, though the subject pains me as much as a boot-toe to the ribs."

"I shouldn't—"

"Aye, ye should. I dinna want any secrets between us."

No good could come of knowing, and it changed nothing between them. Yet . . .

"You were very young when you married, weren't you?" Surely no older than Lydia's twenty years.

"Aye, hardly past my twentieth birthday, and she be only seventeen. I was young, foolish, and determined to have her."

His wide back to her, the leather pulled taut over bulging muscles, he spoke into the fire once more, self-castigation rendering his tone ragged around the ends. He wasn't a man to give his affections easily, and he'd harbored the pain, blamed himself, far too long.

"How did you meet?"

Do you love her still?

Chapter 13

Lydia shouldn't continue prying, but Alasdair needed to speak of this, to finally say the things she'd wager he'd left unspoken for years.

Then, perhaps, he'd seek a divorce, freeing himself to move on, to let go of the past.

One oak-like forearm resting on the mantel, he stared into the flames.

"I met Searón at an inn on a business trip to in Edinburgh, and we wed within a week. She be the daughter of the owner, though we didna see him the first week we be in town. I ken she be a wild lass, but I thought marriage and bairns later on would tame her."

"And they didn't." How could they so quickly?

He shot her a glance so loaded with irony, she winced.

"Nae. Even when she refused to return to Craiglocky with me two weeks later, I still believed she'd honor her vows. She claimed her father be furious we'd secretly married and needed time to find someone to take her place at the inn."

You can't take the whore out of a lascivious strumpet any more than you can strip the ocean of salt.

Bernard rolled onto his back, his paws and belly in the air, and released a soft snore.

Lydia envied the cat his oblivious rest. She ran a hand over Bernard's belly, almost afraid to look at Alasdair, to see the pain his wretched, unfaithful wife had wrought.

"What happened then?"

Unfamiliar anger at the injustice swept her. He didn't deserve to suffer because of his wife's betrayal, and he ought to be allowed a second chance at love. To find someone who'd adore him, faults and all.

"She asked me to return in a month. At first, I told nae one of the union, already suspicious I'd made a huge mistake. I finally confessed my marriage to my parents, swearin' them to silence."

Which explained why, in all the years she'd known the McTavishes, no one had uttered as much as a word about the taboo subject.

"Just over five weeks later, I be able to return, and when I did, prepared to brin' Searón home, she refused to go with me." He curled his lip, more sneer than smile. "She admitted she'd thought I be the laird's son. That I had money and position. She'd nae interest in bein' married to a lowly clansman, and even less interest in livin' in the Highlands."

"How utterly awful. I don't mind telling you, I'd like to pull her hair out." Strand by wiry, orange strand. Almost feeling the tendrils in her balled hands, Lydia squeezed tightly.

Alasdair lifted his head, finally meeting her eyes, raw pain deepening his to slate. "My love wisna enough."

"We can't help whom we love, Alasdair, because love is a gift, freely given." Though not always accepted or requited, and certainly no guarantee of happiness even if one should be fortunate enough to find it. That she knew firsthand.

"Maybe, but I had nae business lovin' the likes of her." Each word resounded more bitterly than the last.

One hand cradling her chin, she quirked a brow askance. "But if we try to control something so special and powerful, attempt to put parameters and conditions around the emotion, then love is stifled and eventually dies. It becomes less splendid and meaningful when we dictate its performance by our expectations."

He half snorted, half grunted.

"My love didna die. It be brutally murdered, inch by torturous inch. Until the hurt became so unbearable, I begged God to feel nothin' at all. And then, at long last, when I did become numb, I missed feelin' anythin' but dinna ken how to be whole again."

How well she understood that.

Her love for Flynn hadn't died a violent death, brutally abused and neglected as Alasdair's, yet her heart had bled for months afterward. Still ached wretchedly at times, truth be told. Usually when she lay, alone and lonely in her silent bed, dwelling on her losses.

Of late, those moments had come more infrequently, partially because she'd been too weary to stay awake after climbing between her heather-scented sheets, and also because of Alasdair's presence.

She'd been wrong to criticize him for his cynicism regarding love. He'd experienced the heartache and irreparable, lasting harm of infidelity, and she'd no right to judge him when she hadn't suffered the same.

No one did unless they'd experienced the like themselves.

"I thought I knew what love was." Lydia offered a self-conscious half-smile.

"Ye mean Bretheridge?"

"Yes. His lordship snared my girlish affection, and I'd convinced myself he meant to propose. I think, too, he thought himself enamored of me, until he met his wife. His feelings for me paled in comparison. I saw that at once." The truth of it had been glaringly, humiliatingly obvious. A blow to her pride and self-esteem as well. "I'm glad he found true love, even though it meant I hurt bloody awful for a time."

A long, long time.

"Yer unusually unselfish, Lydia, yet I canna help but think Bretheridge an imbecile fer choosin' another over ye."

"Ah, but his heart made the decision for him, long before his brain realized what had happened." Not an uncommon occurrence with men from her observations. "I'll not deny I was crushed in the beginning. But time has healed the worst, and now other than my battered pride, I have recovered."

Mostly.

"Nae, ye haven't. Any more than I have. Ye've learned to cope." He shook his head, and several strands of honey-blond hair fell forward. "Ye willna be over him 'til another claims yer heart."

"I imagine the same can be said of you, Alasdair."

He grinned and shook his head. "Nae, I realize what I felt fer my wife was more youthful lust than unconditional love. My parents should've locked me in the Keep's dungeon until my randy days were behind me."

Lydia snorted, loud enough to rouse Bernard. After giving her a haughty look through green-eyed slits, he twitched his nose, put a paw across it, and went back to sleep.

"You'd still be there then, I fear." She giggled at Alasdair's affronted expression. "Your romantic escapades are quite er, shall we say, legendary?"

"Legendary, be they?" He waggled his eyebrows, a distinctly naughty, almost lecherous, grin bending his mouth.

A frisson pelted along her skin, raising the flesh.

"Aye." Dare she voice what she'd heard whispered?

His smug, unrepentant expression decided for her.

She gathered her hair into a rope and smiled naughtily. "Known for your *stamina*. According to the absolutely delighted maids sighing in Craiglocky's corridors and abundant nooks."

Throwing her hair over her shoulder, Lydia giggled again when his face flushed. She'd made him color. Interesting.

"Women talk too much and exaggerate too." His peeved mutter caused Bernard to open a sleepy eye again. "See, even that scraggly excuse fer a cat agrees."

Laughter burbled upward from her chest. Only he could make her laugh at a moment like this. "Why not petition the church for a divorce? Surely there are provisions for such situations as yours. Abandonment and adultery?"

He stared over her head for an extended moment before drawing his gaze to her face.

"Pride. At first, I be convinced she'd return. When she realized how brutal life fer a woman without means could be. Afterward, when I heard she'd taken up with one rich protector after another, I decided I'd never marry again. So there wisna a need to have the union dissolved. Protected me from all the lasses settin' their caps fer me."

Ah, that smug remark was for her benefit.

He jabbed a pickle-sized thumb at his chest, a charmer's smile twitching his lips. "I dinna need to produce an heir, after all."

Lydia slid her feet into her slippers then raised on her toes and blew out one set of candles. The fire burned low, and after banking the coals, she pushed the tall screen back into place. Hands behind her, she leaned against the mantel. "But what if someday you meet a woman who's worth risking marriage again?"

He encircled her upper arm with his large hand, tenderness softening his rugged features.

What kind of dimwitted nincompoop left a man like Alasdair?

"If I were a free man, ye can bet yer lairdship," he whispered fiercely, "I'd not only win the contest and claim ye as my wife, but I'd plunder yer sweet body from dusk to dawn."

Outrageous!

That wicked image nearly buckled her knees, and she clutched the mantel.

"I'm far from immune to ye, Lydia. But I ken my place. And yers. I'd not disgrace or insult ye with anythin' but a ring on yer finger." He lifted her chin, regret evident in his lowered eyes and the crease between his brows. "And that, ye ken, I canna offer ye."

Yes, he could. "Alasdair—"

"Lydia, ye—"

Without preamble, Uncle Gordon plowed into the room. "What be ye doin' here, McTavish?" Disapproval hardened his angular features. "Lydia, yer entertainin' in yer nightclothes? That be indecent."

He had a knack for stating the obvious.

Lydia scooped Bernard into her arms. Hopefully Uncle Gordon hadn't heard Alasdair's declaration. "Yes, Uncle. I am, and if you'd properly delivered my message, Alasdair would've come tomorrow and saved both of us a great deal of awkwardness."

"Never mind that. Ye've other more pressin' worries." Frazzled, Gordon cupped the back of his head and paced to a window to peer out nervously.

She paused in nuzzling the cat and sliced Alasdair a questioning glance. "Whatever has you so agitated, Uncle Gordon?"

He spun around. "Four of Sir Gwaine's men arrived tonight. They mean to compete fer yer hand on his behalf."

"Nae!" The startled cry escaped, as fear slammed into her with a Highland bull's force.

Hadn't Father or Gordon considered the possibility when they dreamed up the confounded competition?

Fiend seize it.

Sir Gwaine MacHardy, a loathsome feudal baron, had attempted to abduct her and force her to marry him for Tornbury's lands. More precisely, the gold discovered a few months past. "I thought MacHardy and his cohorts were still imprisoned."

Ye Gods. *This*, along with everything else?

"MacHardy boasts a few high connections and managed to arrange his release and that of his men," Uncle Gordon said.

"He knows who to bribe, you mean." Father would have apoplexy when he heard. She had to keep the news from him, but how?

"I suppose, Ross, ye be goin' to claim you hadn't considered this possibility." Alasdair looked as if he wanted to snap Uncle Gordon's neck. One of his large hands could easily encircle her uncle's thin throat, and with a quick jerk—

Stop it, Lydia. Uncle Gordon didn't know this would happen.

"I . . ." Uncle gulped and took a reflexive step backward. "I didna think they'd dare."

Lydia swallowed her fear and drew a deep breath. "Well, they have. Now what do we do about it? How do we know they won't attempt to abduct me again?"

Chapter 14

"I'll crack their skulls like quail eggs if they so much as look at ye cockeyed." Alasdair joined Gordon by the window. Nothing remotely untoward went on below.

"That I'd like to see." Flint echoed in Lydia's voice. She had no love for the MacHardys.

"But, we let them compete," Alasdair said, glancing over his shoulder. "Just like all the other entrants. The gesture will be a powerful testament to the Farnsworth's fairness and power by showin' ye dinna fear yer enemies."

But Lydia did dread them.

Her firmed mouth and rapid breath gave her away. However, the brave lass kept her chin up and shoulders squared. Small in stature, she possessed gumption aplenty.

"Very well, but I insist both of you," she pointed between him and Ross, "keep them away from me. And that means making sure they're never alone in my presence. Assign extra guards if need be. In fact, do that anyway. I want MacHardy's men watched day and night. I don't trust them. Now if you'll excuse me, I've had a long day, and I wish to seek my bed."

"I bid ye guid night." Alasdair bent into a half bow as she passed while Ross, much like a nervous crow, kept darting peeks toward the square.

Did the man have a single courageous bone in his spindly body? Amazing that with a spine and character as weak as a cooked noodle, he could stand upright at all.

"I look forward to my lesson tomorrow, Alasdair. 'Till

then." The cat tucked beneath one arm, Lydia glided from the solar.

"What lesson?" A scowl contorted Ross's face.

"Not that it be any of yer business, but I mean to teach Lydia how to wield a blade." Alasdair patted his leg, a dirk nestled in the stocking. "We be startin' with the *Sgian Dubh*."

"Bloody waste of time fer a woman," Ross muttered, still darting leery glances out the window.

Why did MacHardy's men's presence have him as nervous as a trull whose monthlies were late? They weren't a threat to him.

Alasdair followed Lydia to the exit, expecting to hear the subtle slap of her slippers gradually fading along the corridor. Instead, only a cloak of silence met his trained ears. "I expect to see ye in the courtyard at four of the clock tomorrow, too, Ross. Ye need to be able to defend the laird. The men be mutterin' yer a craven."

Ross, his stance wide and belligerent, crossed his arms. "I be afraid my duties—"

"Shaggin' the village whores 'till dawn? Then sleepin' the morn away when ye should be attendin' to yer responsibilities?" Brows arched knowingly, Alasdair shook his head. "Nae, ye'll be there, or I'll inform the laird what ye really be doin' all day. Time to start earnin' yer wages, but more importantly, the Farnsworth clan's respect."

"Mind yer own bloody business, McTavish," Ross said through clenched teeth.

"It be my business, and I winna hesitate to suggest Farnsworth and Lydia replace ye immediately if yer arse isnae in the courtyard tomorrow with the other men."

Ross cut the air with an angry gesture. "To hell with ye. Ye have nae right to interfere. Ye be an outsider, and ye'll be gone in a few weeks. If we be lucky."

"Aye, ye'd like that, wouldn't ye? But I didna plan

on leavin' until a new war chief be selected." And given the Farnsworth troops' inadequacies, that wouldn't be for weeks yet.

So much for Rome. Or Greece.

Or anywhere but Scotland for a goodly while.

Pretty hazelnut eyes flecked with moss green, rimmed in amber and framed by lush lashes, sprang to mind.

Dammit.

Lydia couldn't be his.

He needed to hurl all romantic notions, even his remotest, most secret dreams, off the nearest crag into the roiling waves.

Ross rattled on, whining and complaining like a bairn. "Ye dinna belong here. But the laird has grown so weak and feeble-minded, he's makin' piss-poor decisions. Like considerin' Lydia as laird."

"She'd be a far sight better laird than ye."

How could Lydia, anyone, for that matter, stand his constant sniveling? Did the man possess ballocks? Maybe someone needed to peek beneath his kilt and make sure he possessed a pair bigger than a newborn mouse's.

Alasdair retraced his steps until he stood over Ross. He'd no doubt he could break the defiant little twig with scarcely any effort, but the Farnsworths didn't need any more drama or division.

His chin thrust upward and animosity flaring in his eyes, Ross attempted bravado. "Nae woman can hope to lead this clan properly. They need a mon as chief."

"I may nae be a Farnsworth, Ross, but make nae mistake. While I am on Tornbury soil, my loyalty be to Farnsworth and his daughter. If ye dare to speak ill of either again, ye'll answer to me and my blade. And I winna hesitate to tell them of yer treachery."

Quite enjoying the terror-induced moisture beading

Ross's forehead and upper lip, Alasdair lifted his dagger and feathered his fingers atop his dirk's bone handle.

Ross gulped loudly, his goggle-eyed gaze riveted on the blade.

Alasdair curved his mouth, more of superior smirk than a warm or humorous smile. "Och, and ye should ken, I didna trust ye, so I'll be watchin' ye closely. I winna hesitate to gut ye like the cowardly cur ye be if ye brin' any more grief to Lydia."

Ross's mouth worked, and his eyes bulged for an instant before a sly glint entered them. He cast a brief glance to the empty doorway before eyeing Alasdair. "Lydia, be it now? Ye care fer the chit then?"

"Yer off yer head." One blow would wipe the superior look form Ross's weasely face. "I only be vowin' what any dedicated war chief would."

Careful there lad, or ye'll give yer secret away.

Alasdair wrapped fingers around the knife's hilt. He'd welcome driving the blade into the coward, but now wasn't the time. Instead, he returned it to his stocking.

Ross rubbed his chin, his eyes narrowed to shrewd slits as craftiness replaced his fright. "Aye. Ye do care. Yet I distinctly heard ye say ye cudna offer fer her."

Damnation. The little, whoremongering turd had heard his declaration to Lydia.

What else had he eavesdropped on?

Sloppy on Alasdair's part.

"Why nae, I wonder?" An exaggerated contemplative look upon his face, Ross tapped his fingertips atop his folded arms. "Does my uncle ken? I suspect he'd welcome a match between ye. Would encourage it. In fact, I think that be the real reason ye be here. He'll have a fit when he finds out his schemin' has been fer naught."

His mocking chuckle set Alasdair's teeth on edge, and rather than wipe the gloating sneer from Ross's smug face, as his flexing fingers itched to do, he curled his toes in his boots until they screamed for reprieve.

"That be none of yer business." *Interfering whelp.* "What be yer concern, however, be attendin' to estate business on the laird's behalf. I think perhaps a thorough examination of Tornbury's books be in order as well."

That ought to deter the conniving wretch.

For a moment, Ross looked like he might hurl his haggis onto Alasdair's dusty boots, and Ross took a wide step backward.

"How, then, do ye intend to compete in the contest?" Ross laughed, another derisive crow. "Ye be disqualified. Ye canna contend."

Awfully happy about that misconception, wasn't he?

"My God," Gordon snickered. "What if a MacHardy wins? She'll have to marry Sir Gwaine. Oh, that be rich revenge. And Old Farnsworth will have to name me laird."

Alasdair seized Ross's lapels, yanking him off his feet.

Fear glinted in the silver shards of Ross's eyes, mere inches away, as tremors riddled the runtling from thin shoulder to his dangling legs.

"I qualify. Read the entry form. And I shall win against Sir Gwaine's mewlin' milksops." Alasdair gave Ross a satisfying, teeth-rattling shake.

"Cease, damn ye." Ross clawed at Alasdair's hands, but he wasn't ready to release the cull just yet.

"There nae be anythin' that says the winner has to offer fer her or that the winner canna be married. A careless oversight on the part of the person draftin' the entry form." No doubt Ross had himself to blame for bungling that bit. "It only stipulates Lydia be the prize. A prize that can be declined, which I intend to do."

He thrust Ross away so violently, he stumbled and would've fallen if he hadn't grabbed a nearby table.

The small gold-framed likenesses of Lydia's brothers atop the table rattled and tilted before one toppled over with a hollow *thunk*, then the other followed. The distinct sound of glass cracking rent the air.

"But why win at all then if Tornbury isnae goin' to be yers?" Ross's expression of sincere bafflement earned him a full grin.

Lydia's freedom was reward enough.

Alasdair folded his arms, mindful the movement emphasized his biceps and chest. "I nae be aware Tornbury ever be part of the bargain."

"I, erm, I misspoke." Chagrin blanketed Ross's features, and his sly gaze slid away.

"I'm sure ye did."

With visible effort, Ross collected himself and scraped a hand across his bristly face. "I'd best be to bed myself if'n I'm to obey yer dictates."

Alasdair stepped aside, permitting him to pass.

Ross's clipped speech rang with resentment. "Ken this, McTavish, I nae be a fool, nor as weak and incompetent as ye and the other Scots think I be. I wadna be a bit surprised if the old laird disna name someone else his successor in the end."

"And we both ken who ye want that to be, didna we?" One knee cocked, Alasdair rested a hand on his hip.

Ross was such a transparent, envious arse.

"I wadna hold my breath waitin' fer Farnsworth to change his mind. He'd prefer the seed of his loins lead his clan, even if it be a woman." Alasdair righted the fallen frames, revealing jagged cracks across the fronts. He'd see to their repair at his expense, of course. "Yer covetin' the position grows tedious and be as obvious and offensive as a loud fart in small cupboard."

"We shall see." Curling his lip, Ross stalked past.

"Aye. We shall." They would indeed.

And God help Alasdair for agreeing to teach Lydia how to use a dirk first. The training would require close contact, and frequent touching.

Would she wear skirts or don a pair of her brother's breeches as the Ferguson women typically did?

His mouth went dry as wood ash at the notion of her tight, rounded rump in breeches, and he gritted his teeth against a hot surge in his nether regions.

Maybe *he* ought to pay the village harlot a visit.

Nae after Ross had his wick there first.

So be it.

Alasdair would consider his male discomfort penance for stealing a kiss from Lydia. God, her mouth had been sweet, her innocence blissful.

He blew out the remaining candles before taking a final survey of the courtyard.

Empty and silent.

Nothing for it. He'd start her training on the morrow.

He'd given his word, and with the MacHardys' presence, as well as her oily uncle skulking about, she needed to be able to protect herself. She couldn't very well cart her bow and quiver wherever she went, and besides, that weapon was useless in close encounters.

Too bad she couldn't compete in the archery portion of the tournament.

His steps faltered on the carpeted risers.

Why couldn't she?

It would prove her mettle and skill, boost her confidence, and since he doubted anyone would best her, she'd take the points for that event.

He grinned.

Why, sometimes his keen mind surprised even him.

He'd mention the idea to her tomorrow, quite anticipating her smile of gratification. Hell, he'd take any smile she directed his way.

Hopeless sot.

But how to get Farnsworth to agree?

Alasdair rubbed his jaw and slowly resumed his trek downstairs.

Well, that might take a bit of clever manipulating.

He grinned in satisfaction. The notion didn't appall him. No, not at all.

Farnsworth had thought nothing of using Lydia, or Alasdair for that matter. The chief had gambled on Ewan's loyalty when he'd asked him to send Alasdair. Both lairds presumed his sense of honor and duty would compel him to oblige, but they'd only been partially right.

Lydia's asking and the promise of time away had tempted far more. Yes, indeed, Lydia taking the archer competition might be just the thing.

Served the crusty Scot right, getting a taste of his own behavior. As long as it didn't kill him. Lydia would never forgive Alasdair then. And her approval mattered. A hell of a lot more than it should. More than he ought to have permitted.

Mayhap the time to pursue a divorce had truly come. He certainly had just cause.

Letting himself out the grand entrance, Alasdair searched the crisp, clear sky and breathed in the glacial air. An owl hooted, low and haunting, and a moment later, another answered the eerie call.

First, he must determine if Searón even yet lived.

Where the hell did he start?

Where her *unusual* appetites might be fed. The most corrupt, depraved, and vilest of brothels.

Tree branches rattled and groaned as an icy wind gust blew past, and he shivered, as much from disgust as cold. Frost already covered the courtyard stones, the rooftops, and every other exposed surface.

Slapping his hands against his shoulders, he trotted down the stone risers. He'd welcome snowfall. That'd mean the temperatures had risen.

Warmer climes beckoned him, but he resolutely shoved those dreams into a chilly corner until later.

How much later, he couldn't venture to guess.

Rather than make straight for the barracks, he strode through the arched entry intent on circling to the mansion's back.

Softly whistling a mournful tune—damnation, the same melancholy melody McLeon had been playing as he mooned over a woman—Alasdair surveyed the area with a warrior's practiced eye.

Lydia's second story chamber lay on this side of the house, the farthest from the barracks and guards.

Leaning against an oak's trunk in the garden, he stared up at her window. A dim light glowed between a smallish gap in the curtains, but no shadowy form glided about her chamber.

Likely abed already.

Did she sleep with candles lit throughout the night? If so, what did she fear?

Angling his head for a better view, he studied the structure. The straight stone walls contained no ledges or casings. No easy access to her bedchamber, at least from the ground, even with a ladder.

His gaze gravitated to the roof.

Not there either. Too steep.

And the windows on either side of her chamber were too far away to access her room.

Satisfied she was safe, he straightened and yawned. He'd be bloody tired in the morning.

A movement at the mansion's corner snared his attention. A slender black-cloaked figure hurried through the garden, carrying what looked like valises, and after glancing furtively 'round, slipped through the stone arched gateway.

Ross just couldn't forego his swiving, could he?

Another, shorter figure separated from the bushes bordering the garden's far side, and the moon illuminated a blue robe.

Lydia?

Foolish chit.

What the blazes was she doing out here in her nightclothes and following her randy uncle to boot?

Chapter 15

Teeth chattering, Lydia wrenched her robe tighter as she charged after Uncle Gordon, a wind cold enough to freeze hell chafing at her heels and rudely sneaking up her gown to nip at her bare bum.

Enough was enough.

She'd held her tongue as the rumors and whispers about his unsavory nocturnal habits tickled her ears, but tonight after discovering just how low he'd sunk, she'd determined to put a stop to his actions once and for all.

After leaving the solar, she'd been annoyingly wide awake.

How fickle slumber proved when, minutes before, she could scarcely keep her eyes open or smother her yawns.

She'd made for the kitchen, intending to warm milk and nibble a shortbread biscuit or two. And perhaps, if she timed it just so, she'd have another opportunity to bid Alasdair goodnight as he departed.

A completely platonic, polite farewell, of course. Nothing else. Certainly, there'd be no more kissing between them.

Drat it all. Such a disappointment.

However, the study's slightly cracked entrance snared her attention. Not particularly unusual or alarming; nevertheless, she couldn't shake the impression something was amiss.

Raising her candle holder, she prodded the door open with one foot. No fire burned in the grate, but the scent of warm beeswax and a freshly extinguished candle lingered in the air.

Venturing farther in, she searched the dim corners. The open drapes lent a jot more light; enough to determine she was alone.

Someone had recently vacated the room, hastily, too, given the open door and the chair's odd angle.

Alarm streaked through her.

Had they been robbed?

She pivoted to inspect the desk.

Yes, the drawers, including the one containing Tornbury's money box, hung splintered and askew. The fireplace poker lay beside the walnut desk, as if tossed there in haste.

Unease tickled between her shoulder blades.

She pulled away the money drawer's broken front, not at all surprised to find the cash chest absent. Father and Gordon possessed the keys, but any manner of tool might be used to pry it open, including the discarded poker.

The process of demolishing the drawers must've been noisy, but then again, the stout, three-inch-thick cherry wood door would've muffled the sound. Even a passerby in the corridor mightn't have heard the wood breaking or detected any plundering.

A reddish glint along the upper drawer's cracked bottom caught the corner of her eye.

What was that?

After removing the top estate ledger, she applied a letter opener to the wood slat and managed to pop it loose, revealing a false bottom with a hidden register. If the drawer hadn't been so damaged, she mightn't ever have seen the small gap.

Brows drawn together, she picked up the thin record. After lifting the cover and seeing the detailed entries, she swiftly looked at its front again.

This wasn't the register Gordon had showed Da and her each Friday. Until recently, that was. Because of his illness the ledger hadn't been examined in some time.

A sickening sensation toppled her stomach.

Setting the volume to the side, she opened the familiar ruby leather-bound book engraved with a gold scroll and raised *TF* that Gordon provided for the weekly audits.

After slowly sinking into the comfortably worn high back chair, she drew the candelabra closer then pulled the ledgers together until they lay side by side. Duplicate entries in Gordon's neat script went on for pages and pages, yet Tornbury's official register, the one he produced for inspection, consistently recorded different figures.

God rot Uncle Gordon's treacherous soul to hell's lowest level.

She and Father had been too compliant, too apathetic, had trusted him too dashed much. They'd dismissed his churlishness and inefficiency as trifling flaws, failing to see his true character.

How many other things had he lied about?

Flopping back into the chair, Lydia folded her arms and scowled at the splintered wood littering the pecan brown and camel-toned carpet. She'd wager her virtue Gordon was their thief; the wrecked drawers a ploy to throw them off his scent, the ingrate.

How long had he been stealing from Tornbury?

Quite possibly since he'd become the estate steward.

These ledgers were the most current, but where were the previous years' records stored? She ought to have considered this months ago, but honestly, she never expected there'd be a need.

As much as Da acknowledged Gordon's faults, he'd never hinted of anything untoward in that regard.

Lydia scanned the dimly lit room, self-castigation prodding her. She should've suspected something like this. All the signs had been present, but she'd naively hoped she'd misread them—that Uncle Gordon couldn't be so conniving and dishonest.

Nibbling her lower lip, she tapped her chilled fingers atop the closest register while rubbing her cold feet together.

Better ask Da where the other records were stored. She could claim she wanted to acquaint herself with the estate's bookkeeping then uncover precisely how devious Uncle had been.

By George, tonight she'd send the ungrateful, lying cull on his way. If he left quietly and returned the money, she'd persuade Da not to bring charges against him, but if he kicked up a fuss—

She'd set the magistrate *and* Alasdair on him.

She'd quite enjoy the latter, truth to tell.

Rather like a lion stalking a lizard, the outcome predetermined, but amusing to watch for a brief spell.

Now, running across the frozen grass, crunching beneath her icy soles, she kept her gaze trained on Gordon's skulking form. Even with the full moon, once he passed through the gate into the hedgerow-bordered oak grove, she'd have a hard time catching him, especially if he had a mount waiting.

"Uncle Gordon. Stop."

He stiffened, but increased his stride, not even turning his head.

Oh, he meant to ignore her, did he?

Holding her side against a sudden cramp, she raced after him.

"Stop this instant." She raised her voice, beyond caring she might be overheard. "I know you have been keeping duplicate books and stole the money box," she shouted.

He pivoted so fast, she stopped running and skidded along the frost-slickened ground, nearly losing her footing.

"Wheesht. Hold yer vile tongue." He veered a swift, wary glance around.

"You tried to make it appear as if someone else broke into the study," she gasped, the freezing air stinging her lungs with each hard-earned pant.

Gordon tossed his bags to the ground and stalked toward her. "Those be evil accusations, Lydia."

"They're true, and you know it full well." Holding her ribs, she strove to catch her breath. "Why, Uncle Gordon, after we put our trust in you?"

He glared daggers at her, his lip curled into a hateful sneer.

He despised her.

When had he come to do so?

Surely his coveting the lairdship in recent weeks hadn't fermented this profound hostility. No, instinct assured her his loathing ran much deeper, beyond her personally.

A pitiable, intense bitterness brought on by his status, out of his control and decreed by the circumstances of his birth. Very similar to Alasdair's position actually, but the slight similarity ended there, as had how each man dealt with his lot.

Peculiar, that even now, she could spare Uncle Gordon a morsel of compassion despite his despicable actions.

His type would never be happy. Never find contentment. He thrived on discord. Jealousy and envy constantly stirred his dissatisfaction, urging his malcontent to bitter resentment and ire.

She jerked her chin toward his abandoned bags. "Is the money in one of those? Why would you do something so foolish for a few hundred pounds? Are you in some sort of trouble that you need funds? Perhaps if you'd told me—"

"I dinna mean to answer any of yer nosy questions, lass," he scoffed. He kicked at a satchel. "And I be leavin' Tornbury. Fer good."

A pang of regret pricked her. He was family after all, and they'd so few members left. She'd been a shy, thumb-sucking four-year-old when he'd arrived, skinny, hostile, and full of distrust. And he'd been kind to her. Oh, not in the beginning.

He'd sulked and shouted, disappearing for hours on end. But he'd also brought her a baby rabbit he'd found, and showed her how to skip stones on the river.

Nonetheless, a blackguard such as he couldn't be permitted to stay. "If you return the money, I shall try to convince Da not to bring you up on charges."

That would take some doing. Da abhorred dishonesty and demanded integrity, most particularly from kin.

"However, you must agree to never set foot here again." She jutted her chin upward and crossed her arms. "You've betrayed our trust and are no longer welcome at Tornbury."

He laughed, the gravelly cackle more maniacal than humorous.

Cold definitely wasn't the cause of her skin puckering or the shiver that rattled her from neck to knees.

"Do ye have any idea, how much, and how long I've detested ye, Lydia?"

His words battered her with the force of an open-handed slap.

"Havin' to sit by and watch as yer droolin' father planned on makin' ye laird, when he ken—*everybody* ken—I should be the next laird?" Fisting his hands, he snarled, his features feral and savage beneath the variegated moonbeams streaming through the trees' naked branches.

Hatred fairly oozed from him, wave upon wave of animosity and revulsion. He cast a furtive glance round, his sneer transforming into a sinister smile.

She sucked in a swift, icy gulp of air, pressing her hand to her throat. Her heart vaulted to the pulse tapping frantically beneath her nearly numb fingertips.

Lydia took an involuntary step backward. Then another, this time calculated to put distance between them. Stupid, rash girl for thinking she could deal with him alone.

She dared a swift peek over her shoulder.

Could she outrun him?

In her boots? Yes. But not a chance in her bedroom slippers.

Another rash oversight.

When would she learn to think things through? Consider all the consequences? Examine situations from every angle as a competent chief must? Had she done so, she wouldn't be in this pickle.

"Ye really be a fool, lass, followin' me into the trees," he said, tossing a glance behind him at the towering grove. "Especially when yer nemeses, the MacHardys, be here. At my invitation, mind ye."

She used his gloating to retreat a few steps farther.

Keep him talking.

"Why on earth would you invite them? You know full well what Sir Gwaine attempted. Do you think a few weeks in jail truly dampened his greed?"

Another few steps nearer to the house.

Gordon laughed again, inching closer. "Who do ye think helped them the first time, ye dimwitted idiot?"

That stopped her in her frozen tracks.

My God. He couldn't possibly be that vile.

Anguish lanced her, stabbing her heart and mind in a brutal onslaught, his heartless betrayal rendering her incapable of responding.

Uncle Gordon slapped a hand to his chest and feigned anguish. "Nae, her abductor hasnae been found. She must've caught him in the act of robbin' the place."

He's off his head. Daft as a Bedlam border.

Or desperate. And desperate men knew no bounds.

Where that thought came from, she didn't know, but he definitely behaved like a man with no other recourse.

She needed to stall him, and hope—*pray*—someone had heard her earlier shouting and would raise an alarm.

Not much chance of that with this wind.

Another hellish blast of air slammed into her, turning her blood to ice.

"Even if I disappear, Da will never name you laird, Gordon. He told me so, just this afternoon." She sought something to use as a weapon. A few twigs, one or two decent sized, lay scattered on the stone-riddled ground, but could she reach one in time?

Her attention fixed on him, she edged toward an arm-thick branch.

"I nae believe ye. Ye've poisoned his mind toward me, ye have. He said I be like his own son." Gordon slapped his chest. "When his sons obliged me in cockin' up their sainted toes, I should've been next in line. Not ye, a silly scrap of a lass."

He spat the last contemptuously, small puffs of steam floating from his mouth. How bloody low had the temperature dropped? Low enough she shouldn't be outside in a night robe.

She shook her head, her unbound hair billowing around her shoulders as the wind snatched at it with grasping fingers. "He said you are too rash, too hotheaded, and not strong enough to lead."

"And who filled his head with those lies?" Gordon jabbed a forefinger at her. "Ye did."

"Gordon, *I've* been the one to defend you. I asked that you be given second chances. Sadly, tonight you've proven Da's every fear has been justified."

Uncertainty tightened his features. "Nae. He loves me, as if he'd beget me hisself. He wadna speak against me unless ye influenced him."

"Oh, for pity's sake. Get over your high opinion of yourself." Perhaps the untarnished truth would finally get through to him. "I was being kind earlier. What Father really called you was a temperamental, mewling, teat-sucking bairn unworthy of even the estate steward position, and he should've let your sorry arse rot in prison all those years ago!"

Chapter 16

At Gordon's furious growl, Lydia scooted farther away. Unwise to have let her temper get the better of her and rile him further.

"Ye be lyin', wench." His countenance grew more vicious. "After yer brothers died, he relied on me." He pressed his thumb to his chest. "Me, Lydia, not ye."

Lydia took another covert step backward.

Raising his ire hadn't been the better part of discretion either. She could scream and pray the sound brought help.

"I'm curious." She retreated two more paces. "Why did you persuade Father to host the tournament?"

He chuckled nastily. "All manner of knaves and ne'er-do-wells turn out fer this type of event, and accidents and attacks nae be uncommon."

Gordon whipped his dirk from his stocking, the blade wickedly sharp and ominous in the half-light.

He meant to kill her.

"Alas, she didna even have time to cry out," he warbled in a singsong voice.

Lydia shrieked as a huge form charged through the gate at a dead run, shoving her roughly to the frozen ground as he barreled past.

"Stay down."

Alasdair.

She landed hard on her side, scraping her hand in gravel as her thigh connecting painfully with a skull-sized rock.

"Wrong on that account, ye goddamned sod." Fury rendered Alasdair's voice a harsh roar. "She had time to scream, and ye can bet yer snivelin' hide, these woods be crawlin' with men within minutes. Ye'll regret the day ye ever threatened her."

Uncle Gordon launched his dirk, and the blade hurtled through the air, impaling the tip several inches into Alasdair's shoulder.

Lydia shrieked again. "Alasdair!"

His visage drawn into murderous lines, his pace didn't slow a jot as he yanked the knife free, and after tossing the blade into the shrubberies, let loose a warrior's thundering roar.

Lydia's scalp tingled and her stomach clenched at such ferociousness as she scrambled to her feet. Uncle Gordon had gravely miscalculated, and like any wounded beast, Alasdair would show no mercy in retaliation.

Panic flashing across his pasty face, Gordon sprinted into the trees. Alasdair raced after, his great strides making short work of the distance between them.

As he'd predicted, clansmen and contestants, a few holding lanterns and some wearing only kilts or trews, streamed through the gate. Even MacHardy's men trotted into the grove, though after a few moments, they wandered to a stump, and the tallest lit a clay pipe.

When none of them gave her more than a passing glance, she relaxed a fraction. But only just.

"Miss Farnsworth, what happened? Be ye all right?" Mr. McLeon, accompanied by Lennox, neither wearing a shirt, burst through the gateway.

If she were of a faster bent, she'd ogle their impressive expanse of exposed flesh. Instead, she spared them a cursory glance before seeking Alasdair.

How badly was he hurt?

"Yes, yes, I'm fine. My uncle robbed us, and when I confronted him, he threatened me."

Would Uncle Gordon have really killed her?

Squinting, she peered between the massive trees where the Scots milled about, calling to one another.

Yes, she feared, Uncle Gordon might have, and that raised a whole new set of disturbing questions. First, what had triggered his panicked robbery and flight? The second, why hadn't he taken any more valuables? The mansion boasted many. And thirdly, why make such an irrational move now?

More suspicions crept forth, ones she couldn't face quite yet.

Esme, accompanied by a crookedly bewigged McGibbons, hurried to her side as fast his lopsided gait allowed.

Wearing pink silk dance slippers—utterly ruined from the grass—a feather and ribbon covered lavender and emerald poke bonnet, a Spanish brown and russet pelisse over her robe, and—*egads, were those yellow evening gloves?*—Esme presented quite a comical picture.

Yet, Lydia didn't doubt in her eagerness to help, the poor dear had done her utmost as she speedily donned the mismatched attire to prevent the scandal appearing in her nightclothes would create.

Something Lydia ought to have considered as well, as her disgraceful attire drew the Scots' scrutiny. More than one man grinned and nudged another.

"Lydia, whatever are you doing outside?" Esme sneaked a glance at Mr. McLeon, and the rogue gave her a wicked smile. Up went her button nose. "I heard a scream, and when I found your chamber empty, I about cast up my cornbread for worry."

Esme's attention repeatedly strayed to Mr. McLeon's magnificent bare chest, and the cocky, grinning Scot puffed out his pectorals, his abdomen rippling with muscles.

Even Lydia had to admit he was a fine specimen of manhood, though her stomach didn't flop weirdly, and her unruffled heart beat steadily on while her knees remained firm in his presence.

Unlike when in Alasdair's.

"I confess, I was hasty and imprudent." A mistake a competent laird never made, and Lydia wouldn't make again.

Lacking men's physical strength and brute intimidation, wisdom and shrewdness must be her armaments. In the future, they, as well as cunning and discernment, would be. She was a quick study and learned from her mistakes. There'd be no repeating this blunder.

When Da heard about this . . .

Why must he know?

There wasn't any need to burden him.

Tension eased from her. Indeed, none at all.

Gordon had fled, and even he wasn't imbecilic enough to return. She'd notify the magistrate, have Alasdair increase the guards, and start carrying a dirk with her—the only weapon she was even remotely familiar with.

So far.

Alasdair would teach her how to use a short sword and pistol. She'd no desire to handle other weapons.

He approached, holding his wounded shoulder, scarlet seeping between his thick fingers. "The excitement be over, everyone. Return to yer beds. McLeon, collect yonder bags and take them to the study. Lennox, post a half dozen extra armed watches around the perimeter and one at each entrance to the mansion." His mouth twitched. "But put a shirt on first, mon."

"Aye, sir. Straightaway." Lennox waved to several men and gave them instructions.

Murmuring their consent, the others, including Esme, wandered back to the mansion or barracks.

"I'll ask Cook to prepare hot chocolate for us, Lydia," Esme called over her shoulder before hunching into her pelisse and shoving her hands into the pockets.

"Thank you—"

Alasdair grabbed Lydia's upper arm and towed her to the dry stone fence, out of the others' sight should they have turned around.

A bloody handprint marred her robe, a reminder of his untended injury.

"Never, and I do mean *never*, pull a stupid stunt like that again, lass, do ye hear me?"

He didn't release her, but pressed her into the rough stones, his breathing ragged.

"I beg your pardon?" Lydia tugged free and pushed her hair out of her eyes. "I'll admit I didn't think my actions through, but I also had no reason to believe my uncle would do me harm. And I'll thank you to not roughly handle me."

I've had quite enough of dramatics for one night, thank you.

Shutting his eyes, Alasdair raised his face and sucked in a great breath. The moon played across his strong, slightly damp features. He exhaled slowly and another moment passed before he opened his eyes, staring straight into her soul. The intensity of his gaze mesmerized her.

He'd make a fine laird in his own right. He was powerful, strong, yet prudent and kind. Men respected him, women adored him—that she knew all too well—and children worshipped him. He emanated confidence, but not arrogance. Bravery, but not foolhardiness. Diplomacy and tact, but not weakness.

He was everything she desired in a chieftain, wanted to exhibit herself—was determined to become.

Da knew it well too. He'd said as much about Alasdair. More than once, an almost wistful note in his reedy voice.

"Lass, ye asked me here to be yer war chief, and I mean to see ye safe. Ye acted foolishly and impetuously, and ye ken ye canna afford to do either." He touched her cheek briefly.

"I know, and I promise to use greater wisdom in the future." And she would. She needed to prove to Da, to her clan, to Alasdair, and to herself that she had the makings of a laird.

"Can we please not mention this awfulness to Da? It would distress him, and the doctor said I should try to prevent upsets." Peering up at him imploringly, she grasped his forearm, and he winced slightly.

"I dinna like keepin' things from the chief, but his health must be considered. I'll not mention it, but if he asks, I'll tell him the truth."

Lydia nodded. "Thank you. That's more than acceptable."

"And I want the magistrate notified," he added while gently prodding his shoulder.

"My thought as well. Now let's get you inside, so I can look at your injury."

He grunted and stepped away, taking his body's heat with him. "It nae be more than a kitten's scratch."

The cruel wind wound its frigid shroud around her, playing with loose tendrils of her hair, and ruffling Alasdair's shorter mane. Her nose was so cold, she couldn't feel the tip, and her poor toes had lost sensation some time ago.

"Nevertheless, I'd feel better taking a peek to make sure it doesn't grow putrid. Besides, it's freezing out here."

"Aye, I welcome the cold."

As they angled toward the house, she cocked her head and examined him.

I wonder?

"Alasdair?"

"*Hmm*?" He shot her a perfunctory, too pointedly-bland glance.

His calculated indifference didn't fool her. "What if you weren't already married? Would you still have entered the contest or agreed to train our troops?"

Chapter 17

Hell's bells, nae.

Alasdair was no martyr. No saint either.

Her question had the same effect as a mule kick to the gut, and he had no intention of answering.

"I dinna live my life by what-ifs and what might be, lass. Doin' so, I might miss out on the joys and pleasures at hand."

Not liking the direction the conversation had meandered, Alasdair touched his aching shoulder. The knife hadn't penetrated more than two or three inches, but the laceration pulsed with pain. Ross was bloody lucky he'd escaped, for Alasdair had meant to end the blackguard's life.

Would end it the next time they met.

"Dinna ye agree?" He forced a lighthearted grin and wink. "Seize the moment and opportunities while ye may?"

Lydia chuckled. "Sounds selfish, and I'd say you're studiously avoiding answering my question."

Most women would've pouted or become peeved. Instead, she gleaned onto the truth and, with good humor, persisted.

"Aye. I am, at that." She'd come to know him too well, in these short weeks.

Her head barely reached his shoulder, but the expectant gaze she leveled him prompted the truth. Given her adorable nose glowed rosy with cold, he owed her that much.

Providential he couldn't marry. He'd never be able to tell her no. Not that marriage to Lydia didn't appeal, but if Alasdair ever remarried, it would be because he chose to. Not because of a contest won. That seemed entirely too barbaric.

Something his Norse ancestors might have considered. Fancy that? Him, actually contemplating nuptials again? *Bugger me.*

Farnsworth pushed the mark with his ridiculous stipulation that Lydia marry the victor, no doubt prompted and encouraged by Ross. A clever way to fill his coffers, though. In fact, now that the churl had run, Lydia should stand up to her father, demand he cancel the tournament.

"And?" She brazenly encouraged, her impish smile and twinkling eyes irresistible.

"I wouldn't have defied McTavish and refused to assist ye. He did offer me a tempting bribe, as ye ken. But I wadna have entered the competition."

"I suppose I ought to feign affront or some other missish silliness, but I appreciate your forthrightness. It's rather refreshing, truth to tell." Lydia shrugged, her attention straying to the mist hovering eerily between the trees' fringes.

Did Ross hide there, even now watching them, or had he truly fled?

"Ye need to embrace what's before ye, lass, and if ye aren't happy with yer situation, then figure out what ye need to do to change it. Even a lass has choices." Foremost, she needed to move on after Bretheridge.

She stared at him, her eyes wide and luminous, a touch of vulnerability in their depths. Strength glinted there too.

He cupped her icy, cold-reddened cheek, and her heavy lashes drifted downward, fanning her cheeks.

Perhaps she had started to put the marquis behind her.

Preposterous how his heart fluttered at the prospect. Him a hardened warrior bent on never letting a woman wound him again.

Fool.

"I had such dreams, Alasdair. None of which included being the Farnsworth chief." Remorse and sadness lay heavily in her softly uttered words.

Her glorious hair cascading over her shoulders tempted, and he snared a thick tendril for an instant, savoring its silkiness between his rough fingers. "When dreams die, dinna try to resurrect them. The decay and rot leave a lingerin' stench. Instead, find a new dream and focus on achievin' it. Whether that be the lairdship or somethin' else ye've longed to do."

Ye might take yer own advice, mon.

He had.

By agreeing to serve at Tornbury for a time in order to finally have his trip abroad. He wasn't a man of means or station, and had no illusions about his status. He'd not have another opportunity such as the one McTavish had promised.

It would have to be enough.

It *would* be enough.

Alasdair lived to serve, but for a brief time, he'd be his own master. *If* he ever managed to put Tornbury behind him. That didn't appear to be happening any time soon.

Lydia shivered and hugged herself, her cheeks as apple red as her nose and lips. And her fragrance, that sweet tantalizing essence that belonged only to her, wound its tentacles around his senses.

"Not everyone has the option to pursue their dreams, Alasdair. Sometimes duties and responsibilities must come first."

He wanted to take her into his arms and warm her, except his already aroused body needed no more encouragement to torment him. Just a whiff of her scent, the touch of her small hand brushing against him, seeing her gentle curves beneath her robe's soft fabric, all played havoc on his senses, and even the brittle air didn't cool his ardor.

He speared a glance over his shoulder, just to be certain Ross didn't lurk behind them. "Aye, but ye can plot a course fer yerself too, and still fulfill yer obligations."

Puzzlement knitted her usually placid brow. "You think so?"

They'd nearly reached the kitchen entrance, where a guard already stood, palm resting on his sword. He raised a hand in greeting, and Alasdair automatically returned the salute, wincing as his injured shoulder objected.

"Put a different proposal to yer father. Show him yer cleverness and strength. Do ye think he wants ye to meekly follow his dictates? He wants to respect ye, ken he can trust ye to lead. If ye docilely allow the contest and marry the winner, how can he?" He shook his head and pressed the door handle.

She stepped across the threshold. "What are you suggesting?"

"Why dinna ye have the outcome based on a single event? Archery. And ye compete. I ken ye'd win."

Understanding dawned in her intelligent gaze, and she nodded slowly and tapped her lips with two fingers. A musical giggle escaped her and she wagged her head excitedly. "Aye, the contestants will be furious, but since I'm positive Tornbury, rather than my irresistible allure, enticed them to enter in the first place, I would rather enjoy defeating the lot."

She is irresistible.

"I'd enjoy seein' it, too." And by God, he would.

She would be marvelous. A Highland version of the goddess Diana.

He laughed, imagining the men's disgruntled expressions.

She returned his jovial smile. "It's not really fair, but how often does a woman have the opportunity to best men so soundly?"

There was the confident woman he'd seen slay three Highlanders.

He bent close to her ear as they passed into the darkened kitchen. The air hung heavy with spices, herbs, and yeast.

A single candle burned in a holder atop a thick, scarred table. "Show the laird and yer clan the resourcefulness, the shrewdness, I ken ye have in ye."

She nodded, pushing her hair off her shoulders. "I'll announce the change tomorrow. Da cannot object because I'm still honoring his wishes for a competition. Just not quite what he had anticipated."

Her lips tipped up at the corners, and she pointed to a stout chair by the table. "Have a seat, and I'll see to your shoulder. You'll need to remove your vest and shirt."

Her soft, delicate hands on his flesh might send him careening head over arse into insanity.

Or have him kissing her senseless.

Seducing experienced, eager lasses accustomed to raising their skirts for a quick tup mightn't prick his conscience, but only a cur dallied with innocents.

Most particularly a married cur.

"Alasdair, your shirt?" Holding a damp cloth, she approached him.

Best for them both for him to be away. And swiftly.

"Nae, I'll have one of the men patch me up. I bid ye goodnight, and also ask that ye refrain from wanderin' about alone until yer uncle be apprehended."

How could he wiggle out of her training session tomorrow? They shouldn't be alone together. As if he could prevent that for any length of time. Perhaps invite a few more women to participate?

Aye, that'd do.

Who?

Miss Adams, for starters.

Maybe even a few maids and other female servants?

It couldn't hurt for them to know basic defensive moves. A woman never knew when she might be set upon. And the notion would appeal to Lydia.

He paused at the door, permitting himself to drink in her beauty.

She stood framed in the doorway, weariness apparent in her sluggish blinking and slumped shoulders, yet even in her fatigue, he detected resolution in the angle of her chin and set of her jaw.

"Lass, I'd like to include more females in the trainin'. I dinna see a reason why any who are interested shouldnae join ye. I'll limit the practice to an hour so their chores aren't neglected overly long."

Her face brightened, and she put the cloth aside. "That's a superb idea, Alasdair. I agree. All the women should be afforded the same opportunity."

And that's how it came to be. That the next morning a passel of women ranging in age from fourteen to—well, toothless Mistress Beechum was five-and-sixty if she was a day—came to be sporting a variety of knives, from butter to short sword, under Alasdair's watchful eyes.

Bleary eyes, truth be told, since the clock had struck two before he slipped into a fitful sleep, only to drag his exhausted body from bed at half past three.

Several women fumbled with their inadequate blades. That would never do. Tomorrow, he'd see they each had a knife that they could at least handle with ease.

"Are ye off yer head, mon? Mistress Beechum? She nae have any worry about havin' her virtue compromised. I doubt any mon's sampled her dried up wares in decades." McLeon leaned a shoulder against a post and, arms folded, tilted his head. "But it isnae her charms yer keen on samplin', be it?

His mouth slid into a taunting grin, and Alasdair all but growled, "Wheesht!"

"Crotchety as an old tabby, ye are, McTavish. Be yer shoulder painin' ye? I've me flask if ye need a swig."

"My shoulder be fine. I've had hangnails that hurt worse."

Straight up lie, that.

McLeon's eyes rounded in manly appreciation as he flashed his teeth and angled his head. "Now *that* be worth watchin'."

Alasdair veered a glance to where he looked.

Miss Adams and Lydia, both wearing breeches from God only knew where and far too form-fitting for Alasdair's sadly neglected lower regions, practiced the basic lunge-and-twist maneuver he'd taught them.

Lydia's black leather breeches pulled taut across her slim legs and plump buttocks.

Saints help me.

One of the more robust maids dropped her dagger and another held hers so timorously, she might have gripped a writhing viper.

Hell, McLeon was right.

Alasdair *was* off his damned head.

A few more men, including the MacHardys, wandered over to observe, joined momentarily by several uncouth fellows.

Bloody perfect.

Alasdair and McLeon exchanged a glance, and with a subtle inclination of his head, Alasdair beckoned Lennox.

"Good thing we dinna have to rely on the lasses to protect us. Especially that ancient hag." A MacHardy chuckled, and nudged his cohort nearest him.

"Aye, but protectin' not be what I'd be wantin' them fer." Another crudely grabbed his crotch and rocked into his hand.

Bloody arse.

Mayhap tomorrow, the women's exercises should be broken into smaller groups that could be trained indoors. Say, in the ballroom. Without a bevy of lustful men looking on.

Little good that would do *his* sullen member.

Alasdair whistled, and the women promptly turned their attention to him. "That be all fer today, lasses. Well done to ye."

A fine sheen of sweat on her forehead, Lydia wove between the women, patting their arms and nodding as she strode his way.

How often would she gallivant around in men's wear, for God's sake? *Nae, nae*. She needed to become accustomed to wielding a blade while attired in skirts.

For his sanity and peace of mind.

Half the barracks now gaped at her slender, leather covered thighs and curvy bottom. Jealousy, jagged and hot, tunneled through him as he scowled at the ogling Scots. He couldn't very well pulverize all of them.

I could try.

Tomorrow he'd insist she wear a gown. A big, ugly, shapeless, tent of a thing. In a ghastly shade of cow manure green or drab brown or stone gray.

A nun's habit would suffice nicely.

He clamped his jaw. No blasted nuns in Scotland.

"That was fun, Alasdair, but I fear, I still haven't quite mastered the grip." She turned her wrist this way and that. "I suppose I'll only improve with practice."

The shortest MacHardy, the one with the scar running from ear to chin, licked his bulbous lips. "Me name's Angus Stewart, and ye can practice on me blade anytime, lass." He thrust his hips forward. "I dinna care how ye hold it."

A growl bubbled up Alasdair's throat, but the bevy of objections mixed with a few snickers smothered the sound.

Lydia's eyes narrowed to slits, only the irises visible, as she swung to face the crude churl. She eyed him up and down, despairingly. "Is that so, Stewart?"

She smiled sweetly, wiping the back of her hand across her forehead. Then in a move so adept, Alasdair wouldn't have thought her capable of it if he hadn't witnessed it with his own eyes, she levered her arm, bringing the blade within a hair's breadth of the man's nether regions.

His trews gaped open where she'd neatly slit the fabric.

At the near swipe, Alasdair's groin contracted in male sympathy, and startled oaths and gasps escaped the others. More than one man defensively covered his male bits with both hands, his eyes rounded in horror.

Snarling an oath, Stewart jumped back while his comrades pointed and burst into laughter, shoving and elbowing each other in glee.

Someone muttered, "Guid help us. With knife-wieldin' wenches, we'll all be gelded by week's end."

"I'll be damned." Admiration filled Lennox's voice, and he raised his hand to his forehead in a neat sign of respect. "I salute ye, Miss Farnsworth. Well done, ye. Most fun I've had in ages."

"She almost nipped off yer bitty jewel, Stewart." Wiping his nose and snickering, his rotund companion slapped Stewart's back. "Ye only have the one measly ballock—"

Stewart's hearty slug to his friend's midsection bent him double.

Alasdair cocked a brow at her, and she unapologetically lifted her shoulder an inch. Quite obviously, Lydia professed much more experience with a dirk than she'd let on.

What other secrets did she hide?

Lydia tapped the dagger on her palm. "I think it best if you left." She pointed her dirk tip at each of the MacHardys in turn. "Today. The terms of the tournament have changed to a single event, archery, and you no longer qualify to participate. Unless you possess a bow and arrow?"

Stewart scowled, looking to his comrades for confirmation. "We paid the entry fee—"

"Actually, Sir Gwaine paid your fees, which I shall promptly reimburse. Wait here, and I'll fetch the funds. Mr.

McTavish, please accompany me." She tossed the knife over his shoulder, and it stuck fast in a support beam.

Alasdair released a low whistle.

Luck, or skill?

"McTavish," Stewart mocked in a high-pitched voice. "Yer like a bairn in leadin' strings, doin' the wench's biddin'." He elevated a derisive eye and scratched his filthy neck. "Makes a man wonder what yer after. Or, maybe," his lustful perusal shifted to Lydia's rear end, "yer gettin' what ye want already."

"God's bones, ye'll pay fer yer insolence," Alasdair roared.

Chapter 18

Lydia spun around in time to see Stewart crumple to the muddy stones, his nose clearly broken and blood oozing across his grimy cheek.

Good.

She arched an approving brow. "You need to teach me how to do that, Mr. McTavish."

Without breaking her hand.

"Nae likely, lass." Alasdair rubbed his reddened knuckles, a brazen grin kicking his mouth upward at one side.

"I trust your exertion didn't worsen your shoulder wound?" He should've allowed her to tend it last evening. If infection set in . . .

"Nae a bit." His grin widened.

Not the least repentant, and she didn't blame him. Stewart deserved what Alasdair had dealt him. And more.

"I'm sure you all have someplace you need to be." She waved her hand at the other gaping Scotsmen. "And I'm equally sure this isn't this first time you've seen a man laid out."

Two of Stewart's friends dragged him to his feet where he sagged between them.

Lydia pointed to the fourth man. "You, come with me. The rest of you MacHardys, collect your things and wait at the outer gate. I never want to see any of you on Tornbury Fortress lands again."

Outwardly composed, inside she quivered like newly set

jelly. Still, she'd almost whooped in glee when she heard bone crunching behind her.

What did that make her?

Vengeful? Hateful? A bloodthirsty monster?

No, just human, and very much a woman insulted. Alasdair jumping to her defense had been magnificent. And she was unashamed to admit, she appreciated his championing her.

Minutes later, she handed the other seemingly contrite MacHardy the entrance fees.

He shuffled his feet and wrung his hat in his hands, his auburn hair plastered to his less than clean scalp. "I'm truly sorry, Miss Farnsworth. I said this was a bad idea to begin with. We be owin' Sir Gwaine no allegiance, the way he treats us. He promised us a big purse though, and ye ken, times are lean fer our tribe."

Yes, especially since your lord is a selfish, wasteful sot.

She'd gargle scalding tea if Sir Gwaine actually intended to make good on his promise to pay them.

"He meant to cause ye more mischief, and I beg yer forgiveness for my part in this." Attention glued to the ground, his cheeks flushed bright crimson, his speech surprisingly refined for a man of his station.

Lydia tilted her head. "What's your name?"

He glanced up briefly before his attention swooped downward once more. "Shamus Robertson, miss."

"Well, Mr. Robertson, I could use some ears in Sir Gwaine's encampment. Perhaps you're interested?"

His gaze flew to his comrades, slouching against the entry wall, Stewart cradling his injured nose.

Probably stupid to trust this man, but it couldn't hurt to build allies in the enemy's camp. She'd be out naught but a few coins if he proved a liar.

Lydia folded her arms and jutted her chin. "What of them? Are any trustworthy?"

Skewing his mouth sideways, Robertson sent them another a sidelong glance.

"They'd all do about anythin' fer the right price, but Duff—he's the fat fellow there—has a kind heart and be as honest as any man, I suppose. He be a slow wit though. The other two?" He shook his head. "Even their own mothers wouldn't waste a breath or prayer on them."

"Before I retain you, I must know if money was the only reason you agreed to Sir Gwaine's scheme." She'd expected Alasdair to object, but he simply stood, arms folded across his preposterously muscled chest, and watched the exchange.

Did approval glint in his eyes?

Why did it matter?

She was to be the laird. Making difficult decisions would be a daily occurrence.

True, but even a chief needed prudent counsel and to surround himself—*herself*—with wise and intelligent advisors. Only an arrogant fool relied totally on themselves and ignored practical recommendations.

Something to consider in a spouse, too.

Alasdair would've been a good choice. She slid him a covert glance to find him staring intently at her.

What went on in his mind?

Did he think her rash or unwise? Or did he approve?

His respectful silence boosted her confidence. Exactly what she sought in a mate; someone to support her, but not override her decisions.

Lydia wasn't even quite sure she'd yielded to the impulse to ask Robertson the question, yet something deep in his eyes, a sort of forlorn desperation, had touched her.

Up 'til now, her instincts had served her well. Past time she honed them further. She'd take all the help she could muster to perform her duties.

Robertson sighed and looked past her, a wistful expression on his haggard face.

"I have five bairns, the eldest just thirteen. Their mother—God rest Màiri's sweet soul—died five years ago, and I can barely keep them fed."

Unfortunately, his tale wasn't altogether uncommon.

He shifted his soulful expression to her and lifted a shoulder. "I did it fer the money, my one chance to make a future fer my family if I won. I may not be much to look at, but I ken my weapons. I be a dam—er, I be an excellent marksman, a dab hand at pistols, and an accomplished stalker."

"How came you by such skills?" Lydia placed a hand on her hip and canted her head. Commoners couldn't often boast such talents.

"I be the third son of a wealthy gunsmith, and I had a genteel start to life. We fell on hard times, and at fourteen, I was obliged to set out on my own."

Perhaps Robertson would be more useful here.

"Mr. McTavish, what say you?" She waited for Alasdair's skeptical gaze to gravitate to her. "Mightn't Tornbury have need of another gamekeeper?"

He'd no more know that than she knew if he slept naked.

A most enticing image sprang to mind, heating her face, and causing a humiliating surge of dampness under her arms.

Good God, she'd become a fast chit. Practically a wanton.

Flynn had never inspired lewd fancies, and he'd been very pleasing to the eye. Very pleasing, indeed.

A small frown tugged her brows together. Oughtn't her reaction be the exact opposite? Perhaps she'd not been as entranced with Flynn as she'd thought.

The notion enlightened as well as disheartened.

"Gamekeeper, miss?" Robertson perked up, his entire mien so hopeful, Lydia determined in that moment to find a position for the man, even if she had to contrive one.

Alasdair's blue-gray gaze—more of light slate at the moment, which usually meant his keen mind chugged away—casually scrutinized Robertson. "Aye, though I'd actually prefer him to work with firearms drills. I assume yer father trained ye, Robertson?"

"Aye, sir, he did."

Lydia passed Robertson additional coins. "Return the entry fee to Sir Gwaine, then use this money to hire a wagon to bring your family here. I suggest you not mention any of this to your friends."

They'd relieve him of the money before he blinked.

Fighting tears, he nodded. "Thank you, miss, and bless ye." He jammed his cap onto his head. "I'll be back within th' week with me children."

"I shall look forward to it, and I'll arrange accommodations for you and your family." Feeling more light-hearted than she had in a goodly while, Lydia winked at Alasdair.

His mouth curved into a sizzling smile, heating her from her toes to her hairline.

After an awkward bow, Robertson trotted to the others.

"I wonder what excuse he'll offer Sir Gwaine?" Lydia crinkled her nose. "I hope the baron doesn't give him a difficult time."

"Most likely, that fat, crusty buzzard hasnae a clue what Robertson does, or even who he is, except fer when Sir Gwaine needs somethin' from him." Alasdair took her elbow and spun her toward the mansion.

"Probably true," she managed without sounding like a breathless ninny as another wave of awareness flooded her.

"I wanted a word with ye." His regard slid to her breeches. "I think it best if ye stick to wearin' gowns fer practice. Yer current attire be a might *disruptive*."

Because men can see my legs and bum?

Lydia pulled her arm free. "How so? Men wear breeches,

trews, pantaloons, and kilts. And you don't see women ogling them."

All right, a kilt might be a bit distracting; fine, *verra* distracting—depending on who was wearing it.

Women were simply more discreet in their leering, hiding their lust-filled gazed behind fans and lowered lashes.

"Lass, I ken I have nae right to tell ye what to do, but if ye insist on wearin' those," he flicked a glance at her lower half, his attention lingering a trifle longer than truly necessary, "I'll have to have ye train indoors. I canna have the men unfocused or preoccupied."

Did that include him too? What a lovely, disconcerting thought.

"It nae be safe when they be handlin' weapons," he said. "An accident might occur."

Some validity there, but movement was so much easier, the breeches so freeing, she was reluctant to give them up.

"What say you, that for public training, I wear a gown, but you will also privately school me? I can still wear my breeches for that. I'd like to learn some defensive moves that don't include weapons. Say, some of the wrestling maneuvers I've seen you use."

They stood at the entrance stoop, and Alasdair blinked at her like a simpleton for several lengthy, disconcerting moments.

"Wrestling moves?" he repeated in a strangled voice, sounding like he'd swallowed a pickled egg whole. Or she'd asked him to milk cows, wearing nothing but pink stockings and a silk bonnet.

"Yes," she pressed patiently. "So I can escape or fight if someone tries to seize or ravish me."

He drew in a long, raggedy breath and forked his fingers through his supple blond hair. Wrath darkened his arresting eyes and creased the planes of his face. "I'll bloody well kill any mon who lays a hand on ye, lass. That be why I'm here."

Must he go all dramatic and male bravado on her?

She'd only asked for a simple grappling lesson. Nothing too terribly difficult, but something clever and unexpected to give her a slight advantage.

A few moments ago, she'd relished his brutishness, but this possessive attitude simply irked.

"Alasdair, you aren't my personal guard. It's not your role, as you perhaps ought to know, and you cannot be with me every waking moment."

Or sleeping ones either.

Another wayward memory flickered to her mind's forefront.

The day after she'd arrived at Craiglocky, she'd become lost in the Keep's maze of corridors. She'd happened along the passage outside his chamber as his manservant exited, allowing her a brief glimpse of Alasdair rising splendidly naked from his bed.

Naturally, she'd pretended absorption in the toes of her half-boots until the door clicked shut, but she'd had an extended look at his magnificent form.

Such naughtiness. But deliciously so.

Truly, mythical Roman and Greek gods had nothing on him.

He opened his mouth, and she presented an outthrust palm to him, cutting off whatever he'd intended to say.

"I need to be able to defend myself to the best of my ability, even if I am only a woman. And the truth is, I wouldn't feel comfortable having another man so intimately train me. Besides, you'll leave one day soon."

Too soon for her liking, but he'd already fulfilled his obligation, and she no longer needed him to stay for the tournament.

"Lydia—"

Alasdair's tone puckered her skin.

In anticipation or wariness?

A little of both, truth to tell. And it excited her.

She marched ahead of him, resisting the urge to cover her ears like she had as a child when she hadn't wanted to hear something.

"Why'd you have to be married?" she whispered beneath her breath.

The first man to awaken her feelings since Flynn, a man so worthy of ruling Tornbury beside her, one Da would exuberantly welcome to the clan, and Alasdair wasn't free.

Lydia pressed the door's latch and stood to the side as he closed the remaining distance between them.

Where was McGibbons?

Probably soothing a ruckus below stairs again. The new scullery maid, Jinnah, a buxom beauty with a saucy mouth and impertinent attitude, hadn't quite settled in yet.

Lydia almost snorted.

Actually, McGibbons had revealed just this morning, that Jinnah tearfully confessed to grating soap into the staff's porridge—after being scolded for loitering outside Uncle Gordon's rooms thrice yesterday, and they'd teased her about her obvious *tendré.*

As a result of her prank, the other unfortunate servants had dashed to the necessary all day.

Gordon knew Da strictly forbade dallying with the servants, but unless the chit was as brazen as a doxy, she'd been encouraged to seek him out. Likely not the first time either. All the more reason to be glad Uncle had left—even if his leaving had been unpleasant and upsetting.

And if Jinnah's attitude didn't improve markedly and quickly, she'd be searching for another post. Servants who acted rashly or held grudges couldn't be endured. Tornbury's staff had always gotten on wonderfully well, and Lydia meant for the harmony to continue under her watch.

Alasdair tossed a frustrated look 'round the entry before setting his mouth into a grim line, firmly grasping her arm, and then unceremoniously hauling her into the nearest open doorway.

Though his touch remained gentle, and he strove to conceal his agitation, his rigid posture, flared nostrils, and tense mouth exuded exasperation.

Bother, had he heard her imprudent mumbling?

Well, she *did* wish he wasn't married. That didn't mean she wanted to marry him, only that he hadn't suffered from his wife's despicable actions.

Hogwash and claptrap.

After pushing her ahead of him into the gold and emerald drawing room, he closed the door with a distinct, and somewhat portentous, *thunk* behind them.

Bernard, curled in a comfortable ball on the floral padded window seat, raised his mottled head. After a toothy yawn, he dismissed them, rolled onto his back—all four feet in the air, one fang sticking out, and the sun warming his belly—and went back to sleep.

Must be done working for his keep today, as evidenced by the two mice and the shrew Cook said he'd left on the kitchen stoop this morning.

She rather envied him his life. He didn't have monstrous brutes hauling him into rooms and ordering him about, nor did he have to worry about hundreds of peoples' futures, quite possibly at the expense of his own happiness.

A few feet inside the room, Lydia spun around and planted her hands on her hips. "Pray tell me, what you're doing? Why are you so upset and acting like a barbarian? I but spoke the truth. I'm not your responsibility."

Alasdair leaned against the door, his eyes hooded, and an almost predatory demeanor about his large form. His lips twitched with her last fiery declaration, but he kept stoically silent.

His untamed hair hanging nearly to his shoulders, golden stubble shadowing his face's chiseled planes, and an unfathomable, wild glint in his steely azure eyes, accented his Viking ancestry. All he needed was a battle-axe and round shield to complete the image of a fierce, marauding Norseman.

And she wouldn't mind all that much if he'd laid siege to Tornbury. She feared he'd already done so with her heart. Oh, the plundering hadn't been the overwhelming bedeviling of senses as Flynn's had. No, Alasdair's onslaught had been a subtle, insidious seduction, snaring her before she even realized she'd been led into a trap.

He smiled then, that charming, tempting bending of his strong mouth which, despite her pique, towed at her reluctant heartstrings and sent a frisson of excitement coursing through her pores.

His absurdly broad shoulders and marbled muscles appealed to her femininity. Why must he be so deliciously masculine?

Still, he owed her an explanation for lugging her into the drawing room like an errant child.

"Well?" Widening her eyes, she leaned forward a mite, demanding an explanation, irritated at his highhandedness and her wanton response. "What, you've nothing to say now? After you dragged me in here, like a crazed, uncivilized barbarian?"

"I shan't teach ye grapplin', lass, even if I do fancy ye, and I'd make ye my own if I could."

Chapter 19

If Alasdair wasn't valiantly fighting the grin Lydia's slack jaw and owl-wide blinking eyes produced, a grin she'd certainly take exception to, he would've bitten his traitorous tongue in half.

The lazy cat, his idiotic expression half smug feline smile and half superior scorn, blinked his almond-shaped, yellow-green eyes.

Alasdair hadn't meant to confess his attraction, but when she said she wasn't his responsibility—well, hell— something foreign inside him cracked wide open.

He'd felt it give, rupture sickeningly somewhere behind his ribs.

She bloody well *was too* his concern.

Precisely when she'd become so, he couldn't be sure. But he'd made her his, nonetheless, and the obligation went far beyond his promise to Ewan to help with Tornbury's swordplay and defensive training.

Her welfare, her future, her happiness must be secured.

Except for that wrestling falderal.

Never going to happen.

Never.

He forbade his mind to even tiptoe in the direction of what that would entail.

Only a corkbrain would, for an instant, consider the intimate contact necessary to teach her rudimentary self-defense in wrestling.

By God, he wasn't a bloody saint, though wrapping his

limbs with hers whilst pressing her to the ground did entice in the extreme.

Thank God, he could claim societal restraints and his sore shoulder for rebuffing her suggestion. That she'd suggested it confounded him. Surely the impropriety hadn't escaped her, or was she really so desperate to prove herself equal to a man, she would risk censure?

Honesty forced him to admit that the minute he'd agreed to journey to Tornbury, he'd hoped something more would come of his stay, as impossible and implausible as the notion—no, the fantasy—seemed at the time.

Farnsworth had hinted broadly, and repeatedly, that he'd welcome a match between his daughter and Alasdair. Alasdair had steered the conversation away from the touchy subject, unwilling to betray Lydia's confidence or confess his unavailability.

These past weeks had been every bit as torturous as he'd predicted, but satisfying, too, as he molded the men into warriors. He looked forward to conversing with Lydia daily, experiencing her keen wit, giddy humor, and genial kindness.

And every day his admiration and respect for her had grown as she went about performing the chief's duties with wisdom, fairness, and moderation.

Farnsworth would be hard-pressed to find a man as worthy as she to take his place, and yet the ailing man hesitated to name her laird.

Surely her father's lack of confidence in her abraded, if that's what his reluctance was. Far better permitting her to rule alone than force a union that might render her unhappy the rest of her life and, perhaps, jeopardize the clan.

Alasdair had voiced that opinion more than once, and each time the old laird had given him a smile that could only be described as crafty.

He'd a suspicion Farnsworth asking him to Tornbury had been a calculated scheme, one to throw him and Lydia together once more, and with each passing day, and after every meeting with the chief, that misgiving grew.

The cunning old goat didn't know his efforts to guilt Alasdair into proposing were wasted.

God's toenails, what a complicated, reeking hash.

Alasdair couldn't offer her marriage. Not now. Not honorably. And honestly, asking her to wait until he was free was blasted selfish too, especially since he couldn't dare profess undying love.

Lydia wouldn't believe him in any event, staunch pragmatism having replaced her youthful enthusiasm and buoyancy of a few months ago. Shattered dreams, grief, and unrequited love had pummeled joy and hope from her.

If she'd remained immune to him, he might have been able to move on, leave her and his heart behind when he finally departed, but her murmured comment—one he was positive he wasn't meant to have heard—made him bold.

And perhaps, stupidly optimistic.

Why'd you have to be married?

That short phrase instantly changed his life's course, gave him renewed anticipation, made him willing to gamble on happiness once again, more the fool he.

A happy, expectant fool, however.

Unexpected, and wholly alien giddiness nudged him, and he hid a grin behind his hand on the pretense of rubbing his mouth.

He had something to look forward to, to anticipate if successful. It wouldn't be an easy course by any means. No, in fact, it would be blasted difficult, but Lydia was worth the battle.

He relished a good fight, particularly when it involved something he cared passionately about. Something worth championing. Lydia was that and much more.

His experience with women fairly shouted her interest in him. She mightn't love him, not the all-consuming way she had Bretheridge. Mightn't ever, for that matter. But a match between them would benefit them both, would certainly profit the clan, and neither could deny the physical attraction simmering between them.

If Lydia agreed to his plan, he'd send a missive off to Ewan today, asking him to find Searón, and if she lived, begin divorce proceedings.

Or, mayhap he ought to begin the measures to terminate the marriage straightaway, and if his wife was alive, the process would be that much further along.

Surely a wiser, more efficient course.

He had grounds enough, adultery and desertion, and scant doubt existed that the Kirk wouldn't grant his request.

But what if the church *did* refuse?

On what premise?

No. He refused to consider failure.

He could produce dozens of witnesses to his wife's whoring.

Nevertheless, marriage dissolution took time and money, even in Scotland, and although humbling, he must ask Ewan to extend him the blunt he'd need. Divorce didn't come cheaply, particularly an accelerated one.

He'd determine how to repay his cousin later, after Lydia became laird.

Could he persuade her to wait?

Would her father allow her to? Would his health?

Time didn't favor Farnsworth, and understandably he wanted her married and established as laird before he passed.

Alasdair considered her from beneath his half-closed eyes.

She'd shut her pretty mouth, now turned down at the corners, and stared at her feet. What did she fret on?

His impulsive scheme could work to both their advantages.

Aye, if he spoke with Farnsworth, the laird might be persuaded to permit the match he'd encouraged, despite Alasdair's current entanglement.

Not a particularly vain man, Alasdair wasn't stupid either.

He knew his value to Tornbury Fortress and to the old laird, and an alliance with the McTavishes benefited the Farnsworth clan immensely. Somehow, he'd make the laird see reason. *If* Lydia agreed to the suggestion.

She'd perched her perky bum on the settee's arm, and swung one booted foot back and forth. She didn't respond to his blurted declaration of several minutes ago, just stared at him, her expression a combination of uncertainty and expectancy.

He pushed away from the door, and in three long strides, stood before her. He took her small hand in his, the skin so soft and creamy compared to his tanned, callused paw. "I'm sincere, Lydia. I am keen fer ye."

A tiny frown furrowing her forehead, she stared at their entwined fingers before raising trusting eyes, and saying softly, "I really do wish you weren't married, that we had more time to come up with a feasible plan."

"If I weren't, would ye consider marryin' me?" He brushed his thumb across her delicate knuckles, noting the slight tremble of her hand and lips.

Bloody poor proposal, that.

Her gaze drifted to somewhere over his shoulder, and she raised her fine, raven eyebrows upward in uncertainty.

"I cannot deny you've the making of a perfect chieftain. The men respect you, I trust you, and I think you'd be a fair and kind leader and spouse." A small smile bent her sweet mouth. "And I've no doubt Da would approve. He told me I needed to find a strapping Scot, specifically mentioning the

McTavishes. And he did ask for you by name. I've wondered for some time now if he weren't playing at matchmaker, truth to tell."

"Aye, I've had the same thought."

Farnsworth had made his desires patently apparent.

"What are we to do? His health is so fragile, I'm loath to disappoint him." She pulled a face and kicked at the rug's fringed corner. "What a confounded tangle."

"I suggest we call off the entire tournament. Since the contest games changed, men be leavin' already. After I've spoken to yer father, presented our proposal, we can arrange a marriage settlement."

"Our proposal?" She laughed, that contagious lilting trill that made him grin in agreement. "We cannot, as you must know full well. Have you forgotten you're married? In any event, I'm certain Da would never agree, and I cannot be a party to adultery or bigamy."

Alasdair sighed and shook his shaggy head. "I'm bunglin' this mightily. Let me try again."

She scratched her nose, leaving a small dirt smudge on the tip. "Very well, though I don't know what good it will do."

He took both her small hands in his. "We've both experienced heartache, but I believe we would suit, and in fact get on well together. I respect ye, want to protect ye, and I dinna think ye'll find another man who'd willingly remain in the shadows as I would and permit ye to lead yer clan."

She tilted her head, her gaze more curious than anything. "Go on."

Hope dared flare more brightly.

Alasdair sat beside her then boldly pulled her into his lap.

A startled yelp escaped her, but she didn't try to rise.

A small victory he'd gladly accept.

"I'll petition fer a divorce and hire an investigator to search fer Searón. I can have Ewan pull strings where he may. He's highly connected and may be able to hurry things along. If yer father knows yer to marry me, and I agree to never attempt to wrest Tornbury's lairdship from ye, I think he can be persuaded to wait fer ye to wed. Besides, if we find Searón has died, then there's no need to wait."

She fiddled with his leather collar. "I'm not as confident as you are. Da wants to see me wed before he dies, wants to see his grandchildren. Doctor Wedderburn told me weeks ago my father likely only had six months to live. Surely a divorce takes longer."

Alasdair tipped turned her averted face to his. "He wants ye happy too. Let me at least try."

She dropped her gaze, her mouth stretched into thin pink ribbon. "You won't regret not marrying for love?"

But he was.

"I shan't. I did that once, and the results were disastrous. I'd prefer the respect of a worthy woman I admire, and one I readily admit I canna wait to bed." He was well onto loving her, but she wasn't ready to hear that yet. Not until Bretheridge had been expunged from her heart. "Can ye marry fer convenience rather than affection? At least at the onset?"

She gazed into his eyes, her expression open and honest. That was one of the things he most admired in Lydia. Her sincerity, lack of guile, her willingness to be transparent.

"It would be a brilliant match from the perspective of the clan, and I do hold you in the highest regard, Alasdair." She stared out the window, silent for a few moments before searching his face. "I'm not sure what else I feel for you. Honestly, my emotions are in such turmoil given all the deaths and Da's ill health, but I am afraid you might regret shackling yourself to me or resent my role as laird. In my experience, men don't take well to female leadership."

Alasdair squeezed her to his chest for a brief moment. "Not a bit of it. I like a bossy lass, and I'd never thought to marry again. But the idea of some mushroom like yer blackguard of a cousin, tryin' to wrest the lairdship from ye, makes me determined to see yer rights protected."

She smiled impishly, her eyebrows cocked high on her smooth forehead. "And how do I know you aren't such a man? You could do the same thing afterward, could you not?"

He squinted the merest bit, nodding thoughtfully. "Aye, ye make a valid point. We'll include a clause in the marriage contract that specifically protects the lairdship, yer property, and monies from me."

Lydia angled away from him, one hand braced on his chest, the other on the forearm wrapped around her tiny waist. Her inquisitive hazel gaze, more forest green than caramelized sugar at the moment, explored his face.

God help him, but her tight buttocks rubbing across his groin had his member springing to life, and he gritted his teeth and sucked in a steadying breath.

"You'd do that? Why?" She brushed his hair off his forehead then must have realized the intimacy of the action, and cheeks flushed, dropped her hand into her lap.

"Aye, I would. As fer the why, it's nae complicated nor terribly gallant. I care fer ye, lass, and I think ye deserve yer chance as chief. I've never aspired to the position, but by God, I'd make sure nae one else ever tried to usurp ye. I'd clobber any who dare."

Nibbling a corner of her lower lip, she nodded slowly, a faraway look in her eyes. "It is a sound suggestion, to be sure. I'd need time to deliberate it, nonetheless. I've never considered marrying a divorced man."

Even in eighteen hundred and nineteen a divorce was scandalous, though far less for a man than a woman. "I agree it introduces another set of issues, though nae any that canna be overcome."

Did she think of Bretheridge? Or perhaps, resist relinquishing another chance at love? Quite possibly, Alasdair had spoken too soon, but she knew as well as he, time was against them.

He clasped her hand. "Aye, I understand, but time we may not have."

"I know, but I cannot be rushed in this. Too much depends on my decision."

She obviously loved her father and wanted to please him, but her independent spirit rebelled at being manipulated or forced.

Leveling him an inquisitive gaze, she scrutinized his face with an intensity that touched his innermost being.

"Before I make a decision, I must know the truth, Alasdair. Do you have a single qualm about divorcing your wife, even after all these years?" Lydia hesitated, her focus dipping to her lap before she forged onward. "And, are you prepared, I mean truly equipped, to learn she may have died? It saddens me to think she has, though I don't know her."

"I long ago forgave Searón, Lydia, but it be far past time I was free of her and the memories. Our time together was brief, and I've been fool enough letting her haunt and hinder me this long. Whether you accept my offer or not, I intend to pursue this."

She made a soft noise in the back of her throat, not quite an affirmation, but not entirely disbelieving either.

"Very well. What excuses will we give for cancelling the contest? Won't it reflect badly on Da? On Tornbury?" Her expression cleared, and she swung to face him. "Couldn't we instead allow the tournament and even expand the fete, make the event into a fair and include a bonfire, games, and dancing?"

Excitement fairly bubbled from her, her eyes bright as she squirmed on his lap.

How Alasdair managed a strained smile and nod with his cock pressing instantly against his buckskin, and that Lydia hadn't noticed the involuntary pulses against her rear, had to have been God's grace.

To prevent humiliating himself, he slid her off his lap and onto the cushion beside him. He hooked an ankle over his knee to conceal his obvious arousal, and she curled her legs beneath her bottom, still chattering away.

"We could invite the villagers, tenants, perhaps even nearby tribes. And booths could be set up to sell handcrafts and foods. It's short notice, true, but we could make it an annual event."

Gathering one of her hands in his, Alasdair studied her tapered fingertips before rubbing the rice-grain sized callus on her index finger. Probably caused by the bow string rubbing through her gloves.

Lydia seemed completely oblivious, as she tapped her forefinger on her slender thigh, her expression contemplative. "What do you think?"

"Fer certain, the men who'd journeyed to Tornbury Fortress fer the tournament will be disgruntled, but if we turned it into a May Day event? A community celebration?" He gave an approving nod. A perfect way to earn loyalty and unite her people. "Aye, that's quite brilliant, lass. Verra diplomatic. We can say the tournament terms have been changed due to the laird's ill health, but still offer a monetary reward."

She slid him a shrewd sideways look as she rubbed her arms, as if suddenly chilled. "Naturally, we can't mention anything of our pending *arrangement*. And we've still Da to convince. But if I can assure him marrying you will make me happy and also protect the clan, Tornbury, and the lairdship, he may very well agree."

He'll pounce on the chance faster than a starving flea on a fat dog's arse.

"And will ye be happy, lass? I ken how ye loved yer marquis." He traced her jawline, so velvety, delicate, and fine. But also strong and determined. Like her.

She caught his hand in her small palm and turned her satiny cheek into it.

Dared he hope affection shone in her eyes?

"It will be a different kind of happiness, Alasdair, but no less wonderful. Flynn was my first love. A green girl's infatuation with all that glittered and bewitched a London debutante."

How would she describe her feelings toward him? Best not to push her in that arena, just yet. Take what she offered at present and relish it.

He nuzzled her neck, whispering against her silky, fragrant flesh. "Ye have to promise we'll take a weddin' trip to someplace warm." So he could sample all her charms without a foot of bedding piled atop them.

"Yes," she whispered, offering him her sweet mouth.

Like a ravenous man long starved, he accepted the bold invitation. He kissed her over and over, devouring the honeyed cavern, encouraged by her little mewling sighs and moans.

The door burst open, and McGibbons rushed in. "Miss Lydia. Come at once. The laird fell."

Chapter 20

Alasdair charged after Lydia as she flew up the stairs, taking them two at a time, each stride pulling her breeches taut across her shapely bum.

He was a bloody cad for noticing the temptation during a crisis.

"Did you send for Doctor Wedderburn?" She flung a frantic look over her shoulder.

McGibbons trailed Alasdair, grasping the handrail and ascending the risers as swiftly as his game leg permitted. "Aye. I sent a footman to the barracks and asked Lennox to ride out at once. I also sent Jinnah fer water and cloths. Miss Adams be with the laird."

"What happened? Is Da conscious?" Panting, her breath coming in short rasps, Lydia didn't slow her pace or turn around to ask the questions.

"I dinna ken what happened, Miss. And he's nae awake." His face twisted with pain and a white line bracketing his mouth, McGibbons resolutely continued his labored climb. "Jinnah found him when she went to tend his bedchamber fire. It appears he had a seizure or fainted and hit his head on a table when he fell."

The one thing Alasdair hadn't fully considered was what would happen if Farnsworth died before naming a successor. Best hope he appointed one in his will, or the chaos he'd hoped to spare his daughter would erupt in full force. And even with the McTavish clan here to help maintain order, Alasdair couldn't guarantee they'd be able to stifle an uprising or a coup.

God's bones. What would happen to Lydia then?

At least Ross wasn't here inciting discord, though Alasdair, unlike Lydia, didn't think they'd seen the last of the scoundrel. Another thing Ewan ought to look into. Farnsworth was hardly in condition to do so, and as yet was unware of his nephew's treachery. Alasdair feared Lydia underestimated Ross's threat.

After the attack, Alasdair followed a hunch and began poking around. He bloody well didn't like what he'd uncovered so far. Too early to say anything; he still gathered evidence after all. Nonetheless, if either Lydia's brothers' boat sinking or her carriage losing a wheel had been chance accidents, he was a Turkish concubine.

Add her riding accident and her father's series of misfortunes, not to mention her mother's sudden death, and every single sign suggested the family was systematically being eliminated.

And only one person benefited from their demise.

Gordon Ross.

Was the coward capable of such treachery, or had the deaths and accidents been purely coincidental?

Lydia sprinted the corridor's length, but outside the laird's chamber, she drew to a faltering stop. Hands at her waist, she shut her eyes, her lashes inky wings across her wan cheeks, and drew in several deep breaths. Her chest rose and fell rapidly, and her lower lip quivered.

Brave love.

Alasdair touched her shoulder, and her eyes sprang open, anguish and fear in their moist depths.

He'd never seen her cry.

Not once.

Not a single tear.

And she'd been in situations where even a woman possessing stalwart fortitude would have dissolved into waterworks.

"Shall I wait here or accompany ye inside?" He wouldn't intrude on the family's privacy.

"I'd like you to come too." She slanted a distressed glance toward the carved door. "I may need—"

She needed comforting, had no one, save a cousin and a handful of servants to depend on, but feared asking for support. Feared seeming weak or undignified. Had she imposed that burden on herself because of her gender, or had someone else?

Alasdair reached around her and pushed the latch down, whispering in her ear as he pressed near. "I'll be with ye the entire time. It might nae be as bad as all that."

True. It might be worse.

The door swung open, revealing a chaotic scene.

A smallish table lay sideways near the hearth, a tray and remnants of a meal, a bronze candlestick, as well as several books scattered nearby. A chair had toppled, its riser and a serviette dangerously close to the unscreened hearth.

Nearby, a newsprint partially hid a bedroom slipper and a piece of wood, while an inkpot, its contents pooled in a purple-black circle staining the carpet, lay shattered.

A stray spark might have ignited any of them.

Damned negligent on the maid's part, but shock at her master's condition no doubt made her careless and forgetful.

McGibbons clicked his tongue and shook his head. "What do ye need me to do, Miss Lydia?"

"Would you please await the doctor? Oh, and tell Cook we'll not dine formally tonight."

He dipped his head, his troubled gaze resting on his laird. "Aye. I'll see what be delayin' Jinnah too."

As he limped from the room, Alasdair scowled at the leaping flames. Jinnah had taken the time to feed the fire but not pick up the wood she'd dropped or clean any of the mess?

Her face contorted in worry, Miss Adams pressed a scarlet stained cloth to Farnsworth's head. Congealed blood covered the right side of his ashen face and neck, and had seeped onto the pillowcase.

"Oh, Da," Lydia whispered, dashing to his bedside. "How badly hurt is he?"

"Lydia, it won't stop bleeding." Miss Adams still held the makeshift bandage firmly to a spot above his ear. "This is the third cloth I've used to stem the flow."

"Let me see, please." Lydia bent near and gasped, clapping a hand to her mouth as Miss Adams lifted the cloth. She sat on the bed and took one of her father's hands in hers. The anguished gaze she raised to Alasdair shimmered with tears.

"Nae fear, lass. Head wounds are notoriously messy. The amount of blood doesn't necessarily indicate the injury's severity." Alasdair edged nearer, relieving Miss Adams of the bandage.

She promptly retreated to an armchair a few paces away, her face as ash-gray as the dress she wore.

He'd seen far worse gashes, but Farnsworth sported a fist-sized bump and would likely suffer an eye-crossing headache for a few days.

"He must have glanced off the table's edge when he fell." Lydia rose from the bed and after checking the washstand for water, rubbed an eyebrow. "Esme, might I trouble you to see what is taking Jinnah so long?"

"Of course, Lydia." Giving a weak smile, she slipped from the room.

Lydia bent and gathered the books and newssheet, exposing a lone piece of parchment. Her brows crashed together and a soft gasp escaped her when she read it. She held the paper up, disbelief draining her face of color. "This is part of Da's will."

Hell's bells.

Something smelled foul as a basket of eels gone to rot.

Alasdair checked Farnsworth's two-inch gash, which had finally stopped flowing. Hands on his hips, he, too, surveyed the room. A struggle could account for the toppled furniture. Or, if someone had struck Farnsworth, and he'd fallen on the table.

Rotating slowly, Lydia examined the area nearest her before her attention gravitated to the snapping fire. She crossed to the hearth, dropping the books and newssheet with a thud and crackle on a chair as she passed by. Fireplace tongs in hand, she sank to her knees and pushed the logs back, sifting through the ashes.

Leaning forward, she snatched a charred paper from the grate. "I don't believe it. Who'd burn Da's will?"

She straightened, outrage shaking her voice. "This," she swept her hand over the disarray, "was nae accident."

In four strides, Alasdair was at her side. He gathered her trembling form into his arms, smiling despite the dire circumstances when she wrapped her arms around his waist. "Aye, I fear ye be right, and this confirms what I've suspected for some time."

Tilting her neck, she peered up at him, a hint of accusation in her eyes and tone. "What's that? What do you know that you haven't told me?"

"Liddie lass, be that ye?" Farnsworth rasped, his papery voice scarcely more than a feeble whisper.

"Aye, Da. It's me." She rushed to his bedside. "Ye had a fall."

He blinked in confusion, then winced and touched his head. "Did Gordon leave? I wished to speak with ye both."

Chapter 21

Early the next morning, Lydia paced to the drawing room's window seat before spinning round and retracing her steps, loitering for a few moments before the fireplace to warm her hands.

The day promised to be warm and sunny, perfect for a walk by Galanock Water. A much-needed reprieve she fully intended to indulge with Esme a bit later, and toward that end, she'd worn practical half-boots and a soft gray woolen gown complimented by a rose and black spencer.

Grizelda had twisted Lydia's hair into a simple knot at her nape. She'd even willingly asked Cook to prepare a small picnic to eat beside the river at Lydia's behest.

Nothing fancy. Fruit, cheese, oat rolls, perhaps some shortbread—she did adore the buttery treat—but something to hold her over until dinner.

Her stomach gurgled, and she pressed a palm to her hollow middle. She'd not eaten last night and had nothing yet today, and the organ protested loudly and frequently.

Before she'd broken her fast, she'd sent for Alasdair, interrupting his morning training with the men. He'd come straightaway rather than wait for the exercises to end, which bespoke his concern too. And hopefully his eagerness to see her as well.

If his night had been anything like her sleepless thrashing, his mind would be full of unanswered questions and troublesome suspicions too.

They'd had no chance to discuss their possible union with Da, of course. Not with the doctor fussing over him and Esme flitting about the bedchamber while Alasdair interrogated Jinnah in Da's sitting room.

Once Doctor Wedderburn determined Da wasn't concussed, he'd given him a sleeping draught then drew Lydia into the corridor.

"Grief fer yer brothers and mother has robbed the laird of several years. He still misses her terribly." Eyes rimmed with sympathy and sorrow, Doctor Wedderburn patted her shoulder. "He's nae likely to leave his bed again, me dear. Nae as weak as he be now."

"How can that be? Barely two months have passed. You said Da had six months. Perhaps even a year."

Lydia had shaken her head. No. It was too soon. She wasn't ready. Wouldn't ever be. Da was supposed to have had more time, at least a few more months. Too much remained unsettled.

Patting her shoulder, Doctor Wedderburn's face folded in sympathy. "Ye have me deepest sympathies, lass, and I hope with all me heart I be wrong. But I dinna think I am." He pulled his earlobe. "I ken Bailoch well and have nae doubt his affairs are in perfect order. That should brin' ye some peace."

If only they were.

"But if there be any thin' that needs his attention, I'd nae wait." Doctor Wedderburn had forced a jolly smile, but no cheer lit his eyes or colored his voice. "Och. He might surprise us and recover. Out of sheer orneriness."

Presenting her back to the fire, Lydia drank in her fill of Alasdair, silhouetted in the window. Just gazing upon him brought such peace. Such joy. Different than what she'd felt for Flynn, but far more remarkable and multi-faceted. She couldn't quite label the emotion, actually. The sentiment was beyond mere words' description.

"Last night, Da asked for Uncle Gordon, Alasdair. As if he'd just been there, moments before. Not days ago." She shot a short glance over her shoulder to her father. "We need to discover if he was, indeed, here. *If* he saw Da. I fear my father has become even more confused or perchance has slipped into delusions. Though, I suppose Gordon might have slithered into the house unseen."

Not easily with the extra watch assigned. Someone must've helped him, unlocked a door. Someone capable of distracting the guards. Say, a voluptuous, shameless flirt wearing a starched apron and a seductive smile.

"Does Jinnah truly expect me to believe Da *accidentally* dropped his will in the fire?"

Codswallop.

Disdain dripped from every word, cold as a melting icicle. Lydia folded her arms and rested her hips on the settee's arm. "Why was his will out to begin with? I wasn't aware Da kept a copy in his chamber."

It seemed there was much he'd kept from her, and his wariness nipped, ragged and needle sharp. What else hadn't he trusted her with?

Lydia wanted to shout her frustration before she went mad with the powerlessness she felt, but lairds maintained their outward composure, even if inside they'd crumpled into sobbing heaps.

Alasdair, his expression grave, turned from gazing into the garden with its hexagon hedge maze. The first daffodils, their sunny blossoms a bright spot of color, bravely turned their faces to the austere sky.

"Another question fer which we dinna have an adequate answer, but like ye, I dinna believe the maid's story. I can see the falsehood in her eyes. She be a slippery one, and I'd keep my eye on her. Lies roll off her tongue like warm honey from a spoon."

Uppity and lippy, Jinnah's behavior surrounding Da's accident was wholly unacceptable and the final straw for

Lydia. The maid's story had changed twice more after she first claimed Da threw his will in the fire, because he'd decided to update it.

As if she'd be privy to that information, cheeky chit.

"Well, you may rest assured of one thing, Jinnah will be on her way today. Without reference, too." Harsh, but necessary, else another unsuspecting house retain her for service. Dishonest servants couldn't be borne.

Alasdair crossed to Lydia and, bold as brass, drew her into his arms. He spoke into the top of her head, his voice soothing and reassuring. She could stay like this all day, secure in his embrace, the gossips be hanged.

"As much as I'd like to see her gone, lass, I think we might learn more by lettin' her stay fer a bit longer and watchin' her. Ye ken somethin's afoot."

"Aye." Lydia didn't need to be a genius to know something was horribly amiss. God help her, and her snake of an uncle, if her suspicions were even partially founded.

Did she dare voice her concerns to Alasdair?

It would be lovely to confide in him—to have another to help carry this haunting burden.

His tone contemplative and questioning, Alasdair spoke into her hair. "And Doctor Wedderburn said he doubted a fall caused the knot on the laird's head. I think someone struck him, but I want to keep that to ourselves, fer now at least."

Which was another reason a message had been sent to Mr. Gwyres, Da's solicitor, yesterday, requesting he attend Da today at his earliest convenience and to bring a copy of Da's will.

The room fell silent except for the mantel clock's rhythmic ticking and the fire's usual sputtering chatter.

Standing chest to chest and thigh to thigh with Alasdair, Lydia closed her eyes, soaking in his presence. His breath warmed her scalp as he gently massaged her shoulder and spine.

She could love this man, might already if she'd had the time to really examine her feelings without chaos constantly interrupting. Weeks had passed since she'd mooned over Flynn, and when she did ponder him, familiar pain didn't well within her chest.

She didn't give a whit that people might frown on her marrying a divorced man, except for how it would affect the clan. In any event, Alasdair had already earned acceptance and respect from the tribe. In fact to such an extent, that if she were a lesser person, she might become jealous.

Instead, tremendous pride filled her.

They would lead well together.

How long did a divorce take?

Was she terribly wicked to want the match? Immoral to even entertain the notion? If only Alasdair had approached her after he was free, guilt wouldn't plague her as it did knowing she had become the *other* woman.

But Searón had left him. The marriage had ended long ago, except legally.

"Lydia?"

"Alasdair?"

Her face pressed to the wall of his chest, his leather vest warm against her cheek, she relished his comforting embrace. She gave a small smile, releasing a soft, joyful sigh as she nudged his solid back. "You first."

Chuckling, the deep rumble vibrating his chest, he hugged her a bit closer. "I think it be time to post a watch outside the laird's door too, and although he be fragile, he needs to ken what's happened with yer uncle and about the May Day plans."

She nodded. "Yes, that's wise, I think, although it's sure to cause him upset. And he must name the next laird in his will, and announce his decision soon. He cannot delay any longer. The tribe is restless."

He kissed the top of her head; such a simple, husbandly gesture. "He also must ken we plan to wed, though I only want him to know fer now. I dinna want tongues waggin'. I think it will brin' him peace, despite our havin' to wait on the dissolution."

"Alasdair," she protested softly. "I told you I needed time to think about it, and I've certainly not had a minute yet." Lydia wanted to marry him. At least she thought she did. He certainly had her at sixes and sevens and invaded her thoughts constantly. She huffed an exasperated breath.

"He could die." Lydia swallowed, before continuing, unshed tears slightly thickening her words. "Probably well before you're divorced. Then what happens?"

Alasdair tipped her chin up, looking deep into her eyes, understanding in his. "All else aside, he must name ye laird and reveal his choice. Immediately."

"And if he doesn't name me? Will you still want to marry me?" There, she'd asked it. When had marrying him become as important as the lairdship? It shouldn't be.

Tenderness bathed his features as his azure gaze slowly roamed her face. He brushed a large thumb across her cheek, his mouth turned upward into a smile so gentle, her heart moaned.

"Och, every part of me from me bones to the air I breathe, cries out fer ye, and even though I ken I dinna deserve ye, dinna deserve yer love, I'd forsake everythin' from now until eternity to make ye mine. I love ye, Lydia, have fer months, passionately, wildly, and unendingly."

He loved her? This great hulking, wonderful warrior loved her?

Searón was a complete and utter fool for casting such a splendid man aside, and thank God she had, else Lydia wouldn't have known him. Wouldn't have been able to claim him as hers.

"Oh, Alasdair, I think I love you too."

"Only think? I'd better see what I can do to make ye sure."

Lydia held her breath as he lowered his head. Standing on her toes, she entwined her arms around his sturdy neck and opened her mouth. She'd cherish this bit of heaven in the perdition that had surrounded her these past months.

He slashed his mouth across hers, hot and desperate, pillaging and plundering. And she relished in every new sensation, boldly meeting each stroke of his tongue, slanting her neck to give him greater access.

Yes, she'd marry Alasdair.

Today, if only she could. If he could.

He'd snared her for all time, and she'd wait until he was free, no matter how long it took. Even if it cost her the lairdship.

Prepared to tell him what was in her heart, she ended the kiss. "Alasdair—"

A sharp knock had them quickly separating. He turned toward the fire, and she sank onto the settee, her knees too soft to remain standing.

"Enter." Pretending absorption in a loose thread on her spencer's decorative braid, she drew in a handful of calming breaths before painting a smile on her face and raising her focus.

McGibbons presented a salver, atop which lay a small rectangular paper. "A letter has arrived fer Mr. McTavish, and the laird requests both yer presences in the solar."

"The solar?" Lydia flicked Alasdair a baffled look as he took the letter, the McTavish seal bright against the white surface. "Da felt well enough to venture to the solar? He's better then? He still slept when I peeked in earlier."

"Aye, Miss Lydia, he seems much better." McGibbons grinned and winked his good eye. "Chipper and demanding. Our laird ate a hearty breakfast, called the doctor a fussy old tabby, barked at a footman and a maid, and threatened me with his cane if I dinna promptly get my sorry, ar—er, rear below to fetch ye."

She laughed at McGibbons's comical, put-upon expression. "He is, indeed, improved then."

"I'll read this later. Let's nae keep the laird waitin'." Tucking the missive into his pocket, Alasdair offered her his other hand, and help her to her feet.

Lydia accepted Alasdair's extended elbow. How right the gesture seemed, though he towered over her by several inches, and the breadth of his shoulders easily surpassed hers twice.

Petite, just over five feet tall, her small stature had been a matter of concern to her regarding the lairdship too. However, with a husband as powerfully built as Alasdair, well, he more than made up for her lack of stature or ability to intimidate.

Why, simply crossing a room or the bailey he commanded attention and admiration. A born leader, he was.

Moments later, they entered the solar.

Da, looking remarkably well considering yesterday's events, sat in his customary armchair before the fire. A plaid covered his knees, atop which Bernard soundly slept.

He glanced up as they entered and smiled broadly. "Ah, there ye be."

"Da, should you be out of bed?" Lydia hunted for any signs of discomfort or fatigue. His color looked good, the best it had been in weeks, actually, and his caramel-brown eyes sparkled with enthusiasm.

What was he up to?

"Farnsworth, ye look well-rested this morn." Alasdair took Lydia's elbow and drew her farther into the room.

"Och, I am. Slept like a bairn last night. Me head scarcely aches after that fusspot Wedderburn insisted I drink some foul powder mixture."

He motioned them to the fern green couch. "Sit. Sit. I

have somethin' to tell ye before Gwyers arrives and I sign me last will and testament, once and fer all."

He chuckled, the sound raspier than Lydia would've liked, but surely stronger than she'd heard in a long while.

"Five times I've updated me will in the past year. That be plenty, dinna ye think?"

"Undeniably." And rather horrid that there'd been the need.

After kissing his cool cheek, Lydia sank onto the cushion, and Alasdair took the seat beside her, leaving a respectable distance between them. Too bad they weren't officially betrothed because she might hold his hand then. "We have a couple of things we wish to discuss with you as well, but feared you weren't feeling quite up to snuff, Da."

"Och, I'm fit as a fiddle and eager to name my successor."

Before the contest? But he'd been so adamant she marry the victor, not that she objected, mind you. Quite possibly, word had reached him of the contest changes she'd made, and that he hadn't objected portended well.

Surely angels in heaven danced at this most welcome news. Quite possibly, he wouldn't be upset by what she and Alasdair proposed then either.

Da leaned forward, one hand on his cane, and the other on his thin thigh, his gaze vacillating between Lydia and Alasdair before another huge smile wreathed his face.

He looked so pleased with himself, Lydia couldn't help but smile in return, her heart lighter than she could recall in a very long time.

The moment was at hand, the moment when she'd become the first female Farnsworth chief, and rather than being overwhelmed by trepidation or nervousness, an extraordinary calm beset her.

She'd passed muster, made Da proud, proved her worth to him and the clan.

And she'd achieved the goal alone.

No victorious betrothed or intended to make her wonder if her husband had been, at least partially, the reason Da had at last named her his successor, Lydia Farnsworth, Lady of Tornbury Fortress.

"I ken without a doubt who the next chief will be. That be why I burned the old copy of me will yesterday. I'd already written Gwyers and told him me new decision."

"*You* burned it, Da?" Jinnah had told the truth? Then, why had she made up the other stories? "But why?"

"I had a condition in me previous will about me successor I wanted to make sure would never be implemented. After today, everyone will ken who the next Farnsworth chieftain will be."

Probably the condition about her having to marry the tournament winner. That had weighted mightily heavy on Lydia, and she was heartily glad Da had eliminated that particular.

He relaxed against his chair's padded back, pride crinkling the corner of his eyes. "The clan's future will be assured, and I can rest easy in me declinin' years now."

Not years.

"I be sure that eases yer mind greatly," Alasdair said, his attention trained on Lydia. "To ken yer clan and Tornbury Fortress are in such capable, trustworthy, and just hands. That yer successor will be as diligent and carin' as ye've been."

At his admiring smile, Lydia's heart swelled with love, and—yes, she dared admit—a morsel of pride too.

Alasdair's approval mattered so very much, and she could see the sincerity and respect in his eyes. Her victory was his, and until this moment, she hadn't really considered yet what she'd do if Da had named another his successor.

Da beamed, his eyes bright and excited. "I couldn't have said it better meself. And that be why, ye, Alasdair McTavish, will be Tornbury Fortress's next laird."

Chapter 22

Alasdair managed to keep his slack jaw from smacking his knees.

Only just.

Lydia's tiny, shocked gasp seared his heart, like a dagger's, poisoned, piercing tip.

"Bloody, God-damned hell."

Had he said that aloud?

What did it matter?

Alasdair couldn't begin to imagine what she felt at this moment, and that she didn't rail her outrage spoke of her self-control or complete devastation.

Perchance both.

The laird must be made to change his will once more, must declare Lydia the chief.

Alasdair shook his head to clear his name echoing in his ears, then faced her. Words that, Alasdair didn't doubt for an instant, had rendered her a mortal wound.

Could Farnsworth have truly underestimated or disregarded her ability to rule?

Stone-still, as if carved from marble, she stared at her father, her lips slightly parted in bewildered accusation. Every ounce of color had drained from her exquisite, oval face, now alabaster white.

But it was her eyes that brought the scorching, damp sting behind Alasdair's lids.

The betrayal and hurt radiating from her beautiful, wounded eyes, darkened to the deepest treacle from unimaginable pain—as if her very soul had been sucked from her by her father's joyfully, callously uttered words.

Laird Farnsworth loved Lydia, his affection transparent and sincere. Why strike her so vicious a blow?

If you loved someone, you didn't deliberately hurt them.

He felt Farnsworth's keen perusal rake over him. Watchful and expectant.

By God, Alasdair hadn't anticipated Farnsworth's deception, and Lydia clearly hadn't either.

How gut-wrenchingly unfair.

And damned cruel too, even if her father hadn't intended it should be. The old, conniving coot had obviously plotted this for some time, and Alasdair had unknowingly assisted.

Perhaps changing the contest terms had forced his hand, or his increasingly failing health had precluded delaying any longer. Or maybe, asking Alasdair to train Tornbury's men had been a test of merit, but whatever Farnsworth's reasoning, he'd made a grievous miscalculation.

Under no circumstances would Alasdair accept the appointment.

He would never, as long as his heart pumped blood, deliberately, through actions or words, hurt Lydia.

Farnsworth simply couldn't name him laird, and not only because a chance existed that Alasdair's divorce might be denied.

He'd sooner rip out his heart with a salt spoon than steal Lydia's rightful position. Whether Farnsworth realized it, or even cared, he'd jammed a large, immovable—perhaps unforgiveable and permanent—wedge between himself and his daughter.

A man soon facing death oughtn't to have taken such a risk. He might die before she forgave him.

If she ever did.

Alasdair folded Lydia's icy fingers in his, desperate to

comfort her, to reassure her they'd wade through this mire together.

The old laird could make of that what he wanted, but instead of objecting, the crusty curmudgeon beamed wider. Then winked.

"Aye, she be a verra bonnie lass. Me most precious possession. I've seen the way ye look at her, Alasdair, heard the admiration in yer voice when ye speak of her." Farnsworth bathed Lydia with a doting gaze. "Yer to have another wish granted, me boy."

Emotion riddled his gravelly voice, and he veered his watery eyes in Lydia's direction, but she dropped her gaze, now snapping with scornful anger, to her lap and firmly withdrew her hand from Alasdair's.

"Another wish? Well, isn't that interesting? Tell me, exactly how much of Da's plotting were you privy to?" Hard and brittle, her voice crackled like old, sun-dried leather.

"Ye canna believe I planned this with yer father?" On the heels of his half-arsed proposal yesterday, it did rather look suspicious.

"Didn't you?" Her unrelenting gaze bore into Alasdair, demanding truth.

She'd not give a jot, no mercy. No quarter. No reprieve.

God's toes, Farnsworth had skillfully and strategically maneuvered him into a corner.

They'd discussed Lydia's position, yes.

Several times in fact.

But no mention, not even the merest hint, had ever been voiced that Farnsworth considered Alasdair a candidate for chief.

Or her husband for that matter.

At least, not directly.

Farnsworth had asked what attributes Alasdair thought the new laird should possess and what characteristics and habits ought to be avoided. He'd asked the same about a husband for Lydia.

Damnation take it, had Alasdair subconsciously made himself seem the ideal candidate?

Because he wanted Lydia?

At any cost?

Nae.

True, he longed to marry her, more than anything, but not like this. Not forced. And, by God, not as the man who'd unintentionally stolen her rightful position.

Ironic that last night he and Lydia had eagerly intended to broach the subject of marriage between them with her father. And today under these circumstances, surely as soot was black, she found the notion abhorrent.

Head angled regally, she poked his shoulder. "You haven't answered me, Alasdair. Did you ever have even a single discussion with my father that included the subject of my marriage or status as successor?"

"Liddie lass, leave off yer harpin'. The lad's done nothin' but worry about yer welfare since he arrived. And of course we had those discussions. Many times. Toward that end, and because I mean to see ye married before I die, yer to wed McTavish within the week." He paused, wheezing, after the lengthy monologue. "Ye'll be the grand lady of Tornbury Fortress—"

Her high-pitched laugh bordered on hysterical before she clapped a hand over her mouth and presented her profile, her posture stiff and fragile.

After an extended moment, she lowered her hand. Her eyes spitting righteous fire, she met Alasdair's gaze before gravitating to her father's.

"Nae."

One syllable. Final. Unnegotiable.

And cold as death.

"Aye, ye will daughter, because it be what be best fer the clan. And ye." A flinty gleam entered Farnsworth's eyes, and he thrust his chin out, waggling a gnarly finger at them. "And if either of ye be thinkin' of objectin' or refusin' to comply, ye should ken, I've made a provision to deed Tornbury Fortress to Ewan McTavish if ye dinna marry."

The last words came out strangled and forced as a fit of coughing overcame him. He gave her a woeful look, his expression pitiable. Rather like the urchins roaming Edinburg's streets before they picked one's pockets clean.

Did Farnsworth hope to prevail upon her sympathy or daughterly devotion? Something, Alasdair presumed he'd done in the past with a degree of success.

Rather than respond to his blatant ploy, she lifted her pert nose in scorn. "I'm surprised you don't just post an advert and sell the estate and position to the highest bidder. Me, too for that matter."

Winded, Farnsworth slumped into his chair, his previous frailty enshrouding him. Defeat tinged his weary words. "I'll see me tribe protected from the likes of the Blackhalls, MacHardys, and that craven, murderous nephew of yer mother's, even if it means forfeitin' the laird's position to McTavish."

Alasdair crossed his arms. The wily old *bastart*.

He'd figured out what Ross had been up to, and Farnsworth had manipulated Lydia and Alasdair. Knew that neither would permit Tornbury Fortress's or the lairdship's sacrifice.

Ingenious actually, except for one, small irrevocable detail known only to a half dozen people besides Lydia.

For all his clever scheming, Farnsworth's plan would fail.

"Yes, and you don't believe a mere woman, even your own daughter, capable of doing the same?" Dismay warred with outrage in Lydia's eyes before shifting into defeated resignation.

Tight-lipped, probably to keep the stream of oaths that must be competing for release from exploding forth, she clasped her hands, the knuckles white, and pulled in a ragged breath. "You don't intend to answer, do you?"

Mouth pulled into a thin line, his blue eyes sharp, yet infinitely weary, Farnsworth's half-cocked reddish eyebrow gave him away.

It had cost him greatly to hurt her, and in his misconception that a woman couldn't lead as well as a man, he'd alienated her. In fact, Alasdair would wager his sword, she was more put upon for the reason Farnsworth passed her over, than his failure to name her his successor.

Women had been dealt a piss-poor lot in life.

If she were his wife, he'd treat her as his equal, not as chattel or a possession.

Lydia's rigid posture and carefully controlled breaths revealed just how distressing she found this situation.

So why hadn't she exposed Alasdair's marital state yet? He'd give her that small victory. At the moment, she deserved a triumph.

For certain her father would change his will in her favor. He had no recourse if he wanted to see her married and to assure the land and position remained with a Farnsworth descendent.

Change his will the seventh time in a year.

Surely that set a record of some sort.

If the situation were not so bloody distasteful, Alasdair would laugh.

"Well, know this, Da. In mere days, I'm of age, and I'll marry whom I want, when I want. That is, if and when I decide to marry at all. After this, I owe you no allegiance. Mr. McTavish can rule Tornbury alone, for I intend to leave."

"Nae, ye canna." In disbelief, Alasdair swung to face her.

She snorted, flicking her fingers in his face. "Indeed, I can. And I shall."

She mustn't.

This was her home. The only one she'd ever known. The place was in her blood. Unlike him, away from Scotland, she'd wither and dry up.

Hell, he might too for that matter. Of late, the reckless notion of trotting off to warmer climes didn't appeal at all. If she wasn't with him.

Time to set things aright.

If Lydia wouldn't, Alasdair would. He planted his palms on his knees. "Respectfully, Sir, I can—"

"Sir, Mr. Gwyers has arrived." McGibbons stood at the threshold. "Should I show him up or would you prefer the drawing room or study?"

Given his pallor, Farnsworth didn't have the energy to go below. He craned his neck to see around the chair's high back.

"Aye, up here will do." He'd never make it below, unless carried. "And ask Cook fer a tea tray too with danties. Gwyers always be hungry."

Lydia stood, her face a polite, bland mask. "If you'll excuse me. My presence isn't required any longer, and I've a picnic planned with Esme."

She still hadn't refuted her father's directive, hadn't exposed Alasdair's marriage. They'd planned on telling Farnsworth that very thing last night.

Why the hesitation now? What had changed?

Alasdair slid Farnsworth a covert glance.

He'd an entirely too satisfied expression on his colorless face, and exhaustion lined the sagging folds.

This trip to the solar had cost him much, and he'd pay heavily for the over-exertion.

Did worry for his health mute her?

Lydia marched to the door, her boots clacking on the stone floor between the scattered area rugs. She shot Alasdair and Farnsworth one final accusatory glance before sweeping from the room.

Bernard stood and after yawning and arching his back, hopped gracefully to the floor. Tail in the air, he delivered what could only be described as a frosty feline glare before he presented his rear and pranced from the room.

Even the bloody cat sided with Lydia.

Alasdair needed to speak with her, but not now. He'd give her time to digest this conundrum, to calm a jot so he could explain.

Ancient Mr. Gwyers gave a thin smile as he tottered into the solar, a worn, brown leather satchel tucked beneath his elbow.

At least Alasdair presumed the almost imperceptible upward curve of his almost non-existent lips was meant to be a smile. His demeanor and attire more suited an undertaker.

Gwyers bent into a brief, stiff bow and Alasdair could almost hear the old fellow's bones creaking and cracking as he slowly straightened. The man was seventy if he was a day. Wonder he hadn't retired to a comfortable seaside cottage by now.

Farnsworth made cursory introductions, seeming weaker by the minute. Had his sojourn from his bed simply been for show?

Shuffling to the chair beside Farnsworth's, Gwyers scrutinized Alasdair and sniffed loftily. "Yer to be the new laird, then?"

Chapter 23

Giving vent to her battered emotions, Lydia strode along the corridor then ran down to the ground floor. Rather than collect her lunch or find Esme, she escaped the house through a seldom used side door.

She needed to be alone, Da and Alasdair's treachery having shattered her to the core. And anger, scorching and wrenching, unlike anything she'd ever experienced, bubbled in her veins, shrieked banshee loud in her mind, drove her hurried, stamping steps onward.

How could Da?

God, how she wanted to smash and break something, to scream the oaths thrumming behind her teeth at the injustice.

It didn't matter that she understood Da's reasoning. That he thought his actions best for her and the clan. That he'd weighed his options, took the risk of alienating her to do what he was convinced was all-around best in the end.

Because, despite all of his preparing her, his many assurances that she'd be laird, he had, in the end, found her wanting.

Found her gender unworthy.

Unfit for such a lofty status.

And as awful a blow as Da's disloyalty was, Alasdair's part in the muddle . . . Well, how could she believe anything he'd said?

She didn't want to consider he'd do something nefarious, or that he'd plotted and conspired his way into Da's good graces.

The man she knew at Craiglocky, had come to know so much more these past weeks, wouldn't have done something so calculating and underhanded. That man was honorable and trustworthy; a man of his word with unimpeachable character.

Which brought her 'round to the question she'd asked before.

Who was the real Alasdair McTavish?

This doublemindedness would drive her mad, as her emotions warred with logic against the evidence she'd seen and heard.

Skirting the mansion, she rapidly made her way to the oak copse, intent on the river beyond. The crystal blue sky, only disrupted by an occasional cottony cloud, hinted at spring's early, but most welcome, arrival after an unusually harsh winter.

Overhead, birds tweeted and chirped, while in the distance, the Galanock's soothing waters burbled and beckoned. The river still ran rapid and high, but nowhere near winter's peak runoff.

Lifting her skirts, she ducked her head and increased her pace. Would that she could simply disappear, at least for a time.

At his first opportunity, likely the instant he escaped Da, Alasdair would pursue her, and she wasn't ready to speak with him. She needed time to process this life-altering turn of events. Decide her wisest course of action, which didn't include marrying him any longer.

Her vision blurred as a torrent of tears gushed onto her face. She hadn't cried in a good while, not since Mum died, actually, but today her tears couldn't be stayed. Sobs welled in her chest, escaping in noisy, raspy, wholly unladylike gasps.

Betrayed again.

Only this pain made what she'd endured with Flynn seem a mere knee scrape or a stubbed toe.

Of course, she'd leave Tornbury.

Most probably, she would accompany Esme to America, far sooner than dear Esme had anticipated, to be sure.

Lydia could act as her cousin's companion. She'd be her ruddy housekeeper or laundress if it meant fleeing Scotland upon Da's death.

More on point, putting distance between her and Tornbury's newest laird.

A body could only endure so much, and she'd already been served more than her portion in her short life.

If she possessed a vengeful spirit, she'd have exposed Alasdair—his marital state—right then and there. Nevertheless, as furious as Da had made her, she feared the shock would kill him where he slouched. Still, if Da had cast her to the street or announced she was a gypsy orphan, she would've been less surprised than him naming Alasdair laird.

Now, knowing she wasn't his choice, she could never—*would never*—assume the chief's position, Alasdair had better accept the assignment. She'd never coveted the rank like Uncle Gordon had. Pleasing her father and honoring her brothers' memories had motivated her.

Not anymore.

Wouldn't Uncle Gordon have a conniption fit if he knew she had been passed over as well? The issue of whether he'd been inside Tornbury had yet to be solved too. Surely, if anyone knew whether he had, Jinnah did.

Suspicion tapped constantly. Had Gordon anything to do with the numerous accidents and deaths plaguing Tornbury's residents?

Swiping the tears from her face, Lydia darted along the narrow, often trod path through the glen to the riverbank. A ledge, carved long ago when the water's path had run higher, balanced above the gravelly shore.

Many an hour she'd spent secreted there over the years, especially when upset or wanting to escape her brothers' good-natured, but frequent teasing.

Being outdoors, surrounded by nature, had always soothed her, though as she grew older, the time to indulge that whim diminished. Maybe in America, she'd have the time once more. Except it wouldn't be the same as Scotland, and Esme lived in the city, didn't she?

Lydia squinted, trying to remember.

Esme's family had a country house too. Lydia was certain of it.

A startled rabbit dashed across the path as squirrels scolded and chattered in the tree tops. Spring budded in the Highlands, and soon heather's lavender and pink hues would cover the hillsides and scent the air.

"Lydia, wait." Alasdair called in the distance.

Bother and blast.

She hadn't expected him to seek her quite so soon. The business with the will and Gwyers must have been swiftly seen to. Not a surprise, since Da had already told the grim solicitor what he'd intended.

Determined to have this time by herself, she quickened her steps. Nearly running, she rounded the last corner before the embankment dipped to the river's shore.

Or what used to be the embankment.

Winter's high waters had washed the shoreline away, leaving a low cliff instead of the much trodden, gradual slope to the river.

A startled scream escaped her as she tumbled down the overhang, landing in a bruised and muddy heap at the bottom.

"Lydia!" The ground shook with Alasdair's heavy running. "Where be ye, lass?"

Groaning, she rolled over on the gravel.

Bloody perfect.

What else could go wrong today?

Shoving her tangled, debris riddled hair off her face, she stared at the azure sky. Her cheek stung, and her right ribs and shoulder felt like they'd been kicked by a cow. She held her breath and gingerly flexed her limbs, waiting for any painful twinges.

A watery chuckle burbled upward. She surely had the worst luck.

A massive, manly, indecently broad-shouldered shadow blocked the sun warming her face.

"Tryin' to run away from yer groom?"

That was the wrong thing to say, even if he had meant to lighten her mood.

Lydia sat up, pushing away the hand Alasdair extended. She scrambled to her feet, refusing to look at him. One glance from his gorgeous eyes, and she'd forget her resolve.

His gaze dipped to her throbbing cheek, and he made a soft noise in the back of his throat, reaching to cradle her face.

"Don't."

Swiftly angling toward the rippling river, she brushed her fingertips over the scratch. She fished her handkerchief from her spencer pocket, and after soaking it in the icy water and wringing it dry, patted her face.

"Lydia. Ye must believe me. I dinna ken yer father's intent," Alasdair said, directly behind her, so close his breath warmed her nape.

"He's made his choice, Alasdair. And it wasn't me." She passed the cloth over her heated face again, grateful for the coolness and the chance to compose herself underneath the frilly scrap.

Da never would've chosen her.

She knew that now.

And the irrefutable knowledge hurt. Abominably. More than she would've thought possible.

Deep inside, she'd always feared that truth, had shoved aside her misgivings, convinced herself Da had seriously considered her as his replacement.

What an utter, blind fool.

Lydia swallowed the lump constricting her throat, and faced him. "I suppose I ought to congratulate you."

"I willnae accept the position." Alasdair shook his head, his overly long blond hair held back by a short, black ribbon today.

Not the first style of elegance, even in the Highlands. However, she rather favored the unruly tendrils. The fair mane suited him.

He stared at her, so stern and serious, not the mocking, playful flirt any longer.

Shading her eyes against the sun, she curved her mouth upward into a small, hopefully not pitiful, smile. "Yes. You will accept. I may be crushed that Da didn't pick me, but I won't have our estate absorbed by one as large as your cousin's. I'm sure Ewan would manage Tornbury magnificently, but she warrants her own laird, and if I cannot be chief, there's no one I would prefer more than you."

She meant it too, though each word was another well-placed dagger stab to her dying dream.

Had it truly been her dream or a convenient escape from a heart once broken?

Not broken anymore.

Not by Flynn, in any event.

A perky crested tit swooped onto an old pine stump and tilted its head back and forth, its tiny black eyes curious.

Alasdair watched the bird for a moment, then he too cocked his head endearingly. The gentle entreaty in his bluish gaze pulled at her heart strings. "What about us, lass? Please tell me ye haven't given up. We can work things out."

His gaze hovered on her mouth for before making the slow trek to her eyes. His voice feather-soft, he brushed a fingertip along her jaw. "I dinna want ye to leave. I want ye to spend the rest of yer days with me. If ye'll still have me."

Even now, he charmed and beguiled her, when she had steadfastly determined to not let him woo her into his web again. Easier planned than carried out, especially since she couldn't feign indifference.

Silly, weak, gullible female.

She shut her eyes, as much to obscure his handsome, concerned face as to shield her thoughts.

"I don't know, Alasdair. Last night, even this morning, I was prepared to tell Da we'd agreed to marry after your divorce became final." She cracked an eye open, and the crested tit gave a cheerful trill, uplifting her soul despite her doldrums. "But everything has changed now. His stipulation about wedding within a week does rather tilt the tea pot head over bum. And I'm serious about leaving Tornbury after he dies. I cannot remain now."

Not to watch someone else rule her beloved tribe.

His voice rang with resolve rather than resignation. "I told him I be married and that I sought a divorce, but it would be months until I ken whether my wife lived or the marriage had been dissolved."

Da didn't have months.

She opened her eyes wide. "And how did he take it?"

Alasdair shrugged, and then crouched and gathered a handful of colored stones. "As well as anyone in his position would, I suppose. He wisna happy, but he be more concerned that we make a match and lead his clan together. I left him to plot with his solicitor, so I dinna ken what he decided."

"You will lead the clan. Not I."

She wandered to a frog-shaped boulder shaded by Scots pines, beneath which, a deep pool had formed. Placing her hands behind her, she leaned against the rock's cool expanse, and her stomach rumbled and gurgled.

In her haste to escape the house, she'd forfeited her picnic, and poor Esme undoubtedly wondered where in the world she'd disappeared to. "I think he'd intended to appoint you even before he sent me to Craiglocky on his behalf. The tournament was a distraction Uncle Gordon concocted, though we'll probably never know why. Or why Da agreed, in the first place."

"That be nae why I came to Tornbury, and I think in yer heart ye ken it." He angled so that his shoulder rested against the rock. A tender smile played about the corners of his mouth.

At Craiglocky, he'd not wanted to come here. He'd told her so himself, and he hadn't been playacting. Only the bribe promising him time away from Scotland had motivated him to accept. And as laird, chances were that would never happen now.

Chiefs didn't gallivant around the world for months on end.

His dream would die too, and somehow that was worse given all he'd suffered already with his despicable wife.

A tear escaped, slowly tracking down Lydia's face.

Why couldn't she hate him? Or at least remain impassive?

This traitorous tenderness and compassion left her too vulnerable. Two more fat tears slithered over her cheek, and she swiped them away. At this moment, she wanted to curl in a ball and wail like an infant.

Alasdair caught a tear on his forefinger, his face etched with sympathy. "I'd take yer pain from ye, lass, if'n I could. I wish yer father wisna dyin' and had more faith in ye. That ye'd nae lost yer mum and brothers. And I'd give my sword arm to see ye smile with joy once more. To hear yer musical laugh and yer eyes sparklin' with mirth."

He gathered her hands in his then raised them to his mouth, pressing a warm, ardent kiss to each row of knuckles. "I swear by my dead bairn, I didna conspire to steal the chieftain's position from ye. How can I make ye believe me?"

She sighed and looked beyond his shoulder to the pines waving in the breeze.

Thinking straight while his captivating gaze snared hers proved nigh on to impossible. "I want to believe you. I do. I'm still too raw from Da's decision to make sense of anything right now."

Alasdair leaned in and carefully kissed her damaged cheek then picked a couple of leaves and twigs from the hair tumbling over her shoulder. A crooked grin bent his mouth. "Ye look like a forest nymph, except yer nae naked."

Despite her upset state, a sensual flush swept her.

"I look a wretched mess." Lydia brushed at her ruined dress, the torn braiding on her cuff swinging from her movements. A long slash from forearm to elbow split the rose velvet.

The garment might be salvaged, but a talented seamstress's most skillful stiches couldn't hide the repair. The spencer would never be good for anything more than the humblest tasks.

Much like her lacerated heart.

"Ye've dirt on yer chin and neck yet." Alasdair rummaged inside his vest, and after a moment, withdrew a kerchief and the letter he'd slipped there earlier. He set the missive atop the stone.

"Here, use mine. Yers be stained with blood and soil." He wetted the cloth then stood uncertainly. "May I help?"

"I can manage." She wasn't ready for his touch quite yet. "Just tell me where most of the dirt remains." She nodded toward the note as she accepted his clean handkerchief. "Why don't you read your letter? Is it from your cousin?"

"Aye."

Not that it was any of her business, but she suddenly felt nervous, all warm and squishy, and a change of subject seemed prudent.

Lifting the starched cloth, she hesitated. "Where's most of the dirt?"

"Yer chin, along yer left jaw, and the right side of yer neck. Och, and yer ear." He pointed to a spot below her ear before he stepped away and slipped his big thumb underneath the letter's crimson seal, breaking it.

Lydia attended to her face once more, and after rinsing the cloth, made her way to Alasdair.

He stood, staring into the shadowy forest, the letter dangling from one hand. At her approach, he partially turned, and the devastation ravaging his profile stole her breath.

"Alasdair? What is it? Please tell me." She rushed to him, forgetting her own troubles in that moment.

He didn't look at her, but she clearly saw a tear's damp trail down his rugged cheek.

Clasping his arm, she prodded. "You've had bad news?"

Had there been an accident or death at the Craiglocky?

"The worst and the best at once." He laughed, a sound so laden with pain, she winced.

"My God. What's happened?" She wrapped her arms around his trim waist, desperate to soothe him.

He finally met her gaze, devastation having turned his eyes cobalt with misery. "Searón be at Craiglocky. She be verra ill."

Lydia crinkled her forehead. Which of the two, pray tell, did he consider the worst and which the best?

Revelation struck.

Ah, he was too decent to divorce a sick, possibly dying woman. The situation became more convoluted and intolerable by the minute.

A fish jumped, rippling the tranquil pool. Odd that the water lay in that nook so peaceful and serene, while just inches away, the river gurgled and splashed playfully on its southward journey to the sea.

Well, that was that, then. "I see."

"Nae, ye dinna." He blew out a long breath. "She nae be alone."

"She's not? Who's with her?" Unlikely a loose woman required a traveling companion, unless her infirmity was so disabling, she'd hired someone to see her to Craiglocky.

"A lad she claims be my son."

Chapter 24

Alasdair had thought Lydia's countenance ravaged when she'd heard her father named him his successor, but that expression had been joyful compared to the utter and complete desolation contorting her features now.

A child complicated the situation.

Tremendously.

She shoved a fist to her mouth, shaking her head back and forth, her tasseled curls bouncing from her exuberance. "A son? But how can that be? I thought she rid herself of the child."

"So she told me."

He scrubbed a hand through his hair, dislodging several strands from the ribbon at his nape. Was the child really his or a by-blow? And why bring the lad to Craiglocky now, after all this time? He'd have expected her kind to exploit the child, demand money from him long ago.

His attention slipped to the letter, and he tapped it against his thigh. "I must be away to Craiglocky at once to sort this out."

Lydia wadded his handkerchief in her hands, torturing the poor scrap. "Of course, you must. You—" She closed her eyes for a moment, her breast rising as she inhaled deeply. "You must be overjoyed to know you've a child."

He cupped her shoulders, drawing her near.

She trembled slightly in his embrace, burying her face against his chest, and his shoulder pinched a bit when she bumped his wound.

The cheerful bird eavesdropping on their conversation bobbed its black crested head and chirruped.

In approval?

Alasdair and Lydia had suffered dual emotional blows today, fierce enough to lay even the most stalwart of heart out flat.

He smoothed a strand from her forehead then kissed her satiny brow. Roses and spice surrounded him. "I'm still intent on a divorce, but I dinna have to send someone to locate Searón anymore."

"I'm glad for you, I truly am. And I'm happy she's brought him to you at last. But now that you have a son, well, that changes everything." Lydia peered up at him through still spikey lashes.

"There be no proof the child be mine, but if he be, then I shall do right by him." A son. Despite his misgivings—Searón was a consummate liar, after all—a jot of anticipation swept him.

How did she intend to prove her claim?

His expectancy evaporated as reality struck him full on.

This news would surely kill Farnsworth, no matter what he'd ultimately decided about his successor after Alasdair left the solar.

If he'd gone ahead and named Alasdair laird against his wishes, Alasdair would still refuse the role. Especially now that no guarantee existed he'd be granted a divorce.

If Farnsworth appointed Lydia the chief, with the provision she marry Alasdair in order to inherit, she'd be forced to forfeit the position too.

Perhaps, in the end, the best course was to let Ewan have the estate. Then he could turn around and sell it to Lydia for a pence.

That notion wasn't altogether insane.

In fact, the idea could bloody well be the solution to what had seemed intolerable situation mere minutes ago.

Ewan would do it, too.

He had no wish for the encumbrance of another estate. Not with his dual roles as Craiglocky's laird and his English title, Viscount Sethwick.

At first opportunity, Alasdair would discuss the situation with Ewan, and hopefully, bring good tidings to Lydia when he returned. Best to not mention his plan just yet, on the slim chance Ewan wasn't receptive to the idea.

Alasdair would worry about what to do with the lad after he'd determined if the child was his.

Lydia had missed a dab of dirt near her nostril, and he wiped the small fleck away with his forefinger. Such trust simmered in the gaze she lifted to his; such faith, perhaps even devotion, and deep abiding sorrow as well.

Damn, to be able to erase her hurt, and give her new, happy memories to help mute the prior ones' pain.

A cloud drifted across the sun, casting a brief shadow over them. A golden eagle screamed above, and she glanced at the sky, her pink mouth sweeping upward upon spying the majestic bird.

True, she'd need a season to recover from all she'd been dealt today, but she was strong, resilient, not at all given to womanly ploys and tricks. She didn't abuse her gender's weaknesses. No doubt because she'd been trained as a chief and thought and reasoned like a laird.

He'd do everything within his power, exploit every connection, to ensure she took her rightful place as Tornbury Fortress's laird.

"Alasdair, I know you, and I know you won't forsake the child, even if he isn't yours. But if he is, won't that make acquiring a divorce that much more difficult?"

If she worried about his divorce, didn't that mean she still considered marrying him? That perchance, hope yet existed she'd be his for all time?

"Aye, but nae impossible." Just lengthy as hell. How could he expect Lydia to wait, years perhaps, for his divorce?

Didn't that make him a selfish, unfair arse?

Absolutely, but how could he let her go?

He loved her, craved her presence, needed her every bit as much as food, air, and water. Life without her would be empty, meaningless, a hollow existence. Far worse than when he'd thought Searón had cuckolded him, as well as the ensuing years since.

Her gaze clear and direct, Lydia gave a small, defeated smile. "Perhaps we should face the truth. We won't ever be able to wed. Fate's been against us from the onset."

"I think it best if we wait to worry over that issue until I've seen Searón and the lad. I'll leave within the hour, but I expect I'll return by the end of the week. Or the beginnin' of next." Vise-like dread cramped his gut, far more for leaving Lydia than seeing his wayward wife after eight years.

Who would protect Lydia while he was away? He didn't trust anyone other than himself to properly guard her. Until Ross had been captured and imprisoned, Alasdair couldn't put his mind at ease. He'd ask his men to be extra vigilant.

"I'm positive that will relieve Da. Your decision to return, that is. I'm not sure what reason I'll give for your absence. Unless you want me to tell him the truth?" A hint of anger lingered 'round the tattered fringes of her words. She hadn't forgiven her father yet, and no small wonder. Likely, she wouldn't for some time. Nonetheless, she loved him and wouldn't cause Farnsworth undue distress in his weakened state.

"No sense worryin' him unduly. Simply tell him Ewan summoned me regardin' an urgent matter." Alasdair permitted a ghost of a smile. A long-lost wife and secret child certainly qualified.

Throwing her tangled hair over her shoulder, she appeared deep in thought, her lips pressed tight and her brow furrowed. She cut him a somewhat distracted sidelong look. "Do you suppose McLeon would train my—the men while you're gone? I feel quite certain he and Lennox could manage the task between them. Unless you think they haven't any more need of training. In which case, you needn't hurry back until Da—"

She swallowed audibly. "Well, ye ken."

Alasdair framed her delicate jaw between his forefinger and thumb. "I promise, I'll be back, Lydia. Nothin' can keep me away from ye. Ye must ken I love ye."

Tears welled in her almond-shaped eyes, a shade somewhere between sage green and umber at the moment. As unpredictable as she, they changed color depending on her mood and what she wore.

"I ken, Alasdair." She blinked her tears away. "And I love ye too."

She did?

"I oughtn't to, I know. You're married, and it's wrong. And I did try so very hard not to fall in love with you." She bent her mouth wistfully. "I seem unable to resist you."

He swept her off her feet, lifting her high against his chest and pressed his face into her shoulder's fragrant curve. "Then we will be together. I vow it to ye. Yer my heart, my passion, and I canna live my life without ye."

Lydia twined her arms around his neck, clutching him to her. "I shall wait for you. No matter how long it takes. I shall wait. And no matter what Da decided about his successor, I shall be at your side."

He slid her down his length before capturing her mouth in a blazing kiss. With each nip of teeth, and tangling of tongues against the velvety, honeyed cavern of her mouth, he conveyed his adoration and devotion.

She eagerly returned his kisses, sliding her fingers into his hair and dislodging the ribbon. Holding his head fast, she peppered his face with short, hot kisses, her breath warm and sweet.

Resting his forehead against hers, he ran his hands up and down her spine. "There's nothin' we canna overcome to be together, Lydia. Nothin'. Promise me ye'll take guards with ye when ye leave the house. Until yer uncle be locked away—hopefully, for good—I shall fear fer yer safety."

She nodded slowly, toying with his collar. "I shall, though I don't think we'll see him again. He's greedy, but he was also terrified that night. I'll be bound he's decided to put as much distance between Tornbury, and us, as he humanly can. I doubt he was ever in Da's chamber."

"I wish I could be as certain, but I nae be." Lifting her chin, he touched the small, square tip. "Given the events of today, I'd advise ye to go ahead and dismiss Jinnah at once. If Ross did get inside, she's likely the culprit who aided him."

"All right." A sudden breeze ruffled both their hair, tangling his blond tresses with her dark strands, and she laughed softly before sighing and stepping from his embrace. "We should return. Da may have sent for one or both of us, and you must be on your way if you hope to make Craiglocky before nightfall."

Taking her hand, he entwined her fingers with his as they swung toward the path. "I'll miss ye, lass."

A few feet down from the collapsed former pathway, he leapt onto the embankment.

Lydia accepted his extended palm, and light as a child, he lifted her to solid ground.

"Alasdair?"

"Aye, my darlin'?"

She blushed, a delightful rosy hue tinting her high cheekbones. "I rather like it when you call me that."

"Then I shall every time we be together." Reclaiming her hand, he steered them along the trail. He ought to hurry, but each step closer to the manor meant the sooner he'd have to leave her.

"Alasdair?" she said again, a tinge of hesitancy coloring her voice. "If the time comes and you're a free man, I should like a proper proposal."

Scooping her to his side, he planted a possessive kiss on her parted lips. "And ye shall have one. Complete with me kneeling before ye, worshiping ye like a Roman goddess."

"I'd be satisfied with you actually asking me to be your wife."

From the corner of his eye, he slanted her a doubtful look. "I've already asked ye."

She shook her head, a smile teasing her plump lower lip. "No. You haven't. True, we've discussed it, at length, but you've never actually asked me to marry you."

He opened his mouth, but she quickly placed two fingers over his lips.

"Not now. When we can actually wed. Then it will be real."

Such a little romantic.

He pressed her fingers to his mouth and kissed the pads. "Aye. I'll wait until I be a free man."

An hour later, the sun high in the sky, Alasdair kicked Errol's sides and galloped from Tornbury Fortress. Lydia stood on the stoop, the picture of poised serenity, her hands clasped before her. Nonetheless, her eyes, those mysterious, intelligent pools, gave her distress away.

He would return. No force on heaven or earth could prevent him doing so.

Rounding the bend that would take her from his sight, he glanced over his shoulder and waved his hand high in the air.

She waved back then slowly turned and walked into the house, her dejection tangible even at this distance. She'd not had an easy time of it, far harder than his life. Nevertheless, still she remained sweet and hopeful.

Today, though, might mean the end of her optimism.

Thoughts of her, her breathtaking smile, her lilting voice, the sheen of her raven hair, her incomparable spirit, kept him entertained the duration of his journey to Craiglocky.

As the sun gently kissed the horizon *adieu*, Errol trotted across Craiglocky's drawbridge. Before Alasdair had dismounted, his parents, Gregor, and Ewan appeared at the gatehouse entrance, their expressions disturbingly bland.

So, they'd been watching for him.

Did that bode well or the reverse?

Likely Searón and her son's arrival had set the castle tit over arse in commotion and confusion, since no one but his immediate family knew of her existence.

He'd rather have liked to have been here to see the hullabaloo.

Ewan reached him first, and slapped him on the shoulder. "Thank you for coming straightaway."

"Yer summons didna leave me much choice." Alasdair dutifully pecked the cheek his mother slanted upward. "Mother, Father."

Gregor's lopsided grin seemed half-hearted and forced. "Even I admit I be glad to see yer ugly face."

"Since yers looks almost identical to mine, I suppose I canna take too much offense." Alasdair embraced his twin then stretched his spine. "Well, which of ye has been delegated to fill me in on the sordid details?"

Ewan cupped his nape, veering a wary look. "We thought we all should."

All four, *hmm*? So, they'd needed reinforcements.

Interesting. And troublesome.

"That bad, be it?" Trepidation marched across Alasdair's shoulders.

What had Searón brought with her?

The black death? Typhus? Scarlet Fever?

Mother looped her hand through his arm and guided him up the steps.

His boots echoed hollowly on the centuries old, weather-worn stones. Odd he'd never noticed that before.

"Searón's dying, Alasdair," Mother said softly, leaning into him as if she wanted to offer comfort but wasn't sure it was appropriate or needed. "Doctor Paterson has already been to see her, and there's nothing he can do."

Thank God, they hadn't called her his wife.

Searón had stopped being that years ago, in his mind at least, and apparently in theirs as well.

"I assume she's diseased?" He tried to summon some regret, some sorrow for her, for the pitiful way her life would end. However, relief, profound and immediate was his first response, immediately followed by profound guilt for his selfishness.

There'd be no scandalous divorce now, and by God, no mourning for a year either before he wed Lydia. He'd not pretend sorrow nor bow to mourning protocol. His wife had died, in his heart and mind, years before.

"It's the pox, Dair, and she be far gone. It be a wonder she made it to Craiglocky alive." Gregor searched the castle's bailey, his attention resting on the stable for a lengthy moment. "The boy tied her to a pony, then led the pathetic beast from Inverness, askin' fer directions and beggin' fer food fer her, himself, and the beast along the way."

"Aye. He's a resourceful laddie. Smart and brave too. He said he sold every last possession they owned, includin' his one pair of shoes to buy the animal."

Likely some unconscionable cur had taken advantage of the whelp.

"I presume the child has a name?" Alasdair hid a wide yawn behind his hand. Two hours of sleep didna begin to suffice.

All four stopped and stared.

Father nodded and scratched a bushy eyebrow. "Aye. He be named Alasdair, though she calls him Al. And he be the spittin' image of ye and yer brother as lads."

Chapter 25

Lydia blew out a soft breath and pulled the shawl knotted across her chest a mite snugger as she surveyed the toasty kitchen.

Normally the scent of fresh oat bread and drying savory herbs enveloped her in nostalgic comfort, but today, her mind kept straying to Alasdair.

Gone but a week and she missed him dreadfully. And if she were completely honest, an onslaught of guilt had buffeted her since his departure. The more she considered their relationship, the more self-condemnation assailed her.

She coveted another woman's husband.

Although inarguably justified in seeking a divorce, Alasdair oughtn't to have become involved with her until he'd been made free from that encumbrance.

Not that Lydia placed the blame entirely at his feet, or at his feet at all. To do so would've been most unfair. She'd done nothing to discourage him, and had, in fact maneuvered the situation so he agreed to come to Tornbury.

Then again, life offered no guarantees, did it? And moments ought to be seized and cherished while they may, should they not?

Her brothers' and Mother's deaths—Esme's parents, too—as well as Da's rapidly deteriorating health confirmed that wretched truth.

Should two people, loving one another passionately and completely, ignore the blessing they'd been given? Weren't they entitled to happiness, and shouldn't they seize it while they may?

So says every man and woman trying to justify an illicit association.

Bah!

She vacillated like a clock's pendulum—one moment wreathed in smiles and the next, wallowing in the blue devils.

For now, she'd tuck her guilt into a dark corner, and there it would lurk until Alasdair returned and they better knew what their future together heralded.

If they had a future together.

That dismal thought was promptly shoved into the same dank, remote niche as her remorse.

She twisted her mouth.

He'd not returned at the end of the week or the beginning of the next as he'd promised. No letter had arrived explaining his delay either.

What exactly had Alasdair found when he reached Craiglocky?

Why had his wife shown up after so many years? Probably not for any positive reason.

Was the child his?

Lydia hoped so. She truly did.

To know Searón mightn't have killed their child after all surely brought him peace and joy. Verifying the parentage might prove a trifle difficult, however.

"Would ye care fer a cup of tea, Miss Lydia?" Anice, her graying hair secured beneath a cheerful blue cap, bobbed her head toward the cast iron stove. "I've the kettle on, and I've just sliced some black bun. I'd been saving it for a special occasion, but thought it might tempt the laird. It's one of his favorites."

His very favorite, truth to tell.

Anice's troubled gaze flitted to the full tray Lydia had just set on the table.

"Yes, that would be lovely." Lydia sank into one of the scuffed and scratched servants' chairs paralleling either side of a long table upon which sat Da's untouched tray.

Again.

Despondent and withdrawn, he hadn't eaten enough to sustain a wraith since Alasdair left. Almost certainly that meant he'd left Tornbury Fortress to Ewan McTavish.

In her core, she feared the obvious, that Da had given up. He'd no more fight left in his frail form, no reserves in his defeated spirit.

All his clever planning and engineering had been for naught, and his greatest wish—that his clan and lairdship would carry on after he'd passed—had been thwarted.

It wouldn't have been if he'd named me laird.

Ah, but too much had hinged on that, hadn't it?

Primarily his lack of confidence in her as a female.

Her once vibrant and fierce father had shrunk into the doldrums, a feeble and pasty shadow of the warrior he'd once been.

Only once had she attempted to broach the subject.

He'd shut his eyes, turned his haggard face away, and in a paper-thin voice that the slightest breeze could tear asunder, whispered, "The matter be settled. There'll be nae more discussion."

He wreaked such anger and grief within her, and they warred, ferocious and determined, each fighting for supremacy.

Neither would win.

Lydia wouldn't permit them their hard-won victory.

She would cherish this meager, treasured time with her father.

If she permitted disappointment to turn her surly and unforgiving, regret would tinge every day of her life after he was gone. She refused to entertain that nonsense.

Hope gave her strength.

Not that Da would live; he was in God's hands now, and nothing she could do or say would change the outcome.

Denying he had little time left and crying pails of tears changed nothing either.

Nor did an iota of hope remain that she'd be Tornbury's laird. And honestly, after she'd gotten beyond the initial upset, relief had filled her.

The role wasn't one she'd ever sought.

No, her hope rested in Alasdair's return, and that someday, maybe months or years from now, they'd become man and wife.

Taking in the kitchen's familiar bustle, each item neatly stowed in its proper place, the serviceable, sturdy dishes stacked in the open cupboards, a budding smile tugged her mouth.

Maybe not here, any longer.

Lydia wasn't sure where they'd live, but as long as they were together, did it matter? She loved Alasdair, more than she'd ever loved Flynn. And she would wait. For as long as it took.

Anice sprinkled a dark spice into something delicious smelling in a pot simmering atop the cookstove. She slowly stirred the contents, expertly adding another dash. "Have the last of the contenders departed, then, Miss Lydia?"

"Yes, the last left yesterday." Stating Da's ailing health as the reason, Lydia had cancelled the competition. Its purpose no longer existed, and she wanted the extra men gone and for Tornbury to return to a somewhat normal state.

Most had taken the news in stride.

However, a few of the more belligerent expressed their dissatisfaction. A stern glare from McLeon or Lennox sufficed to send the grumbling discontents promptly on their way, their entry fees refunded and stowed somewhere on their person.

Gordon would've loved to have seen her forced to marry one of their ilk, probably the reason he'd convinced Da to hold the competition to start with.

The McTavish men would remain on for the time being, but they'd leave soon enough too. Ewan McTavish had never promised them to Tornbury for the long term, and Lydia hadn't the faintest notion what he'd decide to do when Tornbury became his.

It wasn't her worry any longer.

The knowledge proved rather liberating. Perhaps she and Alasdair would travel together. Mum had left her a tidy amount, and Da might bequeath her something as well.

If not? She lifted a shoulder. Well, they'd make do.

Perusing the cozy kitchen once more, she smiled at Bernard neatly nibbling a chicken bone in the corner.

Anice pointed her wooden spoon at him. "His treat for bringing me a mouse earlier."

She'd always made Lydia welcome below, in fact had taught her to cook. A footman walked past carrying a pair of silver candlesticks, and two maids bustled about preparing one thing or another. They'd more work since Jinnah's dismissal a week ago, but none expressed discontent. Jinnah hadn't been popular with the other staff.

She hadn't accepted her discharge with good grace either.

Swearing like a dockside whore, she'd tossed a milk pitcher onto the floor. But, she had confessed—quite gleefully, as a matter of fact—that she had retrieved some of Gordon's possessions from his chamber, which explained why she'd loitered outside his door so often. And probably meant he hadn't gone far.

That knowledge had worried Lydia more than a little.

McLeon and McGibbons had waited outside her chamber while Jinnah packed her meager possessions, and then escorted her from the house.

At Lydia's request, they'd followed her, and she'd led them straight to Gordon.

Under Lydia's direction, they gave him a choice. Take the purse she'd sent along and leave Scotland for good, or they'd take him into custody and turn him over to the authorities for robbery, attacking Lydia, and she'd insist an investigation be opened into her brothers' and mother's deaths.

No surprise, he'd eagerly snatched the purse.

According to McNeal, Uncle Gordon's glee turned to fury when they deposited him on a ship, appropriately bound for Australia. A little, well-deserved retribution.

After a word with the captain, and a hefty bribe as well, they'd waited until the ship sailed, taking Gordon from Tornbury once and for all. If he returned, he'd be imprisoned.

"Here's yer tea, Miss Lydia. I already added milk and sugar fer ye." Anice placed a plain white teacup before Lydia.

Steam spiraled upward, eager to escape the brim's confines. She added a fork and another plate holding two slices of the pastry-covered fruitcake and other dainties.

"Thank you, Anice." Lydia took a bite of the black bun, and closed her eyes. "*Umm.* Absolutely delicious. We normally only get this treat for Hogmanay or birthdays. I feel quite special."

"Well, yer birthday be but days away, and since it be a favorite of the laird, I hope he'll eat a bit."

"I do too." Though, honestly, she doubted he would.

Anice hesitated, then wiped her hands on her apron and after a slicing the maids a glance, drew near again. "We all be worried, Miss, and we ken how hard this must be fer ye." She shook her head, a beleaguered expression creasing her full face. "So much death this year. Makes a body want to go to bed and stay there."

Lydia grasped Anice's plump hand. "It is hard, but we shall manage it together. Somehow."

~ ~ ~

Ten days after receiving word of Searón's arrival at Craiglocky, Alasdair leaned a shoulder against the door frame to her room. Arms folded, he frowned, something he'd done a lot these past few days.

An oil lamp burned low on the nightstand, illuminating his wife's wasted, skeletal face, and his son's too-thin countenance as well.

His mouth slightly open, Al snored softly.

Searón and the boy hadn't heard Alasdair's light knock or him entering the bedchamber.

Why should they have?

The entry's long case clock had chimed quarter past five as he'd passed. He'd no business being in their chamber, but he couldn't put them neatly out of his mind.

He was in, what Lydia would describe as, a colossal pickle.

God, he missed her.

Every waking moment and especially at night, when his mind wouldn't cease its incessant rambling.

A neighbor had paid Aunt Giselle a visit yesterday, and her rose perfume so reminded him of Lydia, he'd made an excuse to linger just to inhale the air in her wake, like a hound on the hunt.

She'd heard him sniffing once and given him an arch look that suggested he'd gone daft.

Besotted idiot.

And heartily glad of it.

He'd fully intended to have returned to Tornbury by now, but Searón had slept for three days straight when he'd first arrived. She'd been too weak—starvation and the late stages of syphilis, according to Doctor Paterson—to receive visitors until yesterday.

Yesterday, he'd finally written Lydia a short note, explaining he'd been delayed but deliberately hadn't given a timeline for his homecoming.

He shook his head once, a smile toying with his mouth.

When had Tornbury become home?

Wherever Lydia rested her satiny head was his home.

How fared Farnsworth?

Pray God, he hadn't worsened. Lydia shouldn't have to bear that burden alone, and Alasdair rather chafed at the bit to be on his way.

Today, he'd have the why of everything from Searón, and then as kindly as possible, tell her he'd already decided to end the marriage before her untimely arrival.

He'd provide for Al, of course.

There'd been no question of that from the first instant he clapped his eyes on the lad. And in time, when his son grew more trusting and accepted Alasdair as his father, then Alasdair intended to forge a relationship with the boy.

That meant spending time with his son.

A great deal of time, and toward that end, the lad must accompany him to Tornbury.

If Lydia was amenable to the idea. And pray God, she would be.

Softhearted and kind, he expected she'd accept Al with open arms. If not, Alasdair had a conundrum of monumental proportions.

Though he scarcely knew the little chap, he'd not abandon Al, on the heels of his mother's death. Neither would Alasdair eschew Lydia.

Not again.

Pressing two fingers to the crook of his nose, he rubbed in a circular motion and released a drawn-out sigh.

What if Searón died before the divorce was granted, or she lingered for years? And he'd have to decide what to do with her if she did. And how he'd pay for her care too.

Ewan couldn't be expected to bear the burden. Perhaps a nearby cottage, and Alasdair could hire a companion to care for Searón. The lad too, though Alasdair would prefer the boy reside with him.

Nevertheless, he'd bet his beloved Errol that Al would pitch a fit worthy of Poseidon if he took the boy from his mother's side.

After nursing a bottle of whisky for several hours, Alasdair finally mustered the energy to seek his bed. The luminous night sky, even now, faded around the fringes as dawn opened her drowsy eyes and prepared to rise.

Searón and Al slept the sleep of the exhausted; the slumber one allows when one knows they're safe after having been fearful for a very, very long time.

Al refused to sleep in his appointed room, instead, faithfully lying on the floor beside his mother. He wouldn't share her bed either, he'd defiantly decreed.

"She deserves a clean, comfortable bed to herself fer once."

The boy's words, not Alasdair's.

After the first night, Alasdair had asked that a pallet be prepared for the lad. He'd lose his mother soon enough, possibly any day now, and no harm could come of indulging the boy.

They held hands, even in their sleep.

Alasdair's eyes misted.

Fiercely protective of his mother, Al's need to be near her touched even Alasdair's hardened heart. She'd been a good mother to the lad then. Such devotion was earned, and how she'd managed to nurture her son while living as a harlot, he couldn't imagine.

The boy was his, or else his mother had lain with his twin.

He quirked his mouth upward again.

Except for Al's bright green eyes—Searón's eyes—he was indeed a replica of Alasdair and Gregor as laddies. Right down to his unruly fair hair.

Thrashing about, the boy muttered something in his sleep before calming, and his breathing fell into a regular rhythm once more.

How hard and cruel life had been to Al.

So help him, Searón *would* clarify why she'd kept the boy a secret all these years.

Did the lad understand how ill his mother was? That she lay dying? True, she might linger for weeks or even months, but her fate was sealed.

According to Doctor Paterson, untreated syphilis had attacked her eyes, heart, and nervous system. How the boy managed to get her here was a wonder itself. A miracle, or a testament to his grit and perseverance?

"Alasdair? Be that ye?" Searón stirred, turning her face toward the door, her nearly sightless eyes wide, the pupils button-sized.

"Aye."

"Be it mornin' then?" Her voice a wispy shadow of the carefree girl she'd once been, she tried to sit up, and her labored movements awoke Al.

"Mum?" Alert and instantly on his bony knees, he rubbed the sleep from his eyes with his fists. His bare feet, callused and brown, poked out from under his blanket. "Do ye need somethin'? Are ye in pain? Sick? Do ye need the slop jar?"

His gaze shifted to the medicines crowding the night table.

She weakly patted his tousled head. "Nae, me love. Yer father be checkin' on us. That be all."

Al shot Alasdair a wary glance as he advanced into the chamber.

Silent and keenly observant, Al's gaze remained on Alasdair while he lit a wall sconce and stirred the fire into a blaze capable of removing the room's chill.

Alasdair replaced the fire poker before facing his leery son.

"Al, would ye run to the kitchen, and see if Sorcha has coffee ready yet?" Alasdair's chance for sleep had passed and he'd need a pot or two to keep his wits about him today. "Ask fer a tray to be brought up. And tell her I said to give ye a couple of Scotch eggs and a cup of hot chocolate to hold ye over until we break our fast. Make sure she tops the chocolate with Devonshire cream."

Al lifted his mother's frail hand, her blue veins vivid against her translucent skin. "Will ye be all right, Mum? Can I fetch ye anythin'?"

"Tea and toast, me dear." She smiled and touched his cheek before sliding Alasdair a nervous, sideways glance. "And mayhap . . . a spot of marmalade?"

The hesitancy and wistfulness in her voice roused Alasdair's pity. "Aye, Sorcha makes the best marmalade."

Al kissed Searón's sunken cheek. "I be right back."

Alasdair touched Al's shoulder as he passed. "I need to speak with yer mother, privately, so please knock before ye enter."

"I dinna want ye upsettin' her." Mutiny crumpled the boy's mouth and forehead.

"I shall be fine." Searón managed a weak, but encouraging smile. "Yer da's a kind man. He willna hurt me."

God's teeth.

Had the poor child seen men hurt his mother?

Not unheard of or uncommon given her chosen profession.

He stiffened, flashing her a surprised look.

Yer da?

She'd told Al, then.

How long had he known, and what did the scamp make of it?

Given the curious, yet wary look he scraped over Alasdair, not too terribly much.

Once Al had departed, Alasdair hauled a chair near the bed, so she could see him a bit easier. Doctor Paterson said she was nearly blind.

Alasdair hooked an ankle over his knee and waited.

Eyes downcast, Searón plucked at the bedcovering. "I suppose ye want to ken why I kept yer son a secret from ye?"

Chapter 26

Alasdair cocked a brow, fresh anger thickening his blood, and stiffening his spine and resolve. "Aye. That I would."

He'd been denied the first seven years of his son's life, had grieved the child's loss eight long years.

Searón had much to answer for.

She flinched at his tone's icy bitterness, but nodded, her mouth pressed into a tense ribbon. Her once vibrant red hair had thinned to scraggly wisps scarcely covering her scalp, and her hands trembled. Great grayish-purple rings framed her sunken eyes, giving her a haunted, wraith-like appearance.

She must have contracted the *grandgore* early on to be this far gone already. Doctor Paterson said some contracting the French pox made a full recovery. Others, like Searón, seemed incapable of fighting the disease's progression and effects.

The syphilis contagion attacked those unfortunate souls with a vengeance, cruelly tormenting the afflicted, and bringing an early death.

"I never rid meself of the wee bairn. I cudna." She spared him a wary glance through sparse lashes. "I lied to ye," she whispered.

"Obviously." Cutting and terse.

She winced, clenching the coverlet.

He clamped his hands on the arms of his chair.

Dinna be an utter arse.

Searón's lower lip quivered, and she spoke unsteadily,

her gaze riveted on the coverlet that she continued to torture with her broken and jagged nail tips.

"I ken ye be angry, Alasdair, and ye've a right to be. But I beg ye, dinna make this any harder fer me than it already be. Fer our son's sake, if'n ye canna find a speck of kindness or forgiveness in yer heart fer me. He be a good laddie. Honest and loyal."

Oddly, pity vied as strongly as ire at her deception.

"I beg yer pardon, Searón. I ken this be difficult fer ye. Please go on, and I promise to hold my tongue."

If he had to bite the damnable thing to still its determined, cantankerous flapping.

Scraping a hand across her eyes, she sighed. "Ye ken I wisna an innocent when we wed. What ye didna ken was me da forced me into servicin' some of his lofty customers since I be fourteen. He pocketed the coin and threatened to throw me and me wee sisters out onto the street if'n I didna comply."

"He prostituted ye? His own daughter?" Alasdair reared upward, dropping his booted foot to the floor with a resounding thud. If she'd announced she'd entertained the Pope, he'd not have been more stunned.

She gave a weary nod. "Aye, and he be furious when he returned and discovered I'd married ye and intended to leave."

Neal had been absent when they'd registered, and a foxed-to-the-gills staggering sot most of the rest of the time Alasdair had been at the inn.

Even his father had commented on the oddity of a young lass running the inn with only a cook, a barkeep, and even younger girls waiting tables and acting as maids.

"Da said if I left with ye, he'd let the men have me sisters. Their mum died when Maeve be only months old, and I took care of the both of them. They only be nine and ten when we wed."

A lone teardrop trickled down Searón's gaunt cheek, and she sniffed loudly before snatching a crumpled kerchief from the night table. After dabbing her eyes, she let her head fall back into the pillows and stared at the pleated canopy.

His jaw muscles working as he strove not to swear like a sailor, Alasdair pounded his knee. No doubt, she'd heard worse, but not from his mouth. "God rot his despicable soul."

"I'd just found out I carried yer bairn when ye came back fer me. I planned on tellin' ye, and beggin' ye to take me half-sisters too, but Da let two perverted reprobates take me sisters into a chamber. If'n I left with ye, they'd have their way with the wee girls." Her tears fell swift and hard, great sobs racking her frail shoulders. "I cudna let them, Alasdair. I cudna. I ken what it be like to be violated over and over."

Crimping his eyes shut, Alasdair swallowed the bile burning his throat.

All these years he'd hated Searón, had spared her nary a kind thought, and she'd only been protecting her sisters. Guilt, bitter and galling, wrenched his innards. If he'd tried harder, he might have found her, spared her and his son some of the misery and hardships they'd endured.

Instead, he'd damned her and their son to a reprehensible existence. This wretched wraith of a woman who'd been wronged by every person in her life, except their gentle son.

How could Alasdair contemplate divorcing her now? Bring even more heartache on her tormented soul? Surely God would send him straight to hell to gnaw scorching coals right beside Lucifer himself.

Wouldn't Lydia take that to mean he still loved Searón? She'd be so wounded, thinking she'd been thrown over for another woman. Again. But not for love this time. Never for love.

She'd never forgive him.

Moisture burned behind his lids.

God, how could he let Lydia, the other half of his soul, go?

He must. God help him, he must.

Granted, overwhelming compassion and remorse filled him for Searón, but he didn't love her. Had never loved her the all-consuming way he did Lydia.

His soul had found its mate in her, even if providence had cruelly determined they couldn't be together.

Tears pricked again, and he angled his head away, blinking rapidly.

Several moments passed before Searón regained her composure, and he marshaled his as well.

He'd chosen the path of honor and duty rather than love and happiness, and a part of him had died in the last few moments.

Perhaps if they hadn't a son together, or if she'd been a neglectful mother, Alasdair might've justified setting her aside. But they did, and she hadn't been.

He leaned forward, resting his elbows on his knees. "If I'd ken, I would've helped ye."

"I ken that now, but I be too afraid. Da threatened to beat me until I lost yer bairn. Al be all I had of ye. He gave me a reason to live. After ye left, I contacted me sisters' aunt." A ghost of a smile tipped her lips. "She loathed Da and agreed to take me sisters in."

Furrowing his brows, he tilted his head. "Nae ye too?"

Searón shook her head, her lanky hair dragging across her shoulders. Tugging the soft blue counterpane higher, she sighed. "Nae. She be a poor woman, and nae me kin, after all. Besides, I be grown, and she had nae wish to take on me bairn too."

"So ye were forced to sell yerself?"

She gave a short shake of her head. "Nae at first. I found work as a cook in an inn, but when me condition became obvious, the mistress sacked me. Called me a whore. I almost starved, tryin' to find work after that, me big belly givin' me condition away."

Another blast of guilt pummeled him.

"A madame, Mollie O'Kearne, saw me beggin' at a brothel's backdoor and took pity on me."

He'd bet she had.

Searón curled her lip. "That be what I stupidly thought anyway. She gave me food, said she had a proposal fer me. She'd let me stay, clean and cook, feed me, and after me bairn be born and I'd healed, I could have me pick of customers. Only the cleanest and most refined gentleman, she promised. And only if I be agreeable to the arrangement."

Searón's high-pitched laugh rang out, bitter and hopeless, ending in a rasping sob.

"I take it she didna keep her word." Once ensnared, women seldom escaped prostitution.

"Aye, she did until Al be born a month later." She turned her face to the wall.

"She had a clients' waitin' list, and began pressurin' me to entertain them within a fortnight, claimin' I owed her fer me room and board, and the bairn's too. I resisted as long as I could, but she threatened to sell Al. If I complied, I could keep him with me. Two of the other girls had bairns too, and all of the women took turns carin' fer the wee ones."

Exhaustion engulfed him, and he leaned back in the chair's padding. "So ye were trapped."

"Aye, as surely as a blind rabbit in a snare."

Alasdair couldn't sit still a moment longer.

Searón's vile revelations put everything in an entirely different light. Hands clasped behind him, he paced at the foot of her bed.

"Why didna ye write me? Ye be my wife, and ye birthed my son. I would've come fer ye."

She flicked him a glance, part cynicism and part despair, her lips twitching upward at the corners. "I be too ashamed, afraid ye'd not want me after I'd lied to ye. And I canna write. After three years, I met a man. He be older and married, but he offered to take Al and me to Inverness, to put us up in a cottage."

From harlot to mistress.

For certain a step up in the industry, and Alasdair could hardly fault her for seizing the opportunity. Service one hoary old goat or dozens of rakes and degenerates?

"He be the man that hurt ye?"

She flashed him a startled glance. "Aye, but he only hit me when in his cups—"

Which was probably every time he called.

"—And never in front of Al. I made him go to the outbuildin' and stay there until Perkins left."

What that unfortunate child had seen and heard in his short life.

Her lashes fluttered shut. This short exchange had exhausted her. "Perkins tossed me aside after his wife died, and he wanted to find a young bride. I be sick by then, though I swear to ye, I didna know I had the pox. I had been ill me first year at the brothel, but I thought it be the stress and me unhappiness."

Removing the stopper from a pale blue laudanum bottle she bit her lip, obviously in pain. She poured several drops into a half full water glass, and after recorking the bottle, stirred the contents.

"I went to see yer father three times, tryin' to find ye." It had taken Alasdair two years to put aside his bruised pride and go the first time.

"I nae have seen or spoken to me Da since the day I left." Her hand shaking, she took a long sip of the mixture, grimacing before swallowing the bitter tonic.

So, Neal had lied each time Alasdair visited, gleefully filling Alasdair's ears with disgusting tales of Searón's activities.

All fabricated.

What a warped piece of shite.

Neal could expect a visit, if he still yet breathed. And afterward, he might not have the luxury, so enraged was Alasdair.

"What of yer sisters?" What was he to do now? Set Searón and the boy up in a cottage in Craigcutty? Wouldn't it be better for Al to be surrounded by his family?

Damn, what a calamity.

"Maeve found me late last year. Or rather her husband did at her biddin'." Pink tinged Searón's ashen cheeks. "That be humiliatin', worse than the thin's I be forced to do as a strumpet. Openin' the door and him introducin' himself. I wanted to crawl into a hole and die from the shame."

Alasdair touched the back of her hand. "I be more sorry than words can say."

Wearily shoving her hair off her forehead, she lifted a shoulder. "She and Peg be married. Their aunt died, and on her deathbed, she confessed she ken I'd become a whore and guilt had eaten at her fer nae helpin' me. Though we weren't kin, she kindly left me a small sum, and I've saved every cent fer Alasdair. It be all I have fer him to remember me by."

Weariness etching her face, aged beyond her years from hardship and deprivation, she finished her draught in a single gulp. Eyeing the empty glass longingly, she sighed and set it on the nightstand with a soft, awkward *clunk*. "When I ken I be dyin', I told him about ye."

Alasdair sat on the bed and took her hand in his. "I'm glad ye did. I promise, I shall love him, and he'll never want fer anythin' else again."

Except his mother's love.

Her eyes welled with tears, and beneath her hardened and ravaged features, he caught a glimpse of the girl he'd fallen in love with.

"He sold his shoes to brin' me here, Alasdair." She swallowed, swiping at her damp face. "and I almost told him about the money. But he be so proud of himself fer findin' a way to buy the pony. He needed that accomplishment, somethin' to make him feel worthy and strong."

Clanking and banging, followed by whispering outside the door announced the tray's arrival. A moment later, one sharp rap resounded.

Somewhat surprised, Alasdair glanced to the partially parted royal blue velvet drapes. The sun had risen while they talked, and a new day's fresh, bright sky winked back at him through the opening. The bedside clock's hands pointed to seven.

A second knock echoed.

He looked to Searón.

This was her chamber, and he'd not usurp her right to bid or deny entry, as trivial as that might seem. To a woman who'd never held any power, even the smallest gestures meant much.

She laid her handkerchief on the night table, and after smoothing the counterpane across her middle, folded her hands primly on her lap. "Come in."

"There are several of us, Mrs. McTavish," Fairchild spoke respectfully through the still closed door. "Master Al has a surprise for you, if you're feeling quite up to it."

Alasdair jerked, startled at Fairchild addressing Searón as Mrs. McTavish. She was, after all. Nonetheless hearing it for the first time somehow made it more concrete.

Unchangeable.

"Yes, please." A glint of excitement lit Searón's faded eyes. She adored their son, had sacrificed much for him.

The door swung open on well-oiled hinges, and Al, Fairchild, and Ewan filed in.

His tongue's tip caught between his teeth, Al slowly walked forward, a tray clutched in his white-knuckled hands. Tentatively placing one foot in front of the other, his forehead scrunched in concentration, he slowly crept toward his mother's bed.

A cup of hot chocolate, cream creeping over the brim in white rivulets, two Scotch eggs, toast and marmalade sat upon the tray.

Fairchild followed, bearing a coffee and tea service, and Ewan brought up the rear, carrying a small bouquet of cherry blossoms, complete with an ornate vase far too grand for the humble blooms.

"I brought ye breakfast, Mum." Al placed the tray on a side table then carefully lifted the cup and saucer, his expression woebegone. "I spilt a little of the chocolate, I'm afraid."

"Darlin', isnae that meant fer ye?" Searón beamed with pride.

"Aye, but I ken how much ye enjoy chocolate, and it be a rare treat fer ye. I thought we could maybe share?" Hungrily eyeing the treat, he passed her the cup for the first sip.

Alasdair grinned, relishing the unfamiliar puff of pride his son's thoughtfulness inspired.

Searón had raised one fine boy, and under the harshest, most difficult of circumstances.

Gratitude tightened his throat.

If only he'd known.

Fairchild deposited his tray. "Young master. Cook sent up a full pitcher of hot chocolate for you, and I do believe—" He lifted a lid from a crockery jar and winked.

Fairchild never winked. Ever.

"Ah, yes, Devonshire cream." He replaced the cover. "You may have as much as you please, and should you require more, or additional Scotch eggs, or perhaps oatcakes, I would be honored to hurry to the kitchen to fetch them straightaway."

Nor did he fetch hot chocolate. Or Scotch eggs. Or oatcakes.

And most especially, not in a hurry or straightaway. *Ever!*

Footmen or maids had the privilege of scurrying up and down the three flights of stairs for that sort of thing.

It seemed Al had already wiggled himself into everyone's good graces.

Excellent.

The sooner he felt at home at Craiglocky, the better.

Unless Alasdair dragged him off to Tornbury or stashed him and his ailing mother in an out-of-the-way cottage.

Ill-begotten knave.

Even Alasdair's conscience mocked him at the uncharitable thought.

"Perhaps you'd care to have a seat at the table, young sir?" Fairchild stood at the ready, pitcher in hand. A drop of warm, brown sweetness dripped from the curved spout.

Al nodded and scurried to do the butler's bidding.

"Thank ye, Fairchild." His eyes grew round as Fairchild extended the dainty teacup to him. He cautiously took it in his grubby hands.

A good scrubbing might be in order.

Al clawed at his nape with his free hand, a creamy mustache balanced on his upper lip.

And perhaps a thorough delousing too.

Pushing the laudanum bottle aside, Ewan placed the frilly, pink blossom-filled vase on the ever more crowded night table. "Al had me climbing the cherry tree after these blossoms for you. He said they're a favorite of yours."

Another blush, surely this one of pleasure, tinged

Searón's face. "Indeed, they be. I cudna afford flowers, but tree blossoms be free."

"You're up early today, Ewan." Alasdair eagerly accepted the coffee Fairchild poured him. He took a quick, grateful sip, burning his tongue on the scalding broth.

Served him right for his carelessness.

"As are you." Ewan looked pointedly between Searón and Alasdair.

Alasdair skewed his mouth to the side before taking another, more cautious sip. "Truth to tell I haven't seen my pillow as yet."

Al stopped licking the side of his cup. "Ye didna go to bed yet, ah, sir? Aren't ye sleepy?"

"Ye may call me Da or Father or Papa if ye wish, Al. Or even Alasdair or Dair." He winked. "I usually only get called the last when I'm in trouble."

Al's features slammed closed, as securely as shutters across windows.

Perhaps a mite too soon for that suggestion. "But nae, I haven't slept yet, and aye, I be tired."

"And you won't be seeking your bed either," Ewan said. "I received an urgent missive, which is why I'm up so early on myself."

Alasdair stifled a yawn.

Not the first time he'd gone without sleep, but he didn't favor the wooly head or muddled senses.

"We can discuss it below." His mien guarded, Ewan canted his head toward the door.

"Oh? Somethin' of import, I gather." Something he didn't want to discuss in front of Searón, and which thickened his normally slight brogue.

Hadn't she been entirely truthful?

Was there more to her pitiful story?

Unless . . .

Every muscle taut with dread and anticipation, Alasdair whipped his attention to Ewan. "Who be the letter from?"

Anybody but Lydia. A letter from her could only mean one thing.

Ewan's sliced a subtle glance toward Searón.

Dinna say it.

"Lydia Farnsworth."

Chapter 27

Lydia let fly an arrow, squinting through the moisture blurring her vision as the steel tip hit home. She grasped another from her quiver and soon sent it hurtling through the air to join the others impaling the embankment, their bright crimson and gold feathers the only color marring the bleak horizon.

Low pewter clouds blanketed the drizzly, dismal morning, matching her equally dreary and peevish mood.

Far better to take her crossness and anguish out on the crag than rail her grief in the manor's drawing room where even now, Da lay in internal repose.

As her brothers and Mum had not so very long ago.

After his funeral, she intended to close the room up for good. Three times in less than a year the once cheerful chamber had housed her family's bodies. Never again would its walls resound with their laughter. Death's presence lingered there, and she couldn't abide to set foot in the room ever again.

Even now a pair of devoted clansmen stood at attention, one at Da's head, the other his feet. Honoring their laird one last time as they'd taken shifts 'round the clock the past three days and would continue to do so until his funeral on Saturday, four days hence.

A continuous stream of solemn-faced mourners had passed through the staid room, paying their respects to their beloved chief. For three days, Lydia had somehow dredged composure from some invisible source and answered the anxious questions put to her.

"When will the new laird be announced?"

"Who be the new chief?"

"Are ye the new laird?"

"Do ye ken who the laird named his successor?"

To each, though her cheeks ached and her lips had become stiff from artificial smiles, she'd repeated the same phrase. "Please, have patience. An announcement will be made soon."

Until this morning.

And then suddenly, she couldn't sit beside her father's corpse and feign self-possession any longer.

Nor could she answer serenely when she wanted to shout, "Bloody, bloody, bloody God damned unfair!"

All of it was unfair.

Four nights ago, sitting beside Da, clutching his crepey hand while tears flooded her face, she'd listened, stupefied to his dying wish.

His chest rising in shallow, rattling breaths, he'd labored to get the words out, to tell her his brilliant plan. What his will said, so she'd not be shocked or hurt at its reading. How he'd provided for her.

Lydia had thought she'd guessed his intent, his plan, but he'd fooled her.

Duped them all, truth be told.

Not unkindly or calculatedly cruel, she was certain. As anticipated, he'd named Ewan McTavish laird. A mite less expected, he'd decreed Alasdair war chief—if he'd have the position. But Da's decision to leave her Tornbury Fortress completely flummoxed Lydia.

The chieftain position brought power, prestige, and authority, but not a single pence, sheep, or speck of gold.

Nothing.

Da had bequeathed Lydia everything else, right down to the hens' eggs and cow manure for fertilizer.

What a monstrous, shortsighted jest even if well-intended.

A laird without an estate, and an estate owner without any power.

Why had Da done it?

Hadn't he considered how his decision would affect the clan? For surely he knew the confusion his actions would cause.

Better to have left all to McTavish. That, she'd foreseen and accepted. However, now she wasn't free to leave.

Unless she sold Tornbury.

She snorted and aimed the arrow.

Bless the sly old fox.

He'd known she count herself a disloyal traitor if she did so, because she loved Da so desperately and wouldn't deny him his final wish.

He'd neatly out-maneuvered her, and she couldn't quite decide if his cunningness impressed or infuriated her.

She quirked her mouth wryly.

He wasn't the only Farnsworth capable of cleverness. She might lease the entire estate and retain the rights to the gold-mining.

Or turn it into a school.

She grinned wickedly.

Or a house of ill-repute.

She'd not make any decisions now when her emotions were scraped raw, but neither could she affect subservience or compliance.

And so, Lydia had left the vigilance to the clan, unable to pretend a moment longer that she didn't know who the chieftain was, or that all would be well.

How could it be?

Arching her back, she stretched her stiff spine then rotated her shoulders a couple of times. She'd slept little, and with the house bursting with guests, she craved time alone.

Rather than play the hostess, she'd snuck from the manor before breakfast to take out her frustration on an unprotesting spot of ground.

She reached for another arrow, grasping air instead.

Had she truly gone through a full quiver already?

Sighing, she lowered her bow and searched the road to Tornbury. Absent of riders and coaches at present, but the lane wouldn't stay deserted for long.

No McTavishes had arrived yet either, though within an hour of Da's death, she'd sent word to Craiglocky. Where she'd house them when they did show, she couldn't fathom. The men could stay in the barracks, and if any women accompanied them, other guests would have to share their chambers.

Ewan had responded with a short, polite condolence, and assured her he'd attend the funeral.

He'd not mentioned Alasdair. Not as much as a word.

Lydia captured her lower lip between her teeth as she trudged across the uneven, stony ground to retrieve her arrows.

Other than his letter saying he'd been delayed, she'd not heard from him, and she didn't know what to make of the silence.

She'd thought—*hoped*—upon learning of Da's death, he'd send a note as well, and that he hadn't, worried her. More than the situation with the estate, truthfully.

His silence and delay in returning had her imagination creating any vast number of scenarios. None of which had a positive outcome.

Surely he'd come for the funeral too, and while he and Ewan were at Tornbury, Gwyers would read Da's official will.

A half an hour later, she deposited her bow and quiver at the smithy to have the arrow tips sharpened.

"Good day, Miss Farnsworth." Mr. Robertson tipped his hat, two of his freckled, fresh-faced sons curiously peeking from behind his legs.

They'd settled into their cottage, and he'd begun his duties with a fervor that impressed Lydia. Her kindness had earned her a loyal servant.

"Good day to you as well, Mr. Robertson. Lads."

With a cordial nod, she made her way to the stables to play with Sheba's pups. Beyond lonely, she intended to pick a pup for herself. She'd always wanted a house dog, but Mum fussed about the shedding. Now nothing stood in Lydia's way from adopting one of the precious puffs of fur.

And rolling in the hair if she wished.

There was something to be said for only having oneself to be accountable to.

"Hello, Sheba." Lydia knelt beside the tidy pen enclosing the wobbly pups and their mother and scratched behind Sheba's ears.

Tongue lolling, Sheba thumped her bushy tail before turning her attention to her rowdy offspring. Three puppies suckled while four others clumsily romped, growling softly as they tackled each other.

One sweet-faced female, black encircling her eyes like someone had lined them in kohl, sat politely, her head cocked adorably.

Lydia lifted the pot-bellied pup, and received several licks to her chin. She buried her face in the puppy's soft neck. "Aren't you a sweet lassie?"

Sheba whined and stood, her anxious gaze trained on her baby.

The nursing pups yipped in protest at having their meal interrupted, and Lydia chuckled. "All right. Here she is, but I must warn you, I intend to claim this darling as my own, Sheba. I'm rather lonely, you see."

Dreadfully lonely.

"Da, do ye think I might have me a puppy, someday?"

Upon hearing a child's wistful voice, Lydia spun around.

Alasdair stood framed in the stable door, holding the hand of a miniature version of himself—except for the boy's bright eyes, alight with cautious curiosity.

He'd come.

Her heart leapt with overwhelming joy, and Lydia couldn't contain her broad smile or giddily leaping pulse.

In an instant, her silly fears evaporated and floated away. She hadn't even dared let the thought that he wouldn't return ripen in her most secret musing, and now here he was.

With a lad who had to be his son.

They must've taken to each other quickly for the child to have journeyed here with Alasdair.

Hadn't Searón minded?

Perchance she was too ill to care or voice an objection, or she wanted her son to get to know his father. Likely, that had motivated her to make the unexpected visit to Craiglocky as well, unless it was money she was after.

Alasdair answered with a reassuring smile. "I be sure of it. Why dinna ye ask Miss Farnsworth if ye can play with the pups while I have a word with her."

Big-eyed, his uncertainty glaring, Al shifted from foot to foot in what appeared to be brand new shoes.

Lydia ran her hand down the puppy's spine. "Would you like to hold her?"

The child's eyes brightened even more, and a grin split his face, revealing a missing front tooth. "Aye, m'lady. I surely would."

"Just Miss Lydia will do. May I ask what your name is?" The puppy playfully nibbled and clawed at her shawl.

"Alasdair, Miss, like me da." He veered Alasdair a swift, slightly unsure gaze. "But most everyone, except Mum sometimes, calls me Al."

No doubt the boy was Alasdair's offshoot then, and he'd claimed the boy as his.

Happiness welled within in her at the welcome news.

"A fine, strong name it is too." For the boy and his honorable father. "It means defender of men. Did you know that? And your father is Tornbury's war chief."

At least temporarily.

The boy beamed, proud to his red-tipped, slightly pointed ears.

"Is Ewan with you, Alasdair? Mr. Gwyers is prepared to read the will after the funeral Saturday, and I'd hope he'd be present." And they could get that bumblebroth settled.

"Aye, but he went directly into the house, assumin' ye'd be within." He released the eager boy's hand. "Go on then."

She extended the wriggling puppy, making sure Al had the dog firmly wrapped within his skinny embrace before releasing her.

He giggled and dropped to his knees when she promptly began whining and licking his face. "What be its name, Miss Lydia?"

"Well, she doesn't have one yet. Perhaps you'd like to help me name her?" She pointed at the pen. "There are seven more. You may kneel outside and pet the puppies until their mama is comfortable with you, and if your papa is agreeable, you may select one of the puppies as your very own."

"I can, really?" He carefully maneuvered to his feet, and after returning the pudgy female to Sheba's care, squatted, and watched them.

Suddenly nervous, for Alasdair had wordlessly watched the entire exchange, something reserved and guarded in his demeanor, she brushed black and white dog hair from her torso.

His square chin—very much like his father's—resting on his hands atop the pen, Al asked tentatively, "Da, might I have one?"

Alasdair considered his son's angst-riddled face. "I dinna see why nae. It be good fer a lad to have responsibilities, and a dog makes a loyal and lastin' friend. Do ye think ye be up fer the task?"

"Aye. I be." A shy smile replaced the uncertain frown on Al's face, and he gave a solemn nod before returning his attention to the rambunctious puppies. "Can I have a boy dog?"

"Certainly, you may." At last, Lydia ventured to meet Alasdair's keen, yet warm perusal. How she'd missed his rugged features, his deep voice, his touch. "You wished to speak with me?"

Alasdair nodded, his great stride closing the distance between them. He drew her slightly aside then turned her to face him. Cupping her shoulders, he peered deep into her eyes, murmuring softly, "I came as soon as I be able. Much has happened that I need to tell ye, and it be too important to put in a letter."

See, there had been a logical explanation for his delay.

He pressed his forehead to hers, and his glorious manly scent enveloped her. "I be truly and greatly saddened to hear of yer father's death, lass."

She ducked her head to hide the sudden onslaught of tears his tenderness caused.

A muffled sob dragged her attention to Al, his face crumpled in anguish as he wept into his elbow.

Lydia knelt beside him, and after gathering him into her arms, kissed the top of his surprisingly clean head. Given his mum's profession, she'd half expected him to be a smelly urchin, but the child she held, though definitely thin and wearing well-used clothing, was freshly scrubbed.

"What is it, dear?"

"I . . ." He inhaled a ragged, saturated breath. "I miss me mum."

"Of course you do, Al." She gave him a little reassuring squeeze. Probably the first time he'd ever been away from his mother, and surrounded by people he didn't know with a father he'd just met? Well, she'd be tense and anxious too. "It's only natural to miss someone you love. I'm sure your father intends to return you to Craiglocky shortly, and then you'll see your mum."

Instead of quietening, Al collapsed against Lydia and wailed, a keening, anguished animal-like cry, so distraught her heart stuttered.

What in God's name?

She veered Alasdair a panicked, questioning look.

What had she said to distress Al so?

Alasdair bent to one knee and clamped his huge hand on his son's skinny, shaky shoulder. "I wish I could take yer pain from ye, son."

Realization buffeted Lydia.

"Oh, Alasdair," she breathed, emotion misting her eyes and closing her throat.

He framed her cheek with his other hand, and bent near Lydia's ear. "Laudanum overdose."

Chapter 28

Several hours later, in what served as Tornbury's nursery, Alasdair sat on the side of the bed harboring his small son.

Lydia, holding Al's hand, sat on the other.

Al didn't know Searón had killed herself, and if Alasdair had his way, the lad never would. It served no good purpose and would only increase Al's heartache and taint his memories of his mother.

Far better and kinder to let him think she'd succumbed to her illness. She would've eventually anyway, but Alasdair suspected Searón hadn't wanted Al to see her continued decline as her physical symptoms worsened, and she gradually lost mental function.

More unselfishness, and her sacrificial act in taking her own life increased Alasdair's admiration even as it compounded his guilt.

For though saddened at her tragic end, a part of him had been secretly relieved. And the knowledge simmered away, a relentless and accusing tangled mass churning in his middle.

What kind of a self-centered arse had he become?

One who'd been spared having to choose whether to act nobly and quash his feelings for Lydia, at least until Searón died, or risk jeopardizing his developing relationship with Al by having to explain why Alasdair had put Searón aside and divorced her.

Perhaps that day in her chamber, given his reaction to Ewan's news about Farnsworth, she'd suspected his involvement with Lydia, and had done Alasdair another kindness.

One God knew he didn't deserve.

All these years he'd blamed Searón, seldom had a kind word or thought for her, and she'd been a victim. He couldn't even bring himself to be outraged that she'd hidden Al from him, given she was likely terrified he'd be taken from her.

Still, the boy had already suffered far too much in his short life. He should be permitted the fond recollections of the woman he adored and who'd cherished him.

Enough to make the ultimate sacrifice.

Lydia sighed, and after tucking Al's hand under the bedclothes, bent and kissed his forehead. "Poor dear. I wish I could do something to ease his grief."

"Ye have, by bein' kind and permittin' the pup." Alasdair pointed to the black and white ball of hair asleep on the pillow. Every now and again, the dog jerked, his nose quivering and his small paws twitching.

Al had wept for hours, and only Lydia allowing him to tote a fur-covered ball of energy into his bed had calmed him.

The puppy, dubbed McCuddles after an intense discussion about appropriate names, lay asleep, his snout across Al's neck. The biggest of the litter, McCuddles's name matched his temperament.

Esme had volunteered to sleep in the nanny's quarters while Al remained at Tornbury, otherwise, Alasdair wouldn't have left his son tonight.

"Ring for a footman if the pup needs to go outside, or misses his mother too much, Esme. And thank you for offering to stay with Al." Lydia waited beside the open door as Esme lowered the lamp.

"I'm happy to do it, and it relieves me of having to attempt conversation with house guests. They poke fun at my American accent." She smiled good-naturedly. "I might have exaggerated a southern drawl a mite. Or a lot."

Already smitten with his son, Alasdair brushed a strand of hair from Al's forehead. "If he awakens and can't be calmed, please fetch me."

"Of course, I shall, Mr. McTavish." After settling into a chair near the fireplace, she picked up her embroidery and stabbed the needle in and out, her face puckered in concentration.

In the corridor, Alasdair kept pace with Lydia as she swept along.

"I asked Sorcha to have a tray sent to the study for when we were done, Alasdair. I'm sure you're hungry, and I'd like a word with you before I retire." She'd gone a bit starchy and formal. Because of what she wanted to discuss?

This was the first they'd been alone since his arrival, the first time the house hadn't buzzed with the voices of Tornbury's many guests, and he meant to take advantage of the deserted passage and the late hour.

"I missed ye, Lydia."

She slowed her pace, her features softened as she graced him with a beatific smile and reached for his hand. "And I you."

"Enough to grant me a kiss from yer sweet lips?" Wrapping an arm about her svelte waist, he steered her into a shadowy, corner nook.

He gathered her close, and she came to him eagerly, standing on her toes and twining her arms around his neck.

"Just one kiss?" she whispered against his throat, before throwing her head back in a sensual challenge. The heated look she gave him sent his simmering desire into a full-on blaze of passion.

Groaning, he nibbled a trail from her delicate ear, along her jaw, and down her swan-like throat's slender column before plundering her mouth and ravishing the delicious depths.

Her little sighs and mews of pleasure as her tongue danced with his, drove him on as he pressed her into the wall, his manhood surging into her soft belly. All his concerns faded away, and the yearning he'd kept dammed, waiting to make her his, welled over his carefully constructed barriers.

Rucking her skirts, he feathered his fingers up one silky thigh, their panting breaths mingling. Her legs trembled, surely from want as uncontrollable as his.

No, not up against a wall in a darkened corridor like illicit lovers. When he at last explored the treasures her lovely body had to offer, it would be atop a luxurious bed with his ring around her finger.

Amidst their frenzied kisses, she'd unbuttoned his vest and unlaced his shirt.

"I want to feel your chest." She pulled at his shirt, tucked into his pantaloons, seemingly unware he'd let her gown drop to her ankles once more.

"I want to feel yers too," he quipped while obligingly yanking his shirt free.

No harm in her exploring a bit.

An instant later, her soft fingertips skimmed his chest and ribs and she nuzzled the hair at the shirt's vee. "Alasdair? Can we . . .?"

He claimed her mouth in a kiss meant to express how precious she was before denying her innocent request.

"Nae, my love. Not when we both be tired and overcome with other emotions. I want the first time I take ye to be somethin' ye'll remember the rest of yer life."

She released a soft, frustrated sigh. "You're right, of course. I'm sure society's matrons would frown upon me bedding you with my father laid out below."

More was the bloody pity.

A saucy smile tilted her mouth. "Besides, I'm quite famished. I've not eaten today at all."

Righting his clothing, Alasdair winked. "I confess, I'm starving too, and will need my stamina when the time does come."

Her pretty eyes widened, and she swatted his arm. "You're making me color."

He trailed a finger along her bodice, lingering for an instant where her pulse—as light as a butterfly's wing—fluttered gently against the tip. "I intend to do much more than that, lass."

"Oh, I'm counting on it." She whirled away.

The seductive smile she tossed over her shoulder had him hauling her back into his arms for another stolen kiss before firmly turning her toward the stairs. He threaded her arm through his elbow as he led them below.

"I need to tell ye somethin' too. I winna have any secrets between us."

Descending the stairs, she slid him a sideways glance. "All right. My news isn't unexpected, but I'd rather make sure we aren't overheard. The house is packed tighter than a biscuit tin with guests. Honestly, I'm looking forward to them departing after the funeral and the house returning to its former quiet."

A few minutes later, seated before a toasty fire and having enjoyed a simple fare of cheese, bread, cold meat, pickles, boiled eggs, and fruit spread on a plaid throw Alasdair had commandeered for the occasion, she took a sip of wine and stared into the flames.

Her black gown emphasized her raven hair, with just a hint of coppery highlights apparent in the candle and firelight.

"Da told me he named Ewan laird."

Fiend seize it.

Alasdair made a frustrated sound in the back of his throat. He'd anticipated just such a thing, but for her sake, had hoped Farnsworth wouldn't actually go that far.

She shrugged and tilted her head sideways. "He left me everything else. At least he said he did. We'll know for certain after Mr. Gwyers reads the will."

Wine flute half raised, Alasdair cocked a brow. "Everything?"

"Yes." She lifted her glass in a silent toast. "And he named you war-chief. If you want the position."

"War chief, huh?" Laughing softly, he shook his head. "That crafty old buzzard."

She frowned and inched her adorably stubborn chin up a notch. "I don't think it's very humorous, and not very respectable, considering he's lying just a few rooms away. And I'm still miffed at him about it, truth to tell."

"Dinna go all prickly on me, sweetheart, and dinna be mad at yer da either." He set his wine aside and after bundling her against his chest, rested his head atop hers. "He ken the title be next to useless without the estate, and I'll bet he ken Ewan wouldn't want it. He provided a way fer ye to wait fer me to divorce Searón."

Her brow furrowed in confusion. "I don't see how."

"I canna speak fer my cousin, but I be fairly certain, ye just say the word, and he'll transfer the title to ye." He traced her ear with a finger, enjoying her little shudder of pleasure.

Angling her head, she narrowed her eyes the tiniest bit. "Is that what you want, or would you prefer he appoint you? Once I put my pride aside, I realized it would be a wise move."

"Nae. A woman be every bit as capable of leading a tribe as a man, and a lass such as ye will be brilliant in the role." He brushed her cheek, affectionately.

And she would be too. As a female chief, Lydia could do much good for womankind.

"And I'd be honored to be war-chief under ye, lass." He tipped her chin so that she had to meet his eyes, then waggled his eyebrows, whispering naughtily, "And over ye too."

Rather than bluster and blush at his innuendo, Lydia coyly elevated a sable brow. "I should hope ye'd eagerly do anything yer chief requests of you."

"Aye, it'll be my pleasure. And yers."

"Such a wonderful promise."

The kiss she gave him had him reconsidering his earlier honorable notion about waiting a respectable time after Farnsworth's burial. Several lengthy, and satisfying minutes later, she curled into his chest, her arms about his waist.

"Now, what is it you wanted to tell me, Alasdair?"

Second thoughts plagued him. What if she refused him after he told her? He could lie or omit parts, and Lydia would never know the difference.

He would know, and his honor wouldn't permit him that escape.

"Ye should ken that I wronged Searón. Not intentionally, but wrong her I did by speakin' so vilely of her to ye when I didna ken the truth." He tightened his embrace, forcing himself to tell her the rest. "If she hadn't taken her own life, I wouldn't have divorced her. We'd have to have waited to marry until she died."

He waited tensely, afraid of her reaction, but also determined she know the whole of it. She'd be stepmother to Al and mustn't think poorly of his son's mother because of the things Alasdair had told Lydia, even if he thought he'd spoken the truth.

His hardened heart and bitterness had prevented him from considering any other possible explanation for Searón's actions, and he'd regret his callousness for the remainder of his days.

Lydia stiffened and drew away. She searched his face, a concert of emotions—confusion, worry, sorrow—shadowing her fine features. "And what could've so thoroughly changed your mind?"

In short order, he told her everything.

"Please tell me ye understand, lass. I love ye so much it hurts to breathe, and knowin' I'd wound you, crushed my soul. I'd rather put a knife to my chest and carve my heart out than ask ye to wait, but I couldn't abandon her again. Especially after she'd given me a son."

With every minute Lydia remained statue-like, staring into the flames, his meager hope waned.

He'd known he risked losing her by telling her all, and still, he wasn't prepared for the anguish.

Her profile silhouetted by the fire didn't reveal her thoughts. Didn't give him a single clue whether he'd destroyed the precious gift they'd been given.

How he'd go on, knowing she'd never be his, he couldn't begin to imagine.

He'd damned sure leave Scotland.

For good.

A tear leaked from her eye, and he slumped in defeat, shutting his eyes against the agony fracturing his soul. His sword and dagger wounds had been insect stings in comparison. Death was preferable to this pain.

"My heart hurts so unbearably for her and Al," Lydia said, her voice choked with compassion.

Alasdair popped his eyes open in disbelief.

She wiped another tear away, then several more. "So wretched unfair, the poor thing. How she must have suffered. And you too, all these years."

The tiniest seed of hope dared to sprout. "Yer nae angry?"

Lydia jerked her head up, her expression incredulous. "Of course I'm angry. I'm furious, but not at you. I'd like to tar and feather Searón's father. Indeed, I would."

For emphasis, she punched the pillow beside her.

"That makes two of us." He brushed the moisture from her soft cheek with his thumb. "Then ye'll marry me? When yer out of mournin'?"

Mischief and love fanned the corners of her sparkling eyes. "I distinctly remember asking for a proper proposal, but since we're both sitting on the floor, you may proceed from here."

Alasdair came to his knees, and taking her hands, pressed them to his heart while framing her face with his other hand. "I love ye Lydia Alline Therese Farnsworth, and I'd live the rest of my life the most privileged of men if ye'd consent to be my wife."

Her gaze dipped to his mouth, and her small tongue peeked from a corner of hers. "No, I don't believe I shall, after all."

"Pardon?" Had she said no?

Truly?

Lydia maneuvered to her knees as well, and after gently closing his slack jaw with her forefinger, grinned. "Well, since you think a woman is equal to a man, I've decided I shall propose to you."

Alasdair's heart resumed beating, a trifle uneven, but thumping away, nevertheless.

He'd never underestimate this unpredictable, enchanting woman again.

She took his big hands in her small ones, his tanned and rough, hers smooth and creamy. "Will you, Alasdair . . .?" She wrinkled her nose then shook her head. "I don't know your full name."

He squeezed her fingers. "Alasdair Graham Erik—"

"Never mind. I've decided to take another tact."

Of course she had.

God help him.

"Because I cannot imagine living the rest of my life without you by my side, because you are the first thing I think of when I wake each morning, and the very last thought that drifts through my mind before I fall asleep, because I do not want to lead the Farnsworth clan without you by my side, because I love you so much, it is a sweet ache that I never want to cease—"

"For the love of God, lass! Aye. I'll marry ye. Now stop talkin' and kiss me."

"Only if you promise to make me a woman tonight."

Alasdair nipped the sensitive hollow where her graceful neck met her shoulder. "Aye, lass. I canna refuse ye anythin'."

And as the fire popped and crackled in the hearth, with practiced hands and tenderness, he granted her request, taking them both on a shattering, soul-melding journey of exquisite bliss.

"Alasdair," Lydia cried, on the precipice of her release, "I love ye."

"And I ye, sweetheart." Groaning, straining to contain his own powerful explosion, until she reached the ultimate summit, he plundered her mouth and passion carried them tumbling over the glorious edge.

Epilogue

Tornbury Fortress
May 1, 1820

Lydia gritted her teeth, squeezed Alasdair's hand, and closing her eyes, bore down. Sweat trickled down her face in sticky rivulets, and soaked her nightgown.

"How much longer?" she panted.

Her pains had started before dawn, and the sun had set some time ago.

Cradled between Alasdair's massive legs, his broad chest supporting her, she strained to bring their child into the world.

He'd insisted on being present for the birth, and truth to tell, she welcomed his strength and presence. He'd been a pillar of calmness and encouragement. In part due to the infrequent sips from the silver flask within arm's reach. But now she grew weary.

"Soon, sweetheart," he encouraged.

Another contraction interrupted the weak smile she'd summoned.

Not bloody soon enough.

God's toenails, teeth, and bones!

Alasdair dabbed her forehead with a cool, damp cloth, and looked at Doctor Wedderburn and Midwife McCreary busily puttering about the bedchamber in last minute preparation for the bairn.

The doctor smiled reassuringly and lifted the sheet covering Lydia's lower half. "Ah."

Ah?

What the devil did 'ah' mean?

Ah, the baby's about here? Or ah, my God, there's a problem?

"Push, Mrs. McTavish. Yer bairn's nearly here," Doctor Wedderburn urged.

Oh, thank you, God.

Lydia closed her eyes and pushed again, swearing a most unladylike oath under her breath.

If he'd ever birthed a child, the Almighty would surely forgive her.

Alasdair chuckled, and she elbowed him in the stomach, finding great satisfaction in his grunt of pain.

He deserved to suffer a little for putting her through this, the oaf. Given his great size, she probably birthed a toddler.

A moment later, the babe finally slid free, bringing almost instantaneous relief.

Midwife McCreary scooped the baby into a towel.

"A bonnie, wee girl, Mr. and Mrs. McTavish."

Wee?

Not by half.

The bairn let loose a gusty, angry wail.

Midwife McCreary chuckled, as the infant kicked up a royal fuss. "Oh, and she be a feisty one."

Alasdair's, "Like her mother," earned him another well-aimed elbow to his gut.

Lydia held out her arms. "Let me hold her, please."

"I needs clean her up, and ye needs deliver the afterbirth first." Wiping the crying newborn's face, Midwife McCreary offered an apologetic smile.

A jovial smile crinkling his eyes, Doctor Wedderburn nodded toward the squalling babe. "The next laird?"

"If she chooses to be." Alasdair pressed a kiss to Lydia's crown, and for the first time, she noticed his shuddery breaths and felt the dampness on her scalp.

She looked over her shoulder. "Alasdair?"

Tears swam in her brawny, warrior husband's eyes.

"Ye were magnificent, darlin'. So strong and brave." He bent and gave her a tender kiss on the mouth. "Thank ye fer the braw daughter. My heart be so full, I'm fair to burstin'."

Who knew the birth of his daughter would bring this war chief to tears?

Doctor Wedderburn peeked above the sheet and winked. "I never heard of a man wantin' to be present fer the birth, but then, I never had a lady laird afore either. I canna say it didna do ye good to have yer husband present."

Lydia tiredly turned her lips upward. "We scandalized the tribe when we wed a mere two months after Da's death. I suppose having my husband attend our bairn's birth will give them more to titter about."

"Nae, it only shows how much we love each other. And they think it's terribly romantic." Alasdair eased from behind her. He smiled tenderly as he fluffed her pillows before lowering his head to give her a reverent kiss.

An hour later, once again resting in Alasdair's arms, the bairn nestled in the crook of hers, Lydia counted their daughter's fingers and toes. "Little Eilean. She's perfect in every way, isn't she?"

"Aye, she be at that." He touched her hand, and she wrapped her tiny fingers around his big forefinger.

A soft rap sounded at the door.

"Al and Esme, I'd guess. You'd better let them in. I'm sure they're dying to meet her."

"Have I told ye I love ye today, Mrs. McTavish, Laird of Tornbury Fortress?" Alasdair whispered in her ear.

Lydia raised her mouth to his. "Yes, but tell me again and again and again. And every day for as long as we have together."

If you enjoyed *Scandal's Splendor*,
be sure to read Collette Cameron's
Castle Bride Series,
now available from
Soul Mate Publishing at Amazon.com:

HIGHLANDER'S HOPE

Not a day has gone by that Ewan McTavish, the Viscount Sethwick, hasn't dreamed of the beauty he danced with two years ago. He's determined to win her heart and make her his own. Heiress Yvette Stapleton is certain of one thing; marriage is risky and, therefore, to be avoided. At first, she doesn't recognize the dangerously handsome man who rescues her from assailants on London's docks, but Lord Sethwick's passionate kisses soon have her reconsidering her cynical views on matrimony. On a mission to stop a War Office traitor, Ewan draws Yvette into deadly international intrigue. To protect her, he exploits Scottish law, declaring her his lawful wife—without benefit of a ceremony. Yvette is furious upon discovering the irregular marriage is legally binding, though she never said, "I do." Will Ewan's manipulation cost him her newfound love?

Buy now at:
http://tinyurl.com/pq4dhds

THE VISCOUNT'S VOW

Part Romani, noblewoman Evangeline Caruthers is the last woman in England Ian Hamilton, the Viscount Warrick, could ever love—an immoral wanton responsible for his brother's and father's deaths.

Vangie thinks Ian's a foul-tempered blackguard, who after

setting out to cause her downfall, finds himself forced to marry her—snared in the trap of his own making. When Vangie learns the marriage ceremony itself may have been a ruse, she flees to her gypsy relatives, declaring herself divorced from Ian under Romani law. He pursues her to the gypsy encampment, and when the handsome gypsy king offers to take Ian's place in Vangie's bed, jealousy stirs hot and dangerous.

Under a balmy starlit sky, Ian and Vangie breech the chasm separating them, yet peril lurks. Ian is the last in his family line, and his stepmother is determined to dispose of the newlyweds so her daughter can inherit his estate. Only by trusting each other can Ian and Vangie overcome scandal and murderous betrayal.

Buy now at:
http://tinyurl.com/oyd98a5

THE EARL'S ENTICEMENT

She won't be tamed.

A fiery, unconventional Scot, Adaira Ferguson wears breeches, swears, and has no more desire to marry than she does to follow society's dictates of appropriate behavior. She trusts no man with the secret she desperately protects.

He can't forget.

Haunted by his past, Roark, The Earl of Clarendon, rigidly adheres to propriety, holding himself and those around him to the highest standards, no matter the cost. Betrayed once, he's guarded and leery of all women.

Mistaking Roark for a known spy, Adaira imprisons him. Infuriated, he vows vengeance. Realizing her error, she's appalled and releases him, but he's not satisfied with his freedom. Roark is determined to transform Adaira from an ill-mannered hoyden to a lady of refinement.

He succeeds only to discover, he preferred the free-spirited Scottish lass who first captured his heart.

Buy at:
http://tinyurl.com/lfddq59

Also read the other books in the
Hightland Heather Romancing a Scot Series:

TRIUMPH AND TREASURE

A disillusioned Scottish gentlewoman.

Angelina Ellsworth once believed in love--before she discovered her husband of mere hours was a slave-trader and already married. To avoid the scandal and disgrace, she escapes to the estate of her aunt and uncle, the Duke and Duchess of Waterford. When Angelina learns she is with child, she vows she'll never trust a man again.

A privileged English lord.

Flynn, Earl of Luxmoore, led an enchanted life until his father committed suicide after losing everything to Waterford in a wager. Stripped of all but his title, Flynn is thrust into the role of marquis as well as provider for his disabled sister and invalid mother. Unable to pay his father's astronomical gambling loss, Flynn must choose between social or financial ruin.

When the duke suggests he'll forgive the debt if Flynn marries his niece, Flynn accepts the duke's proposal. Reluctant to wed a stranger, but willing to do anything to protect her babe and escape the clutches of the madman who still pursues her, Angelina agrees to the union.

Can the earl and his Scottish lass find happiness and love in a marriage neither wanted, or is the chasm between them insurmountable?

Buy at:
http://tinyurl.com/qa579mf

VIRTUE AND VALOR

Bartholomew Yancy never expected to inherit an English earldom and had no intention of marrying. Now, the Earl of Ramsbury and last in his line, he's obligated to resign his position as England's War Secretary, find a wife, and produce an heir. Only one woman holds the least appeal: Isobel Ferguson, an exquisite Scotswoman. Brought to Scotland to mediate between feuding clans, he doggedly woos her.

Disillusioned with men pursuing her for her attractiveness, rather than her unusual intellect, Isobel has all but abandoned any hope of finding a husband in the Highlands. Not only does she believe Yancy no different than her other suitors, he's a notorious rake. She's been told he's practically betrothed. Therefore, his interest in her cannot possibly be honorable, and so she shuns his attentions.

When Isobel is mistakenly abducted by a band of rogue Scots, Yancy risks his life to rescues her. To salvage her compromised reputation, her brother and father insist she marry him. Yancy readily agrees, but Isobel—knowing full well she's fated for spinsterhood by refusing his offer—won't be coerced into marriage.

Can love unite a reluctant earl and a disenchanted beauty?

Available now on Amazon:
http://tinyurl.com/ph6ba3h

HEARTBREAK AND HONOR

Abducted by a band of renegade Scots, Highland gypsy Tasara Faas blackens her rescuer's eye when the charming duke attempts to steal a kiss. Afterward, Tasara learns she's the long-lost heiress Alexandra Atterberry and is expected to take her place among the elite society she's always disdained.

Lucan, the Duke of Harcourt, promised his gravely ill mother he'd procure a wife by Christmastide, but intrigued by the feisty lass he saved in Scotland, he finds the haut ton ladies lacking. Spying Alexa at a London ball, he impulsively decides to make the knife-wielding gypsy his bride despite her aversion to him and her determination to return to the Highlands.

The adversary responsible for Alexa's disappearance as a toddler still covets her fortune and joins forces with Harcourt's arch nemesis. Amidst a series of suspicious misfortunes, Lucan endeavors to win Alexa's love and expose the conspirators but only succeeds in reaffirming Alexa's belief that she is inadequate to become his duchess.

Available now on Amazon:
http://tinyurl.com/zrvno3t

SCANDAL'S SPLENDOR

A determined Scottish lady

Seonaid Ferguson, a lady of Craiglocky Keep, is through with London's Marriage Mart. After learning she has the second sight, the haut ton attempts to exploit her abilities. Even though it means she condemns herself to spinsterhood, Seonaid sets a desperate course to rid herself of her gift turned curse. As she rushes home from England, a snowstorm strands her in a crowded inn with the last man she ever wished to see again. A handsome French baron who once thought her a courtesan. And just her misfortune, only he stands between her and certain harm.

An honorable French nobleman

Jacques, Monsieur le baron de Devaux-Rousset, ventures to Scotland to oversee his new investment; a silver mine near Craiglocky. Only a handsome profit will save his family's destitute estate in France. But when the mine is beset with one problem after another, Jacques must instead search for an heiress to wed. He certainly should not be falling in love with the lovely, spirited sister of Laird Ewan MacTavish, a lass whose dowry is insufficient to restore his ancestral home. Nor should he consider, even for a moment, her risqué, but deliciously tempting scheme to rid her of the second sight.

A danger most dire

Matters are torn from their hands when a dangerous adversary vows to expose Seonaid as a witch, just as Jacques's problems at the mine escalate into deadly violence. Is it by chance, or a dark design, that both of them are beset at once? Dare Jacques and Seonaid throw caution aside and forge a future together?

Available now on Amazon:
http://tinyurl.com/m2x28hs

CPSIA information can be obtained
at www.ICGtesting.com
Printed in the USA
BVOW06s1141220917
495650BV00010B/40/P